The We

A Halle Puma Story, Book 1.

Is Emma ready for a bite?

Emma Carter has been in love with Max Cannon since high school, but he barely knew she existed. Now she runs her own unique curio shop, and she's finally come out her shell and into her own.

When Max returns to his small home town to take up his duties as the Halle Pride's Alpha, he finds that shy little Emma has grown up. That small spark of something he'd always felt around the teenager has blossomed into something more—his mate!

Taking her "out for a bite" ensures that the luscious Emma will be permanently his.

But Max's ex has plans of her own. Plans that don't include Emma being around to interfere. To keep her Alpha, Emma must prove to the Pride that she has what it takes to be Max's mate.

Warning: This title contains explicit sex, graphic language, loads of giggles and a hot, blond Alpha male.

Sweet Dreams

A Halle Puma Story, Book 2.

Sweet dreams can easily become nightmares...

Getting attacked by some crazed she-devil, complete with claws and fangs, certainly wasn't on Rebecca Yaeger's agenda when she agreed to attend a local masquerade. In a few slashing moments, Becky learns things about her friends and the man she loves that she never would have suspected.

When Simon rescues Becky from an unprovoked attack by one of his Pride, he finally confirms what he's long suspected: she's his mate. Carrying her off to his home and dressing her wounds gives him the chance he's been waiting for—to taste her and mark her as his. And she's far sweeter than anything, or anyone, he's ever had before.

Just as their problems seem a thing of the past, a strange illness begins to haunt Becky, threatening to turn their sweet dreams into a nightmare.

Warning: This title contains explicit sex, graphic language, Godiva chocolates and a tall, dark and handsome shifter.

Cat of a Different Color

A Halle Puma Story, Book 3.

He'll do whatever it takes to protect his mate.

Dr. Adrian Giordano is quite happy with the way his life is going. His two best friends are happily mated, and he's still sanely single. He has friends, a thriving business, and the occasional Saturday night date. Then Sheridan Montgomery comes to town. His inner Puma responds to the husky-voiced snow princess in a way that tells him his life is about to be turned upside down.

Sheri can't believe her luck could be this bad. Instinct tells her Adrian is her mate, but the last thing she wants to do is drag him into her messy life. She's on the run from a big bad wolf—an ex who won't take no for an answer. Worse, if he catches her, he's got the teeth (and the Pack!) to take what he wants.

She doesn't stand a chance alone, but with her friends— and the persistent Adrian—by her side, she might just survive.

If her ex doesn't eat the yummy Dr. Giordano for lunch, that is...

Warning: This title contains explicit sex, graphic language, a handsome, dark-eyed shifter and a couple of bites to remember.

Look for these titles by
Dana Marie Bell

Now Available:

Halle Pumas Series
The Wallflower (Book 1)
Sweet Dreams (Book 2)
Cat of a Different Color (Book 3)
Steel Beauty (Book 4)
Only in My Dreams (Book 5)

True Destiny Series
Very Much Alive

Gray Court Series
Dare to Believe

Print Anthology
Hunting Love

Mating Games

Dana Marie Bell

A SAMHAIN PUBLISHING, LTD. publication.

Samhain Publishing, Ltd.
577 Mulberry Street, Suite 1520
Macon, GA 31201
www.samhainpublishing.com

Mating Games
Print ISBN: 978-1-60504-765-2
The Wallflower Copyright © 2010 by Dana Marie Bell
Sweet Dreams Copyright © 2010 by Dana Marie Bell
Cat of a Different Color Copyright © 2010 by Dana Marie Bell

The Wallflower, ISBN 978-1-59998-918-1
First Samhain Publishing, Ltd. electronic publication: April 2008
The Wallflower in Hunting Love, ISBN 978-1-60504-106-3
First Samhain Publishing, Ltd. print anthology March 2009
Second Samhain Publishing, Ltd. print publication: June 2010
Sweet Dreams, ISBN 978-1-60504-132-2
First Samhain Publishing, Ltd. electronic publication: August 2008
First Samhain Publishing, Ltd. print publication: June 2010
Cat of a Different Color, ISBN 978-1-60504-239-8
First Samhain Publishing, Ltd. electronic publication: November 2008
First Samhain Publishing, Ltd. print publication: June 2010

Contents

The Wallflower

Dedication

To Mom, for always helping me look on the bright side and cheering me on even when you weren't certain you knew what you were cheering about.

To Dad, who grinned so wide I thought his face would crack when he heard I was going to be published. Yes, I promise I'll write a fantasy story one day, just don't expect me to leave out the romance.

To my grandmother, who's read every word I've ever written and loved it even when we both knew it sucked. I love you, Memom!

To my husband, Dusty; you've made all my dreams come true. (Other than the cabana boy one. But that's okay. You're not getting your big-breasted masseuse either, so we're even.) Thank you for believing in me. I love you, sweetheart.

Special thanks to A and BR for reading this, helping me fix it and polish it up, and for cheering with me when I got the contract. Also thanks to JG and JW for the technical assistance.

Prologue

"So, have you heard? Max is back." Marie watched with a friendly smile as Emma carefully wrapped her purchase. Emma felt her heart give a little jump at the news, though it wasn't the first time she'd heard it. The knowledge that the hunky Dr. Cannon had moved back home for good after ten years away was hot gossip to all the women who trooped through her store.

"Of course I know." Livia eyed Emma with a gleaming smile before turning back to Marie. "Are we almost done here?" Marie Howard was there to pick up a hand-crafted mirror with beautiful hand-painted tiles. Livia was there, even though she hated both Emma and Becky, because she was friends with Marie. As far as Livia was concerned, they were directly responsible for her breakup with Max.

Livia Patterson was one of the town beauties and knew it. Fine boned with alabaster skin, she had just the right dusting of rose at her cheeks to set off her pale blonde perfection. Add blue eyes the color of forget-me-nots and a tall, wispy build, and she was the epitome of the fragile blonde. The woman could brawl like a linebacker when the time came; she could shriek, and bats for miles around fell dead to the ground; but man if she didn't work the whole Penelope Pitstop thing, and men fell for it. They loved that whole delicate flower of womanhood crap she managed to pull off so flawlessly. Not that Emma envied her or anything. Not really.

Men looked at Emma and saw sturdy womanhood. Hips

made for birthing, plain brown eyes and nondescript brown hair, at five-foot-two inches Emma would never, literally, be able to stand up to Livia. Add in the fact that most of the town thought she was in a gay relationship with Becky and her social calendar remained depressingly empty.

"Apparently Max is planning on taking over Dr. Brewster's practice; he and Adrian will be partners," Livia cooed.

"So you've already spoken to him?" Marie's expression of polite curiousness didn't quite mesh with her tone of voice. Emma didn't dare look too closely, but she thought Marie was almost exasperated with her friend. Everyone knew how hard Livia had once chased Max. Maybe she thought she could get the old fires burning once again?

"Yes, Max just bought his parents' old house. I can't wait to get in there and redecorate." Emma could practically see Livia rubbing her hands in anticipation. "Of course, nothing in this shop will do. No real craftsman things. I want genuine antiques, not knock-offs." Livia's contemptuous gaze raked the store, and its owner, with equal derision.

When Livia's back was turned, Emma, in a fit of childishness, mimicked the blonde as closely as possible. Marie wound up choking on a sip of tea as Emma put her hand on her hip and mouthed along with Livia's words. "Of course, everyone knows Max would never set foot inside Wallflowers. Does he even know you exist, Emma?"

Emma tapped her nail on her chin thoughtfully as Livia turned back to her. "Yes, actually, I believe he does. Something...something to do with...punch. Cherry punch, if I recall correctly." That had been the incident that broke up Max and Livia; Becky had spilled cherry punch all over Livia's white prom dress in retaliation for some comment of Livia's concerning Emma. Max had, apparently, taken Emma and Becky's side and had broken off his relationship with Livia. Livia had hated Emma and Becky ever since. Emma was pretty sure Livia was the one who kept the whole gay couple rumor alive.

The look on the blonde's face was filled with hatred until she smoothed it out, once again the cool, delicate woman most of Halle knew. She smiled at Emma with pity. "I hear Jimmy left town recently. What's wrong, Emma, didn't he like sharing you with Becky? Or perhaps you couldn't talk her into a ménage a trois?"

Emma smiled back, hiding the hurt over Jimmy with practiced ease. They'd known before he left that their relationship wasn't going anywhere, and it wasn't Jimmy's fault. "So you've been invited to Max's housewarming party?" Sometimes it helped to have friends in odd places; Max's best friend had become one of her best artisans and closest friends. He'd made Marie's mirror and supplied quite a bit of glass wall art for the store.

Livia's eyes flickered; she knew nothing about the party. Emma mentally chalked up a score on her mental scoreboard. On the downside, Emma hadn't been invited either, not that she'd expected to be.

"That party is supposed to be a surprise." Livia waved her hand airily. Emma merely raised an amused eyebrow, not deceived in the least. "Oh, well, hopefully you won't spill the beans to Max. Oh, wait. When, exactly, was the last time *you* spoke to Max?" Livia smiled coldly.

Emma clapped in mock approval. "Wow, Livia. Way to express your inner twelve year old."

Grinding her teeth on a fake smile, Livia turned to Marie. "I'll wait for you outside. The atmosphere in here is so cloying and sweet. I really don't know how you can stand it." She stepped outside and sat on the bench Emma and Becky had put out front, looking dainty and sweet as she waved hello to her friends and acquaintances.

"Sorry about that, Emma. I forgot how much she dislikes you."

Emma turned and looked at Marie's apologetic face. She grinned. "It's no problem, Marie. If she actually came in here to buy something I'd take great pleasure in charging her double."

Marie laughed just as Becky stuck her head out of the curtained-off back room. "Has the wicked witch ridden off on her broomstick yet?"

Emma waved towards the picture window. "Not quite. She's flying our bench at the moment."

Becky carried out the mirror with a sigh. "Here you go, Marie. Hope you and Jamie like it."

"Oh, I'm sure we will," Marie replied, her eyes glued to the boxed up mirror. She paid, chatting quietly with Becky and Emma, then left the store with a cheery wave. The two women could see her giving Livia something of a hard time as they crossed the street, but quickly lost sight of them.

"So. Max is back in town." Becky leaned back against the counter, obviously hiding a grin.

"Yup."

"You going to make a play for Dr. Yummy? I mean, since you've had a crush on him since, what, grade school?"

"Given half a chance? Maaaybe."

The two women looked at each other and laughed; they both knew Emma didn't stand a chance in hell of catching Max Cannon's attention. She hadn't done it in high school, and she certainly hadn't changed all that much since.

What would a man like Max want with someone like her?

Chapter One

"God, he is *so* fucking hot."

Emma Carter looked out the front window of Wallflowers and watched the most bodacious backside it had ever been her pleasure to see saunter down the street. Said backside was encased in a pair of tight blue jeans, causing many a female to send a prayer of thanks heavenward for the makers of Levi's. Sunlight gleamed on his golden blond hair, hair that brushed his wide shoulders, just long enough to make a stubby ponytail. Even under the bulky leather jacket you could tell he was built, his body muscular without being a temple to the god Steroid. And he had the brightest, clearest blue eyes in the state, not that she got to look at them often. He usually had them trained on someone else, like one of the sleek, beautiful women who flocked around him all the time. God, he was gorgeous. His face was almost too beautiful to be real; the only thing that marred his perfection was a small scar just along one side of his nose, barely noticeable unless you looked for it. When he spoke to her, which hadn't happened in more years than she cared to count, Emma kept her eyes trained on that scar.

When the finest ass in the world turned the corner, Emma and Becky leaned back with identical sighs. "All I want for Christmas is a piece of that." Becky sighed again, her green eyes gleaming with laughter. Her untamable brown curls danced around her head in wild abandon as she shook herself all over like a wet dog. Becky was too thin, bones showing through at wrist and ankle, and if Emma didn't know for a fact that she ate like a horse she'd have worried she was anorexic. But Becky had been cursed with a metabolism that just wouldn't quit, forcing her to eat more than most people just to maintain her weight. Emma had the opposite problem. The best that could be said about her figure was Marilyn Monroe had also been a size twelve. No matter what she did, Emma couldn't seem to drop weight. Neither woman envied the other.

"What, not a piece of Simon Holt?"

Becky blushed bright red. Dark-haired, dark-eyed, sinfully handsome Simon had featured in more than one of Becky's drunken fantasies. Emma slicked a hand through her hair. "As for me, Max Cannon could be naked and tied up with a bow under my Christmas tree and the first thing he'd probably say is, 'Hi, Edna, right? Could you untie this please? I have a date tonight'."

Both women looked at each other and giggled, then got back to work.

Emma was so proud of what she and Becky had accomplished. Friends since grade school, both women had been wallflowers. Boys didn't go for the frizzy, too-skinny Becky Yaeger or chunky, dull Emma Carter. Especially when there were girls like Livia Patterson and Belinda Campbell, both beautiful, blonde cheerleader types, around.

Both Becky and Emma had decided to go to the local college and major in business, while a number of people, including Max and Livia, had chosen to go out of state for college. After graduation, Emma had taken the inheritance from her maternal grandmother and used it to buy the building that now housed Wallflowers.

Wallflowers was a business that catered to people who enjoyed hand-crafted, artisan-made pieces. Emma loved it. Their eccentric store carried hand-carved cuckoo clocks, paintings, old-fashioned mirrors, masks, plaques...anything that could be used to decorate a wall. Becky had come up with the idea for the business and talked Emma into it over a long night of burritos and margaritas.

Emma paused to look around their "parlor". An antique rug covered the distressed hardwood floors. A small Victorian sofa covered in soft cream brocade graced the center of the floor. A Queen Anne coffee table in rich cherry wood sat before it, a silver tea service placed on it. Two Victorian chairs in that same cream fabric faced the sofa, creating a cozy little conversation group that the two women, and the occasional customer, used frequently. Against one wall was a gas fireplace with an ornately carved mantelpiece. On that mantelpiece were silver-framed photos, all of them either black and white or sepia toned. In one, Emma was dressed in a Victorian dress of ivory lace, a black cameo at her throat, her hair done up, a sweet smile on her face. In the other, Becky was dressed as a Wild West saloon girl, her frizzy hair teased out and feathers stuck in every which way. Her dress was pulled up on one side to show black boots and striped stockings. Neither photo had a place of prominence, both intermingled with other pictures. Unless you stood and went through the pictures thoroughly, you'd never find them.

A cherry and glass counter, as Victorian as they could make it and still have it be functional, graced one wall. On it sat an old-fashioned looking cash register; hidden underneath the counter was the credit card reader.

They'd done their best to have the atmosphere of a by-gone era and still keep the place warm and inviting. A fire crackled merrily in the fireplace on this cool October evening; the walls had a lovely cherry wood wainscoting, with rich rose floral wallpaper above it. It was very feminine, and both women loved it.

They'd had the store now for three years, and while they knew they'd never be rich off it, they also knew they'd never been happier.

Emma sighed, a smile of satisfaction on her face as she finished polishing the old, gilt-edged mirror they'd hung just behind the counter.

Life was good.

Dr. Max Cannon's life sucked. Once again he crossed the street, determined to avoid Livia's obvious attempt to get his attention. He'd been back in his small hometown for three months now, but she couldn't get it through her overly highlighted head that he just wasn't interested. Hell, the woman's vision was perfect and yet she'd tried to schedule three different eye exams in the last three months! Thank God his partner Adrian was willing to run interference, or Max might have been forced to some extreme measures. Until he had a Curana who could safely deal with the woman, Livia was going to continue to be a serious problem. He ducked into the workshop of his best buddy and Beta, Simon Holt, determined to get away from the blonde barracuda bearing down on him.

"Hey, Max."

"Simon."

Simon's deferential nod was all that it should be from his Beta. "Hiding out from Livia again?"

The laughter in Simon's voice nearly had Max growling. "She's getting persistent."

"Have you told her to fuck off yet?"

Simon's approach to the pushy female was beginning to appeal. The idea of her as his mate made his skin crawl. The Puma inside him yowled in protest. There was no way in hell he'd make her his Curana.

"No, but I'm getting there."

Simon pointed discreetly towards the workshop's front window. "Incoming."

Max gritted his teeth just as the door opened.

"Max, how nice to run into you!"

Soft, perfumed arms tried to circle his neck. In a swift move, Max glided away, turning to face the woman who'd tormented him since his return to Halle. "Livia."

It wasn't a greeting; it was a warning. Her eyes flared briefly with fear before she laughed it off. "I just wanted to remind you about the masquerade party over at Marie's. You'll be going, won't you?"

"Yes."

Livia frowned, her expression turning hard and calculating. "Most of the Pride will be there."

Max nodded; as Alpha he was well aware of that. Marie's father, the old Alpha, still held the annual masquerade at his house just outside of town. It was his pride and joy, that house, and he loved to entertain. His daughter, safely mated to Jamie Howard, acted as his hostess since the death of his mate some four years ago. Human and Puma mingled at the masquerade, the humans totally unaware of the Pumas in their midst. The Pride did its best to make the event a night to remember, for both races, and Jonathon Friedelinde did an excellent job of that. It was also the event at which an unmated male could unofficially signal his interest in a female. Hence Livia's interest in his attendance; if she could get him alone long enough, get him to signal in some way that there was a spark of interest, she could force him into a declaration he didn't want to make.

"Who are you taking?"

The question was asked with a seductive coyness that nearly made Max shudder. He suppressed it; he couldn't afford a sign of weakness. "At present, no one."

The chill in his voice should have made her back off. Instead, the stupid woman took it as a challenge. "Oh?" Her lashes fluttering coyly, she reached out with one manicured finger. When her blood red claw touched his chest, Max snarled a warning, his eyes flashing gold as the Puma warned her off.

With a gasp she backed away. Her head dipped in submission, an instinctive response to the Alpha power Max now exuded. It surrounded him in an unseen cloud, forcing all before him to do his will. Max rarely found himself in need of it, but today she'd pushed too far. She slowly backed away from him as a growl rumbled in his chest. He kept it going until she was completely out of Simon's workshop, pissed beyond belief at her persistence.

"Okay, I gotta admit, that was probably more effective than 'Fuck off, you skanky ho'. Think she got the message?"

And that was why Simon was his Beta—he'd flinched but stood his ground, something none of the other Pumas could do. Their reactions were more akin to Livia's when he chose to exercise his power.

He was also one of the few people Max trusted completely. If anything were to happen to Max, Simon would become Alpha.

Max turned with a laughing snort to answer his buddy's question when Simon's phone rang. His Beta punched the speakerphone button, still grinning at Max. "Hello?"

"Simon?" The voice on the other end of the phone drawled Simon's name with an amused authority that had Max's eyebrows rising into his hairline. He waited for Simon to put the woman in her place.

Simon rolled his eyes. "Hey, Emma."

Max blinked. Emma? Emma Carter?

"Your stained glass Madonna is late. Reverend Glaston is getting antsy."

Max blinked again. That sexy voice was *Emma?*

"I've been...distracted." That last was said with a quick glance at Max. He'd been the one keeping Simon busy. As Beta, Simon took care of a great deal of Pride business, something Emma wouldn't know about.

"Well, could you please ask your *distraction* to go home so you can finish the reverend's window?"

Her tone of voice raised Max's brows back into his hairline. His Beta's reaction had his jaw nearly dropping open.

"Emma," Simon nearly whined, "I've been working night and day, here. Give me a break!"

Emma?!? Plump little wallflower Emma?

"Just who have you been working, Simon Holt?"

Emma, who couldn't look him in the eye, making double entendres?

"No one, damn it! I've been working on...other things." Again, Simon shot Max a quick, furtive look.

Emma? *Emma* had his Beta shaking in his sneakers?

"Well, get your *thing* back under control and finish the reverend's window, okay?"

The irreverent authority in her voice stirred his interest. A vision of a dark-haired girl in a sunset colored prom gown flashed through his mind.

"Damn it, Emma!" Simon sighed, leaning back against his workbench. "Where's Becky?"

The entreaty in Simon's voice barcly registered. Max was waiting to hear Emma's voice again.

"Oh, no, don't think you can get out of having that window finished today by sweet-talking Becky. I'm on to your tricks, buster."

Simon winced. Max's cock twitched.

Emma?

Hmmm. *Emma.*

"Okay, okay. I'll have the damn window done today. Anything else, Little General?" Simon's shoulders were quaking with laughter, his voice filled with respect. Max frowned at the affection in his Beta's voice.

"Mm-hmm. Becky and I will be going to the masquerade. Just thought you'd like to know."

Emma would be at the masquerade? Suddenly he was dying to see her. How had she turned out? Was she as sexy as her voice implied?

"Oh, yeah." The purr in Simon's voice had Max frowning. The small, predatory smile had his eyes flashing gold in protest as a wave of possessiveness rose inside him. The owner of that voice was *his.*

"Mm-hmm. See you later? *With* the window?"

"Count on it. Bye, Emma."

"Later, Simon."

Simon hung up the phone, that sexy smile still on his face. When he turned back, Max had himself back under control, merely raising a brow at Simon.

Simon flushed. "What?"

"When are you delivering that window?"

Simon looked over at the window waiting for its finishing touches. "Probably just after lunch. Why?"

"I'm going with you." Max grinned.

Simon straightened up, frowning slightly in confusion. "Why? I thought you had some other things to deal with."

"I want to check something out." At Simon's raised brow, Max's grin widened.

"Man, I'm not sure you want to go there."

Max's grin faded. "Why not?"

"Because Wallflowers has been known to suck the testosterone out of every single male who's ever entered."

"Huh?"

"It's pink. And frou-frou. And lacy. And *pink.*"

Max laughed as Simon shuddered. "If your masculinity can handle it, so can mine."

Max watched his friend work on the stained glass window, his mind once again turning to Emma.

He hadn't seen her in eight years. She'd been seventeen, just about ready to graduate, smiling and laughing at the prom in a way he'd rarely seen her do. She'd been striking in her dress, a one-of-a-kind done in the colors of a rich autumn sunset, a strapless number in reds and golds with a sweetheart neckline and flaring skirt. He'd had a hard time keeping his eyes off her, but he'd been with Livia, and Max was not a man who cheated. By the time he'd broken up with Livia it was time for him to leave once again for college. Between earning his

24

doctorate in optometry, his internship and residency, and learning from Jonathon how to run the Pride during his summers off, Emma had been quickly forgotten. Going out of state for college had been the right choice for him, and he'd been lucky that Jonathon agreed with him. Now, with his partnership with Adrian and Jonathon's official retirement he could finally start looking for his Curana. And he had a feeling he knew just who he wanted for the position.

She'd been sweetly innocent back then; slightly overweight, but with serious curves. It had been that innocence, and Livia, that had held him back.

She didn't sound so innocent now, and Livia was nowhere in the picture.

It was definitely time he got better acquainted with little Miss Emma.

Emma watched as Simon's shiny red pickup truck pulled up to the curb of Wallflowers. She grinned, knowing Becky had hidden in the back office to avoid meeting up with Simon. Simon was the only person on the face of the planet who made Becky lose the power of speech. In an odd, karmic sort of way, Emma had no problem handling the hunky Simon, laughing and chatting with him with ease.

Emma watched Simon climb out of the truck. The passenger side opened up as well, and a familiar tall blond got out, a grin on his face, his unbound hair blown about by the cool autumn breeze.

Emma was horrified. *Oh, no. Not* him! She took a deep breath to steady her nerves. She was no longer the shy teenager he'd once known; she was a grown woman with a shop of her own. She could handle Max Cannon.

Then he grinned at something Simon said, and her hands began to shake. She took another quick breath and blew it out, trying desperately to steady her racing heart.

The two men wrestled the stained glass window out of the

flatbed of the truck. With care, they got it to the door of the shop. Emma rushed to open it just as the reverend arrived.

Reverend Glaston smiled at the two men. "Hello, Simon, Max. Is that the church's window?"

Emma smiled at the reverend. He was a kind soul, with smiling whisky brown eyes and balding gray hair. He never failed to make Emma feel comfortable, and she was counting on that now to get her through *his* presence.

"Sure is, Reverend. Let's get it inside so I can show it to you."

Simon's deep voice reverberated through her, making her shiver a little. If she weren't so hung up on the blond hunk behind him, she'd have made a play for Simon a long time ago. Although, considering how Becky had always reacted to him...

"Becky? Can you come give me a hand with this?" Emma yelled into the back, struggling to hide her grin when Simon's gaze glued itself to the curtained off area that led to their office. *Okay, maybe I wouldn't have gone after Simon.*

She heard Becky's muttered oath as she stomped into the front room. Simon's gaze never left Becky as he and Max maneuvered the window into the store. His dark brown eyes heated as Becky scowled at him and took a step back.

"Becky?" Emma asked, waving her forward. With a false cheerfulness, Becky smiled at Emma, then joined her by the propped up window.

"Emma?" Emma turned to Simon, who was staring at her now. "You remember Max, right?"

He's kinda hard to forget, Emma thought as Max stepped forward.

"Hi, Emma."

She looked up, getting a quick peek at the face that had starred in every single one of her naughty fantasies before lowering them to the scar next to his nose. "Hi, Max."

He cleared his throat, a sound filled with amusement. She

glanced back up at him to see him staring at her with a raised brow. Looking down, she noticed he'd held out his hand. With a false smile she took it, pumping it up and down twice before dropping it like a hot potato.

Her heart fluttering from just that simple touch, she turned to Simon, the lesser of the two threats. "So, Simon, are you ready to unveil your masterpiece?" Her smile for him was genuine; she truly liked Simon. His work was exquisite. On top of that, he had one of the best senses of humor she'd ever seen. It felt like having a brother, something she'd never had the pleasure of experiencing, being an only child.

He lifted one brow, grinning at her. "Yes, Little General. Right away, Little General."

Putting her hands on her hips, she glared at him. Although, from the twitching of his lips, he wasn't all that impressed. "*Now*, Simon."

She could hear the reverend coughing on a laugh behind her. Simon just rolled his eyes and began unwrapping the window.

When it was finally unveiled, Emma was astonished. It was easily one of Simon's finest works. The Madonna sat, her blue robes gently waving around her, a small Mona Lisa smile on her face as she stared down at the dark-haired baby held gently in her arms. The Madonna was beautiful, but it wasn't a classic beauty. It was the gentleness in her face, the love she so obviously bore her child that made it so special. He'd managed to capture that special smile that new mothers everywhere gave their newborns, and it took an otherwise normal face and made it radiant.

"My God, Simon. It's gorgeous," Max breathed from right behind her.

"Thanks." Simon's eyes didn't rest on the Madonna, though; they were on Becky, who stared at the Madonna with something akin to awe. "Becky?"

Becky's gaze went from the Madonna to him. The reverence

on her face seemed to stun Simon, who drew in a quick breath.

Emma felt Max stir behind her. When one of his hands came to rest at her hip, she nearly jumped out of her skin. "Well!" She clapped her hands, moving away from the dangerous heat of the man behind her to go to the reverend. Not surprisingly Becky, after nearly jumping out of her skin, refused to meet Simon's eyes again.

"What do you think, Reverend?" She put on her best salesman's voice, for once not flustered to be using it in front of real people.

The reverend's slow smile was all the answer she needed.

Hot damn, Max thought, watching the little dynamo that was Emma in action. *Why the hell didn't I stop here sooner?* He'd been busy setting up his practice, true, but you'd think he'd have made the time to stop by. Be neighborly.

When Max had stepped out of the truck, he hadn't really been expecting much; after all, most women couldn't live up to the voice Emma had. It was slightly husky, like she'd spent the night moaning in some man's arms, a visual Max could do without. She managed to infuse it with an authority that had his Beta jumping to do her bidding, something that spoke to the Puma in him. Max wondered if she'd try to take the lead in bed, as well. A challenge, that; he loved taking a strong woman and reducing her to a quivering, begging mass of bliss.

Her straight, dark brown hair was caught up in a ponytail that hung to just between her shoulder blades. Big brown eyes dominated her face, artfully made up to accentuate them. Her lips were slicked with a pale rose. Her features weren't classically beautiful, but something about the animation in them drew Max like nothing else ever had.

And her body...

Hell, her *body...*

The top of her head barely reached his shoulder, something he normally wasn't attracted to, but on Emma it aroused protective instincts he didn't even know he possessed. She had the most sweetly rounded ass encased in tight black jeans and the most magnificent breasts Max had ever been privileged to watch bounce under a lacy rose camisole. With a real waist and hips a man could grab on to for the ride of his life, she reminded him of an old-fashioned pin-up girl, all soft curves and feminine strength. Then she turned, laughing up at something Simon said, sensuous and innocent at the same time, and Max was a goner.

Holy. Fucking. Damn.

Emma. Little Emma Carter sure as hell had grown up.

His hands burned to touch her again. That fleeting touch she'd allowed him had merely whetted his appetite. He longed to rip that camisole off her body and feast at her breasts, hear her moans as he slipped her jeans down those incredible, edible legs, her soft cries as he feasted on her juices.

She would scream his name as she came.

He would tie her to his bed, torture her into ecstasy, and then start all over again. He'd bend her over the arm of his couch and take her from behind over and over until she begged him to come, biting into her shoulder and marking her as his for all to see. The thought of slipping his cock into that luscious ass nearly made him come right there in the middle of her store.

When she laughingly hugged Simon, he nearly went for his Beta's throat.

Mine!

Only Simon saw the way his eyes gleamed gold, heard the low, purring growl that erupted from his throat before he could stop himself. Sucking in a breath, Max turned away, desperately trying to get himself under control.

He'd been told he'd know his mate when he met her; now he knew what they meant. He'd spoken to Emma when she'd been a teenager, felt a little spark of *something*, but had dismissed it as nothing serious. Just young lust. Now he knew what that spark had been and wanted to kick his own ass. Not all Pumas got lucky enough to find his or her mate; to know he'd not only met her, but walked away from her, hell, *forgotten* her, galled him.

He forced himself to look around her shop, at anything but the laughing group of people around the Madonna, before he walked over there, plucked her up and carted her out of her shop to somewhere private.

She'd done well for herself. Emma's stamp, mixed with Becky's, created an atmosphere both women seemed at home in. He could see women flocking to the store, much to the horror and amusement of their male companions. He walked over to the mantelpiece, seeing a silver picture frame his mother would probably appreciate as a gift for her birthday. Something about the picture in it drew his attention. He leaned forward, trying to see why the Victorian lady in it looked so familiar when he felt a small hand touch his arm.

"Is everything okay between you and Simon?"

That husky voice, combined with her soft touch, had his cock once more threatening to burst out of his jeans. He looked down into her face and saw nothing there but concern. Before she could move, he put his hand over hers, trapping her at his side. He was ridiculously pleased when she didn't try to pull away. "Everything is fine between me and Simon." *As long as he keeps his paws off of you.*

She looked away, back towards the group, and bit her lip. "Can I talk to you for a moment?"

Her voice was hesitant, shy in a way she wasn't when she talked to Simon or the reverend, but her expression begged him to say yes. A fierce wave of protectiveness rose in him, and his hand tightened over hers. He nodded.

He allowed her to pull them to the side, quiet and private but still in plain view. She looked up at him again, obviously uncertain before she focused, damn it, back on his scar. "Um, do you have any idea how Simon feels about Becky?"

She peeked up at him again before dropping her gaze once more. A flush rose in her cheeks and she bit her lip again.

He took a deep breath, striving to control the possessiveness that roared through him. "Not a clue."

Her softly muttered "Damn" had him nearly smiling, it was so filled with aggravation, but the possessive monster in him couldn't get past her possible interest in his best friend. "He's not for you." He could feel wisps of his power flowing out of his control, trying to force her to acknowledge the truth of his words.

Emma looked him full in the face for the first time since he'd entered the store. He knew he sounded like a caveman, and probably looked like a jealous jackass, but he couldn't help it; little Emma did that to him.

Then she laughed at him. Not one bit intimidated, frightened or cowed.

"Not me, you idiot." His eyes widened in astonishment as she turned back to the group around the Madonna. "Becky. She's had a thing for him since high school, but she can't seem to act on it and he's never shown any real interest." She looked back up at him. "Until recently, that is. So, I wanted to know, you being his best friend, if you know how he feels."

He felt his whole body tense at the devilish calculation on her face. "What are you planning?" He maneuvered his body, and hers, until they were in the corner, effectively cutting her off from the crowd behind them. His power was back under control, but his curiosity was roused.

She puffed out an impatient breath, focusing once more on him. Some of her shyness had evaporated, but in its place was an irritation he wasn't used to seeing in feminine eyes. "Becks and I are going to the annual masquerade. Mr. Friedelinde invited us, for the first time. I'm hoping I can get either Simon or Becky moving in the right direction, but I don't want Becky hurt or embarrassed if Simon isn't really interested." She looked up at him, her little chin tilted as she demanded a response.

"So. Is he?"

Max turned back to look at his Beta. From the way Simon was sniffing the air around Becky, he'd say Simon was *very* interested. He looked down at Emma, who was tapping her foot impatiently. "Yes."

Relief flickered across her face and her body relaxed as if he'd lifted a weight off her shoulders. "Thank God. They'd be perfect together."

"What makes you say that?" Truly curious, he watched as she turned thoughtful.

"Simon knows he can have any female he wants just by snapping his fingers, but Becky backs away from him every time he approaches. He's never quite certain where he stands with her. He gets bored so easily with the ones that fall in the palm of his hand that he winds up dumping them pretty quickly. He can't predict what Becky will do, so she'd never bore him. Also, Becky loves his work and understands how much time and devotion it takes to make the kinds of things Simon does, so she wouldn't resent that if she knew he'd be coming home to her. She would challenge him; keep him on his toes, while he would cherish her like she should be cherished. No one's truly loved her before, or shown her her own worth." Emma focused on him again, her expression gleefully vengeful. "But if he hurts her, I'll scoop out his nuts with a grapefruit spoon."

The change from dreamer to avenger had Max grinning even as his balls drew up at the visual image she'd created; although, from the way Simon was acting she had nothing to worry about. "Remind me not to get you mad at me."

"Oh, no, I'm not the one to be afraid of." She motioned him closer with a crooked finger, and he obligingly bent closer, getting a whiff of her rose scented perfume as he did. "Becky had a friend in college who showed her how to use a goat emasculator," she whispered softly in his ear.

Max reared back, staring at Becky and then back down to

the innocent looking little devil nodding solemnly in front of him.

He threw his head back and laughed harder than he had in months.

Max climbed into Simon's truck with a grin.

"What the hell did Emma say to you to get you to laugh like that, anyway?" Simon asked, his tone aggravated.

Max shook his head. "Nothing you'd be interested in, I'm sure."

"Try me," Simon snarled.

Max snarled a warning to his Beta, who had the grace to look guilty.

"Sorry."

"Want to tell me what that was all about?"

Max wasn't asking, and Simon knew that. He sighed. "Becky. She won't talk to me, barely looks at me and leaves the room the minute I enter it. Hell, if she can arrange it she makes sure she's gone before I get there!"

"So you're not interested in Emma?"

The look Simon shot him was part amazement, part horror, and Max relaxed, his fears that Simon was interested in Emma eased. It was the look a brother would give someone if asked if he thought his sister was hot.

"Emma wants to do something to bring the two of you together. I thought I'd verify that it's what you want before I start helping her."

"Man, if you and Emma can get Becky to agree to give me a chance, I'd be forever grateful." Simon shook his head, frowning ferociously. "I have no idea what I did to turn her off me so thoroughly, but if something doesn't give soon I'm going to lose it." Simon looked thoroughly miserable. "I'm pretty sure she's my mate."

Max mentally rubbed his hands together in anticipation.

Dana Marie Bell

"We'll see what we can do."

He ignored Simon's sideways glance, his Beta's slow grin too close to a smirk. "Emma sure grew up pretty, didn't she?"

Max tried his best, but he couldn't hold back his grin. "Yes, she did."

Simon nodded his approval. "She'd make a great Curana."

Max smiled. The idea of Emma as his Curana, ruling at his side, mated to him for all eternity appealed mightily. Not one to waste time when he wanted something, he began outlining his plan to win over their women.

Chapter Two

Emma turned the sign over to "Closed", pulled down the shade and locked the door, sighing in happy exhaustion.

The reverend had *loved* Simon's Madonna. She wondered if she was the only one who'd noticed the Madonna looked something like Becky. It had been the only thing that had given her the courage to approach Max; that and the look on Becky's face when she'd stared at Simon. Of course, the way Simon had followed Becky's every move hadn't hurt, either.

Max had been surprisingly easy to talk to, once she got over her initial shyness. His nearness had sent her heart pounding, tying her tongue in knots, as usual, until his ridiculous announcement that Simon wasn't for her.

Duh. Simon was for Becky.

She pulled the creamy, lacy shade down over the big picture window, effectively closing her in the twilight gloom of the shop. Becky had already rung out the register and was happily doing the accounts in the back, a pot of coffee and a huge container of Kung Pao chicken at her elbow while Emma finished closing down the front.

Emma loved this time of the evening. The streets were quiet, except for a few people heading either home or to their favorite restaurant for dinner. The soft light of early evening cast a glow over everything it touched, making it seem softer, more romantic. With a sigh, Emma headed into the back to gather up her coat and purse. With a wave to Becky, who waved her fork back with a grin, Emma slipped out of the back of the store.

"Emma."

Emma shrieked, staggering back and pulling her can of mace out of her pocket before realizing that the man standing in the shadows was Max. "God damn it, Max!"

"Sorry." He didn't sound all that sorry; he sounded like he was trying not to laugh. "Don't break out the grapefruit spoon just yet."

Her heart was still beating a mile a minute. She put the mace away and glared at him. "What?"

"Well, jeez, is that any way to greet someone who's here to help you?"

Putting her hand to her chest, Emma glared at him in the dim light. The son of a bitch *was* laughing at her. "Help me with what?"

"Getting Becky and Simon together, of course."

"Huh?" He looked entirely too smug as he moved closer to her.

"You want to get Simon and Becky together? I can help you with that." He picked up her arm and placed it through his, trapping her hand beneath his own. Suddenly he frowned and looked around. "Where is Becky, by the way?"

"She's still inside, working on the accounts," she answered absently, momentarily distracted by the feel of his arm under her own. It felt like it was hewn from rock, strong and solid and probably immovable.

His face blanked. "You came out here, at night, by yourself." It wasn't a question, it was a statement. He sounded like he couldn't quite believe his ears.

"Yeah. I do that every night. I'm parked right over there." She pointed with her free hand and gently tried to extract her other one from his suddenly iron grip. Becky lived in the apartment over the shop while Emma lived in an apartment in a complex on the other side of town. When Becky was done with the accounts, and her Chinese, she'd probably head upstairs to her tiny apartment and veg in front of her TV.

"You carry mace. I assume that means there's some crime in this area."

She nodded slowly. "There's crime everywhere, even here, what with the college nearby."

He was beginning to worry her. His face was still blank, but something about his eyes had changed. They glittered strangely, almost as if he were angry. She decided not to tell him why she carried the mace.

"Have you been attacked out here before?"

Emma winced and quickly tried to cover up the telltale sign by babbling. "It's perfectly safe out here, and Becky keeps an ear out for the sound of my car. Any minute now she's going to run out here ready to annihilate anyone who's bothering me, so you might wanna let up on the death grip!" Her wince was now one of pain as his hand squeezed hers in a vice-like grip.

He let go and stared down at her. She could have sworn his eyes were gold in the moonlight before he blinked, the illusion fading back into his normal blue as he prowled around her, circling her like a predator. "Who hurt you, Emma?"

"What is wrong with you?" Emma took back her hand and rubbed it, wondering if she'd have a bruise. She glared up at him, waiting for an answer.

Max's frown was fierce. "I want to know who hurt you, Emma. I want to know now."

The note of command in his voice was one she'd never heard from anyone before. He compelled her to answer him in a primal way, forcing her body back against the brick wall of the shop with his own, looming over her in a way that both frightened and soothed her. Part of her wanted to bow down submissively and answer anything he asked of her. It took every ounce of her will to sniff and reply, "I have no idea what you're talking about."

She saw the shock on his face as she turned her head away, dismissing him. She ducked under his arm and started walking towards her car, her back stiff, her chin high. "You know, not every woman appreciates the caveman routine. Why don't you try it out on Livia? I'm sure she'd appreciate it!"

She gasped as her body was yanked back into the hardness of his. She could feel him in every atom, as if he was deliberately imprinting himself there. "If I'm reacting this way, how do you think Simon will react when he hears Becky's here alone?"

Emma gulped. *Becky who?* Involuntarily her hand came up and grasped the arm around her waist, her nails digging in with pleasure at the strength in it.

"Um, I don't know?" God, her brains were completely scrambled if that was the best she could do. "Hit her over the head with a club and drag her off by her hair? Not that he'd have all that far to go; she lives over the store, for God's sake."

He leaned down, his lips tickling her ear, his hair brushing hers, blending with hers. His other arm came around her waist, pulling her tighter into his body. She felt completely surrounded. She could feel his erection against her lower back, hot and hard as an iron bar, and gulped. "Why do you carry mace, Emma?"

"Why do you care, Max?" She tried to ignore the feel of his lips as he—

Did he just kiss my ear?

"Emma. Tell me what I want to know."

"And you'll go away?" She tried to ignore the incredible feeling of him gently rocking her in his arms. *Yeah. That's it, I'm gonna start struggling any minute now. Any minute...*

"Hell, no." He laughed gruffly. He put his chin on the top of her head and continued to rock her. When her stomach rumbled embarrassingly beneath his hands, he stilled. "Emma? Am I keeping you from your dinner?"

"At this point, you're keeping me from my dinner AND late

night snack."

"Hmmm. In that case, I suggest we go out to eat. Maybe after I feed you you'll be more willing to tell me what I want to know." He sounded positively cheerful as he grabbed her hand, whirled her around and half dragged her towards his blue Durango.

"Gee, Captain Caveman, care to slow down? I didn't agree to go out to dinner with you."

He huffed out another laugh and opened the SUV's door. "In you go!" He gently lifted her into the seat. "Food. Then fight. Okay?" And with a smile he pushed her legs inside the SUV and shut the door.

She considered opening the door and hopping out, but part of her (okay, the majority of her) wanted to see what the hell Max was up to. Plus, hello! Dinner with Max! Could there be a downside to this?

She snapped on her seat belt as he got into the car. She hadn't enjoyed sparring with someone this much for a long time. "Don't think you're going to get what you want just because you buy me dinner."

"I wouldn't dream of it," Max purred, starting the SUV.

"Oh, boy," Emma muttered as Max, with another choked off laugh, drove out of the parking lot.

Max pulled the SUV up to his favorite restaurant, Noah's. He slid out, fully intending to open Emma's door and assist her down but she beat him to it, hopping out of the cab of his SUV with ease.

"Didn't your mother ever teach you to let the man open your door for you?" he asked, amused, as he followed her to the doors of the restaurant.

She rolled her eyes at him over her shoulder. "It's not like this is a date, Max." She flipped her ponytail back over her shoulder with a defiant flick of her wrist. "It's more like a kidnapping. With food."

He had to press his lips together to keep from laughing out loud. "Do you want my help with Simon and Becky, or not?"

"At the rate they're going we'll be ninety before they get together, so, yeah, anything that will help speed that up would be good."

He managed to reach the door before she did, opening it up and placing a hand at the small of her back as she sailed through. He kept that hand there, reveling in the feel of her strong, sleek back as he maneuvered her towards the hostess.

"Max! Wonderful to see you."

Max smiled what he called his social smile at Belinda Campbell, hostess at Noah's. He ignored her curious stare with ease, all of his attention focused on the woman beneath his hand.

"Table for two, Belinda."

"Coming right up, Max." Her full red lips curled up with a hint of contempt. "Business dinner, Max?"

Max looked up at Belinda through his lashes, his eyes flashing briefly gold in warning. "Pleasure."

Just as Emma said, "Business."

Max turned his attention back to Emma, noted the way her chin was tilted, and grinned. She was still pissed off about being "kidnapped". "Perhaps both."

Belinda's brows rose in disbelief as she gathered their menus. "Right this way."

As she sashayed across the restaurant to Max's preferred table, Emma whispered, "Gee, I get the feeling she doesn't like me."

"I wouldn't worry about whether or not Belinda likes you," Max whispered back as he helped her out of her light jacket and assisted her into her chair. Bending over, he whispered into her ear, delighted when she shivered. "Worry about whether or not *I* like you."

He sat himself across from her, enjoying the flush high on

her cheekbones. When she cleared her throat and snapped open the menu between them, he nearly growled in frustration. Watching her face, her expressions, the way her eyes lit up or went dreamy, was becoming an obsession.

The more time he spent with her, the more she fascinated him. She amused him with her wit, aroused him with a glance, frustrated him with her avoidance, and forced him to deal with her in a way very few people could. When he'd used his power to force an answer out of her in that alley, she'd actually walked away from him, back turned, head held high.

He still couldn't decide if he wanted to fuck her or spank her for that.

If he played his cards right, he'd get to do both.

"So, the seafood alfredo is supposed to be really good here," Emma croaked, her eyes glued to the dinner choices on the page in front of her rather than the dinner of choice sitting across from her.

After a brief hesitation, Max answered, his tone light and easy. "I'm more of a traditionalist myself. I think I'll go with the manicotti." He put his menu down, then gently pried hers out of her hands. "Salad or soup?"

"Um, salad, I think."

Max nodded with satisfaction. When the waiter appeared, he quickly placed their orders, going with wine to drink, chardonnay for her and merlot for himself.

She crossed her arms and glared at him. "What if I wanted something else to drink?"

"I thought, with your scare in the alley, you wouldn't mind something to help you wind down." He smiled, sensuous and predatory, nearly causing her to fall off her chair. "Relax, Emma. Enjoy the moment."

Without thinking, she blurted out the first thing that popped into her head. "Are you flirting with me?"

He blinked, then laughed, low and soft, taking her hand in his and gently stroking her palm with his thumb. She could feel the sensation of his fingers all the way down to her womb. "What do you think?"

"I think I'll need more wine," she deadpanned, completely flabbergasted.

Max Cannon was flirting. With *her*.

When Max chuckled, she tried prying her hand out of his, with no luck. Deciding to completely ignore his heated stare, she tried switching topics. "So, how do you plan on helping me with Simon and Becky?" She raised her brows in silent command, demanding he answer her while trying to hide the fact that her insides were melting into a puddle of aroused goo.

He leaned back with a sigh. "Actually, I was hoping you had one, and I could just lend a hand."

"I know Simon is going to the masquerade on Saturday night; do you know what costume he plans on wearing?"

Max frowned at her, thinking. "Technically, the costumes are supposed to be a secret."

"You're going as Zorro."

"Where did you hear that?"

"Livia and Marie were gossiping in the grocery store while I was there." Emma grimaced, remembering how Livia had treated her that day, with a mixture of false pity and contempt. Livia and Belinda were best friends, which meant that Livia would shortly hear of her little "business" dinner with Max, which meant Livia would be confronting her sometime in the near future. Emma sighed; dealing with Livia in a snit was never a fun time.

He shook his head. "Listening to gossip, Emma?"

His face was mockingly sad, the hint of laughter finally clueing her in. She could practically hear the little light bulb go off over her head. "Let me guess. *Simon* is Zorro."

"Got it in one."

"Wow. Livia's going to be disappointed." Emma tried to control her giggle, but it slipped out anyway.

"I think I can live with Livia's disappointment." Cradling his glass in one hand, her hand still firmly clasped in his other, Max took a sip of his wine, looking extremely pleased with himself. "Let me guess, she immediately bought a Spanish senorita?"

"Complete with Spanish comb, mantilla and fan."

Max confined himself to shaking his head as the waiter arrived with their food. After the waiter left, he let go of her hand so they could both eat. "So, what are you going as?"

His tone was casual, but his look was anything but. "I'm not sure. Becky and I haven't had a chance to go shopping yet."

Max's fork paused. He looked at her, his face filled with unholy amusement. "I have an idea."

Emma raised her brows in enquiry as she licked a bit of alfredo sauce off of her fork. "What idea?"

Max gazed at her mouth, his eyes darkening with obvious desire. "Hmm?"

Emma snapped her fingers at him. "What idea?"

He looked up, the heat in them nearly scorching her. "I have several ideas," he purred. "Which would you like to hear first?"

Emma opened her mouth, but nothing came out. With a startled snap, she shut it, turning her attention once again to her dinner to avoid the satisfied male smirk across the table.

After a few minutes of silence, Emma felt like she once again had the power of speech. "So, what's your idea?" When he looked at her like he wanted to devour her, Emma quickly clarified, "For the masquerade!"

"Becky goes as a female Zorro. If Becky's uncomfortable with that, we can have Simon change his costume so the two of them match."

Emma sat back in her chair, frowning in thought. "Becky's

been talking about doing a lady pirate—"

"No."

Emma blinked slowly, unsure whether or not to be pissed or amused at the firm order. "Okay," she drawled, "and your suggestion would be?"

"How about a saloon girl?"

Emma choked on her wine. "Um, saloon girl?"

"Yes. Simon can dress as a cowboy. Is there a problem with that?"

Emma bit her lip. "Maybe." She latched onto the first thing she could think of to change his mind; Becky would *never* wear the saloon girl outfit in public! She kept the picture of herself in that outfit all the way in the back on the mantelpiece. "Becky's self-conscious about her lack of...attributes."

Max looked confused. "Attributes?"

Emma could feel herself turning red. "Boobies," she hissed, looking around to see if anyone heard her.

Max choked. "She's worried about her breast size?"

Emma nodded, shushing him with her hand.

Max sighed. "Okay, how about a flapper? Simon can pull off a gangster look, I think."

Emma thought about dark, dangerous looking Simon and nodded. Suddenly she flapped her hands at him in excitement as she remembered a costume she'd seen on-line. "Oh! What about a fallen angel? I saw this really sexy number that would look incredible on Becky!"

"Have you ever looked at men's devil costumes? They're cheesy." Max frowned in thought. "No, we need something they'll both be comfortable in."

Emma grinned. "I saw bat wings he could wear over his shoulders. Put him in a trench coat with the wings, leather pants, bare-chested..." Emma waved a hand in front of her face, making Max scowl. "Believe me, women will pass out from the heat."

Max picked up her hand and stared into her eyes. "Really?" he asked softly. With careless elegance, he took her hand to his mouth, gently nibbling the back of her knuckles.

Once again Emma felt her cheeks heat. "Stop that!" She snatched her hand back and put it in her lap for safe-keeping. She cleared her throat and willed herself back into the costume conversation. "Becky has a romantic streak a mile wide. Maybe we can work with that."

"Hmm. How about Robin Hood and Maid Marian?"

"Done to death."

"Which leaves out paired vampires?"

"Yup. You know, maybe Lady Zorro isn't such a bad idea, after all. And even better, Becky knows a bit about fencing, so she'll be comfortable wearing a sword."

"She can use the sword on Simon if he doesn't get the message?"

"Something like that." Emma sat back with a sigh as the waiter appeared. Both decided on dessert, Emma going for the French silk pie and Max picking raspberry cheesecake. Max had coffee; Emma took another glass of wine.

"The only other thing Becky's interested in is Trinity from the Matrix. Think Simon wants to be Neo?"

Max shook his head. "As alluring as Becky would be in a leather cat suit, I think Simon would prefer Zorro."

"Okay. Then it's settled. I'll see about getting Becky's costume."

"Don't worry about it. I'll pick up Becky's costume when I pick up your costume."

Once again she was ready to throttle him. "And what costume will I be wearing?"

Max grinned. "It's a surprise."

"A surprise?"

Max picked up her hand and nibbled on her knuckles again, effectively shutting down her brain in the process. "Mm-hmm."

"Oh."

With a look of satisfaction, Max put her hand back down on the table. "Are you going to finish your dessert?"

Emma looked down at her pie, suddenly no longer hungry. She took a deep breath and asked the question she knew she was going to have to ask before they ever entered the restaurant. "How will I find you at the masquerade?" At his raised brow she added hastily, "If we're supposed to make sure Simon and Becky find each other, we need to make sure we can find each other too."

"Don't worry, it won't be a problem."

Max's purr sent a shiver through her. "Okay." Emma bit her lip, wondering if she should ask her next question. "Will your date mind you helping me out? I mean, I wouldn't want to make things awkward between you and your current girlfriend, whoever she is."

"Do you think I would ask you out to dinner if I was seeing someone, Emma?"

Emma raised her eyebrows, clearly amused. "Well, if you'd *asked* me..."

"*Emma.*"

"I mean, the food part of the kidnapping was kinda nice."

"Very well. Would I be trying to seduce you if I was seeing someone?"

Emma opened her mouth to make the comment that first sprang to her lips, but seeing the serious expression on his face she bit it back. Instead, she went with her second thought. "I don't know. You've been gone a long time. For all I know, you're gay."

It was Max's turn to open his mouth and have nothing come out.

Emma lifted her hand to the waiter. "Check, please."

"I'm not gay." Max stalked to the Durango, trying to decide if he was insulted or not.

Emma shrugged carelessly. "Bi then."

"Emma!"

He was forced to stop when she collapsed against the side of the car, giggling like a schoolgirl. The only thing she managed to gasp in between bouts of giggling was, "Oh, God, the look on your face!"

Max shook his head, wondering, knowing she had no idea how few people dared tease him. How the hell had he missed this woman all those years ago? He could have dated Emma back then instead of Livia. He'd have had Emma all these years, laughing at him, teasing him, driving him insane. The thought of his own blindness where she was concerned made him grit his teeth in frustration.

No more. Never again would he allow himself to do without Emma.

Crossing his arms, he leaned against the car door and waited for her to stop laughing. "You finished?" he asked indulgently, his heart beating a strange tattoo at the sound of her laughter.

She wiped the tears away with a final giggle. "Yeah, I think so."

"Good." With a swiftness only another Puma could match, Max snatched her close, bent down and kissed her. She barely had time to gasp.

That small gasp of surprise gave him immediate access to her mouth. He stroked inside her, slow and deep, just like he wanted to take her. He savored her taste, wine, chocolate and woman, and his head reeled. When her lips finally began to move against his, he moaned, his cock twitching like she was stroking him there with her wet heat. Her tongue dueled with his with a shyness that once again brought out his protective instincts. Without thought, he turned her so that her back rested against the Durango, his broad shoulders and back hiding her from the view of those in the restaurant.

No one but him would ever get to see her passion again.

He wanted to open the door, lay her down on the seat, and strip her naked. He wanted to be sheathed so far in her body she'd be able to taste him in the back of her throat. He wanted to mark her with his scent, his seed, and his teeth so badly he shook with it.

But they were on a public road, outside a very public restaurant; he couldn't do any of the things he wanted to do so badly, except...

With a snarl he lifted his mouth from hers and buried it against her throat.

"Max," she whispered in that soft, husky voice.

He suckled at the sensitive juncture of her throat and shoulder until she lay quiet and panting in his arms, her face buried in his shoulder. Gently he scraped the area with his teeth to prepare her. One hand slid down to cup her ass, reveling in the feel of her full curves; the other held her to him with a grip of iron, hard around her back. He had to concentrate not to dig his claws in and knead. He pushed between her legs with his knee until she was practically riding his thigh. With a rumbling purr he bit down, drawing blood and injecting her with the enzyme that would change her, marking her for all time as his. Her cry was muffled by his shirt; feeling her shivers he realized she was climaxing from the effect of the bite, riding his thigh as his essence and hers mingled.

He lapped at the small wound, not surprised to see it was already closing. With his mark on her and her orgasm, some of his own urgency left him. She was his.

Chapter Three

Emma was still reeling from whatever the hell it was Max had done to her with his bite when he gently helped her into the Durango. Her hands were shaking so badly she couldn't even put her seat belt on without help.

She'd never come so hard in all her life. And he hadn't even gotten her naked. She desperately tried to ignore the little voice that asked, *if it was that good upright and clothed, how would it feel with him naked and inside me?* She shivered.

"Are you okay?"

Emma tried to ignore the way her cheeks were heating, instead focusing on the purring amusement she could hear in his voice. "I'm fine," she squeaked. Clearing her throat, she tried again. "I, um..." Her voice trailed off as Max took her hand in his, placing it on his hard thigh. She had to clear her throat again, shaking her head violently to see if she could get her brain cells to start working again. "Ah, Saturday...when will you be picking up the costumes?"

Max smiled lazily. "I'll head to the costume shop tomorrow and get them, don't worry about it."

"When will you drop them off?"

Max was silent for a moment, obviously thinking. "Would Becky wear a costume from a secret admirer, or would it be better coming from you?"

Emma bit her lip, her attention once again focused on Becky's problem rather than the tall blond problem at her side. "I'm not sure. If I told her I'd gotten the costume, she might feel more comfortable about wearing it."

Max smiled. "We'll do that, then." His shoulders went back and his head tilted as he looked down at her briefly, the determination in his eyes completely wiping out the earlier humor. They seemed to gleam gold under a passing street lamp before he turned back to the road. "Now you're going to explain to me why you carry mace in your pocket." That odd note of command was back in his voice as he drove away from Noah's, demanding a reply.

Emma shrugged and ignored the urge to put her head down. "No reason, I just think a woman alone should carry protection and I don't like the thought of guns."

"Don't lie to me, Emma."

Emma's chin tilted up. "I'm not lying." She sniffed. "I don't like guns."

"Emma," he growled.

"Oh, pooh, you don't scare me, so stop growling," she yawned. She turned to look at him. "Anyway, should Becky carry her own rapier or would it be better to have her carry a toy?"

Max's jaw was moving, like he was grinding his teeth. "I can find out. Would you rather tell me, or let me go looking?"

"Wow," Emma breathed. "I've heard of that, but never actually seen it."

He looked at her quizzically out of the corner of his eye. "Seen what?"

"You actually talked through clenched teeth. I didn't think anyone really did that, you know?"

He pulled over and put the car out of gear. "Emma, why don't you want to tell me what happened?"

"Oh, gee, maybe because it's none of your business?"

His utter stillness surprised her; she wasn't even certain he breathed for a moment. When he turned his head with exaggerated slowness, she realized she'd finally succeeded in pissing him off. "Everything about you is my business, Emma."

She was shocked at his dangerous tone of voice. "Max?"

"You're mine, Emma, and I protect what's mine."

Her jaw dropped in disbelief. "What?"

He put the car back in gear, taking off with a squeal of tires. "You heard me."

"Uh, excuse me, but one kidnapping with food does not make Emma your property!"

"You bear my mark."

She blinked, totally confused. The feral light in his eyes hadn't lessened. The Durango was roaring as Mad Max drove like a bat out of hell for the outskirts of town. "What the hell are you talking about?"

"I bit you."

"And? You think you're the first guy to give me a hickey? *Shit!*" Emma made a grab for the door as Max took a turn at high speed.

"I don't think I need to hear about you and other men right now, Emma."

"Okay, okay! Could you slow down, please?"

Max took looked away from the road long enough to see her glaring at him. With a rough sigh he slowed down. "Look, I know you're confused."

"No, I think you're the one who's confused. Have you forgotten to take your medication today? Is that it? You turn into psycho-boy while in college?"

Max ran an impatient hand through his hair. "This isn't the way I wanted to do this," he muttered gruffly.

"Look, I promise I'm not jealous that the voices only speak to you, okay?"

Max pulled off the main road and onto a side road, shaking

his head. "Emma, we need to talk."

The tone of his voice made her sit back. He sounded...odd, like he knew whatever he had to tell her was something she wouldn't want to hear. "We talked. We talked all through dinner. Why are we out in the middle of nowhere to talk, by the way?"

He sighed. "Because there are certain things you may want to see that I can't show you in the middle of town."

"Uh-huh. I think your thing can go without being seen tonight."

The Durango jerked to a stop. There was a stunned silence for a moment. "I can't believe you just said that."

"I can't believe you can't believe it." Emma folded her arms under her breasts and scowled. "What's the matter, Max, never been turned down before?"

"Why are you being such a pain in the ass?" Max turned to her, frustration written all over his face. "I offer to help you, buy you dinner, kiss you senseless and bring you to orgasm, oh, no, don't bother lying about that either," he yelled as she opened her mouth, "and all you do is give me grief!"

"You felt me up without permission, kidnapped me, practically attacked me on the street, *bit me*, then act like a crazy man, drive like a bat out of hell out of town, and you want to know why I'm giving you grief? You're lucky I haven't broken out the mace, pal!"

"All I want to know is who hurt you!" he yelled at the top of his lungs.

"It happened two years ago, Max! What are you gonna do, hunt the guy down in jail and beat him up?"

"Ah-hah!" Max's finger waved in her face. "Someone *did* hurt you!"

"Argh!" Emma's hands flew into the air in frustration. "All right! I was mugged, okay? It was a college student, he's in jail, I had a broken wrist but he got a broken nose, end of story!"

Emma glared at him, her arms crossed over her chest. If he made one wrong move, hell, one wrong *sound*, she *would* mace him!

He grinned as the temper visibly drained out of him. "Did you give him as much grief as you've given me?"

"*More.*"

"God, you are so beautiful when you're pissed." He grabbed the back of her head and gave her a quick, hard kiss. "Okay, warrior princess, now that you've told me what I wanted to know I'll tell you what you want to know. Okay?"

Emma took a deep breath and debated whether or not to kiss him back or clobber him. "It better be good."

Max leaned in until her lips were once more beneath his. "And then I'm going to take you home and fuck you raw." As her eyes widened, he added, "And, baby, that will be better than good."

She was completely speechless as he got out of the SUV in a slow glide that had her thinking of silk sheets and heated skin. She gulped as he prowled around the hood of the Durango, moving like sex in jeans. His heated gaze never left her face.

"Oh, boy," she whispered as he opened her car door. He smiled when he saw her seat belt was still on.

He reached in slowly to unhook her seat belt, brushing his arm deliberately against her breasts. Her nipples hardened, rasping against his sleeve as he removed his arm just as slowly. His smile, sexy and satisfied, showed he'd felt it.

Suddenly, she had to know. "Max?"

"Hmm?"

She ignored the hand he held out to help her down. "Why me?" He looked confused. "I mean, you just came home three months ago and can still have any woman in Halle. Why are you trying to seduce *me*?"

"The real question in my mind is why I didn't try it sooner."

Emma stared into his eyes, reading regrets past and a determination that almost alarmed her. When he cocked his brow questioningly, she took his hand and let him help her out of the Durango. She took a deep breath to steady herself. "Okay, what's the big deal?"

Max's lips twitched.

Emma crossed her arms and tapped her foot. Her chin lifted as she waited for an answer.

Max reached out and gently stroked the bite mark on her neck. "Do you remember how you felt when I bit you there?"

Remember? My legs still feel like rubber. She nodded, doing her best not to let any of that show in her face while secretly locking her knees. She must not have succeeded because Max's smile heated. "That was me marking you as mine."

Emma rolled her eyes. "Didn't we have this discussion, Captain Caveman? A hickey does not make me yours."

"But in this case, it does." When Emma shook her head, he nodded. "There's a special enzyme that's only released when I bite someone. I released it into you, Emma. You're my mate."

"Doesn't it take three bites to turn me, Dracula?" She didn't even bother trying to keep the disbelief out of either her face or her voice.

"If I was a vampire, yes, it would." Max grinned, his eyes glinting oddly in the moonlight.

"Oh. So I'm going to start baying at the moon, then." She nodded sagely.

"No, baby, you're going to purr," he purred, licking his mark with a rough, raspy tongue.

Emma shivered. "You know, this has to be the oddest way a man's tried to get in my pants in ages."

He snarled warningly, the sound oddly cat-like and strangely familiar. "Didn't we say we wouldn't discuss you and other men?"

"Max, you're not making any sense. Now, let me call Simon

and we can discuss getting your Thorazine prescription renewed..."

Max strangled a laugh, lifting his head from her neck. "Look at my eyes, Emma."

She looked. Then she blinked. She opened her mouth to say something, *anything,* but nothing came out. His eyes had turned to pure molten gold, shining in the moonlight with an eerie luminescence that one only saw in the eyes of...cats.

"Contact lenses?" she asked weakly.

He shook his head and blinked, his eyes that quickly turning back to sunshine blue.

"You're a, what? Werecat?"

"Puma, actually."

"Puma," she repeated weakly, dropping back to lean against the Durango's door. "And you bit me, so now I'm going to roar at the full moon?"

He sighed. "Actually, Puma's can't roar, we're missing the necessary parts. Specialized larynx and hyoid apparatus, to be precise. And we can change at will, we aren't ruled by the moon."

"Oh." Emma's head was reeling. "Can you show me?"

Max frowned. "Show you?"

"Yeah." Emma straightened up, half terrified and half excited at the prospect of seeing him change. She waved her hand at him commandingly. "Change. Become a cat."

"Now?"

"Yeah, now! What, you need to wait for the full moon? I thought you said you could change at will?"

"Emma—"

"I mean, why tell me this at all if you weren't willing to, I dunno, *prove* it or something?"

"Emma—"

He was starting to sound all snarly again. "So c'mon, Lion-O, hop to it." She clapped, loud and sharp. "Chop-chop!"

"Emma!"

"What?"

"Have you ever seen a cougar in Levi's?"

"No."

"Neither have I." He looked like he couldn't decide if he wanted to laugh or yowl.

"You mean you'd have to..." Emma eyed his jeans speculatively.

"*Yes.*"

"Oh."

"And if my ass is naked, baby, you'd better believe yours will be too."

Emma put her hands on her hips and glared at him. "Isn't this why you brought me all the way out here, to show me your Incredible Cougar Act?"

"Puma."

"Whatever."

"No."

"Then why?"

"I figured if you screamed no one would hear you."

Emma blinked. "Gee, Max, you're all heart." He had the grace to blush. "So, because you bit me, and released your enzyme thingy in me, I'm going to change into a puma?"

Max nodded.

"Does it hurt?"

Max shook his head. His eyes had glued themselves to her neck, the hunger in them getting stronger by the second.

"When?"

"When what?" he asked absently, his hand drifting down to her arm before moving to stroke the bite mark.

"When will I change, Max?"

"I changed within the first forty-eight hours after I got bit."

Emma gasped in sympathetic horror. "Is that why you left

and never came back, Max? Because you got bit?"

"No, I was bit because I was next in line to be Alpha."

Emma shook her head. "Okay, now I'm *totally* confused. Maybe I've got food poisoning from my seafood alfredo and I'm actually in the hospital having hallucinations and heaving into a bucket," she muttered.

Max laughed as he focused once again on her face. "Want me to prove you're wide awake?" One hand snaked out, gently cupping her breast. His thumb raked across her nipple, shooting sparks straight down to her clit.

"Oh boy," Emma whispered. "Okay, I'm awake." She pulled reluctantly away from his caressing hand, determined to focus on the whole Emma-as-a-cat thing. With growing confusion, she rubbed at her forehead. "Can you please explain before my brain explodes?"

"Jonathon Friedelinde was Alpha before me. His daughter didn't show Alpha tendencies, so a competition was held to determine who was strong enough to be the next Alpha. Simon and I overheard Marie and some of her friends whispering about the competition and we both entered, not knowing what the hell we were getting into, or what the prize was. Jonathon forgot to make the contest Puma only, which I pointed out to him with great, annoying frequency until he relented and let us in." Max shrugged. "I came in first, Simon came in second. What really bothered some people was the fact that Simon and I were both still human when we won, against some who'd been Pumas since childhood."

"So you knew about the Pumas even before you entered the contest?"

"I was friends with Marie for years, saw her change once."

Emma stared at him in growing horror, thinking of all the ways a Puma could rip into a man. "You could have been killed!"

Max seemed completely unconcerned. "If it had been a duel to the death, yeah, we both would have died. Instead it was a test of endurance, intelligence and cunning, and probably the most fun either of us has ever had. And sometimes I think the only reason we won was because no one was allowed to shift."

"What was the test, paintball? Capture the flag?"

Max grinned. "Something like that, but a lot more complicated." Max reached out and wrapped his hand around the nape of her neck, seemingly unable to go for any length of time without touching her somehow. The gesture was surprisingly comforting. "Jonathon bit us both that night, to our surprise. I was twenty, Simon nineteen."

She reached up and gently stroked his cheek. "And confused as all hell, I'll bet."

He leaned into her caress, his eyes closing in pleasure. "We got used to it, and as soon as Jonathon stepped down I came home and named Simon my Beta."

"Beta?"

"Mm-hmm, my second-in-command."

"You said I'm your mate," Emma whispered as Max pulled her into his arms.

"My Curana."

"Your who-wadda?"

She could feel Max's laughter rumbling through his chest. "My Curana. Mate to the Alpha. It's supposedly a name derived from the Portuguese word for cougar."

"Oh."

Emma allowed Max to pull her head gently to his chest. She snuggled into his warmth, inhaling his unique scent, oddly comforted by his presence. "So," he rumbled, "we've done the dinner and fight." He leaned down and kissed the top of her head. "Come home with me, little Curana. I want to make love to you. I want to be inside you the next time you come."

Emma shivered as she heard the low, rumbling purr emanating from him. "Max?"

"Hmm?" His hand started to stroke up and down her back,

gently nudging her towards the SUV.

"Will I have to use a litter box?"

"Emma!"

Chapter Four

Max took his time driving her home. He wanted to savor having her next to him for as long as possible. "Do you open tomorrow, or does Becky?"

Emma turned towards him. She'd been far away, and he'd left her to her thoughts. After all, he'd dumped a remarkable amount of information on her in a short amount of time, and she'd handled it remarkably well. He was so proud of her he was ready to burst with it.

"Actually, I close tomorrow and Becky opens. Becks closes Saturday."

Max smiled in pure anticipation. "Good. We can take our time tonight. Adrian's got the early morning, I have late shift."

Her shiver of response was enough to send heat flooding his system.

"Emma?"

"Hmm?"

He was truly curious about her responses, so he asked, "You took everything I told you really well."

"I've never understood the woe-is-me thing. I mean, the hottest guy in town just told me he wants me badly enough to bite me and make me like him, and now he wants to drag me home and ravish me. I'm going to, what, run screaming into the night? Oh, no! I'm a Puma now! My life is over! Sob!" Emma rolled her eyes. "I mean, don't get me wrong, it's still freaking me out a bit, and it's probably going to cost me a fortune in bikini waxing, but it's not the end of my world."

Max nearly ran off the road. "You get a bikini wax?"

"Wouldn't you like to know?"

"Hell yes."

Her laughter filled up all the empty places inside him he hadn't even known were there.

"If Simon and Becky get together, does that mean he'll bite her?"

Max nodded. "If he wants to mate her, he'll have to bite her. And from what he told me, he wants to mate her."

Emma gave him a speculative look out of the corner of her eye. "How many women have you bitten?"

"As a mate, or to turn?"

Emma growled, startled at how possessive she felt. "How many mates do you have?"

"Only one, Curana." He took his hand off the steering wheel to stroke the back of her neck soothingly.

Emma still glared at him. "And how many women have you turned?"

"Two, not counting you."

"Oh?"

Max grinned at her possessive tone. "One as a favor to Jonathon, one because it was the only way I could think of to fix a problem she had. And, no, I can't explain it further than that; it's not my secret to tell."

"Did you have sex with the women you turned?" His slight wince was all the answer she needed. "Who?"

"Emma..."

"*Who?* Livia."

Max sighed. "Livia."

Emma groaned. "How did I know you were going to say that?"

"What can I say? I was young and stupid."

"Was she the favor or the problem?"

"Jonathon asked me to turn her. Maybe he thought, since Marie and I didn't hit it off, that Livia would turn out to be my mate."

"Especially since the two of you were already doing the mattress mambo?"

Max flushed. "We broke up soon after that."

Emma remembered the circumstances of the break up, and winced. "So it had nothing to do with how she insulted me," she muttered, not thinking about how that would sound.

"It had everything to do with how she insulted you." When she looked at him, confused, he smiled. It wasn't pleasant. "She was very good at hiding how much of a bitch she really is. I broke up with her that night over what she said about you, and what she wanted to do about Becky's punch stunt." He shuddered. "She's been on my tail since I got back into town. So far nothing I've done has gotten her to leave me alone." Max's smile was cheerful. "But I have the feeling you won't have that problem."

Max turned into his driveway and pressed the button to open the garage door. He lived in a lovely historic house his parents had left to him when they retired to Florida. The home was craftsman in style, built early in the twentieth century, and had been lovingly restored by the entire Cannon family. The dark gray gable roof was set off by rich mahogany brown shingles and bright white trim work, with rich red fieldstone set around the base of the house. The front had that beautiful pillar and post design, with a covered porch that wrapped around to the left side of the house. The elder Cannons had added on a two-car garage and utility room to the right side of the house. They'd made the extension look like just another part of the house by having the garage entrance on the side rather than the front. The windows along the front matched the rest of the house. Emma had never been inside, but she'd always admired it from afar.

Max pulled into the garage and turned off the Durango. He reached up and pressed a button, closing the garage door behind them. He turned to her with a solemn joy that startled her.

"Welcome home, Curana."

Emma opened her mouth to reply, but he was already getting out of the SUV. She hopped out on her own, ignoring the amused shake of his head. He waited for her to round the hood of the car before opening the door into the utility room.

She started to step through the door but he startled her. With a swift move he picked her up, ignoring her gasp of surprise. He carried her into the utility room. "Get the door, will you?"

She reached out with a foot and kicked the door shut.

He laughed. "The other one."

She leaned down and opened the door into the rest of the house.

He carried her into a kitchen straight out of her fantasies. It was laid out in a u-shape with simple arts and crafts style cherry cabinets with silver handles. Stainless steel appliances gleamed in the gentle light Max had left on, their lines set off by the beautiful black granite countertops. Cherry hardwood covered the floors from the kitchen into the breakfast area off on the right where a round table and four Shaker style chairs sat. The windows in the breakfast nook ran nearly floor to ceiling, with a simple geometric design set into the top panel. He'd painted the walls a rich sage green and the traditional trim around the windows a bright white.

Without pausing, Max carried her through the kitchen, past the breakfast nook and into the great room. The sage green walls, cherry floors and white trim carried through into this room. A vaulted ceiling with skylights gave the room the feeling of being huge. A large reddish brown leather sofa dominated the great room. It rested on a bold area rug done in a geometric pattern of reds, blacks and greens. It faced a set of built-in cherry cabinets along one wall that doubled as the entertainment center with bookshelves on either side. The fireplace, on the opposite wall, was decorated with the same fieldstone that was outside the house. She caught a glimpse of the huge double doors at the front of the house before Max carried her past the fireplace down a short corridor and through another door.

A king size cherry wood sleigh bed dominated the room. It was covered in a crazy quilt of geometric designs in bold blues, reds and blacks. He'd painted the walls a warm terra cotta, with framed black and white prints by Escher, whimsical brain twisters that would normally capture her attention but, now, barely registered.

She could make out the master bathroom through the open doorway, barely. The cabinets in there appeared to match the ones in the kitchen, but the room was dominated by the massive oval tub, surrounded by rich, highly polished tumbled stones inset with black ceramic diamonds. The same tumbled stone was on the floor. The room had been painted a dark red wine color.

Emma realized Max had stopped moving. Looking up at him, she found him staring down at her with a quizzical look. "Well?"

Emma blushed. She'd been rubbernecking in Max's house, trying to take in everything at once. "It's incredible."

He smiled with satisfaction. "If there's anything you want to change, you'll have to let me know." Gently he placed her on the quilt. "This is now as much your house as mine."

Emma's mouth fell open as he toed off his shoes and socks. "You're kidding me, right?"

Max began unbuttoning his shirt, diverting her attention from his whole "*Mi casa es su casa*" attitude. "I was in Simon's shop when you called about the Madonna, you know."

"Oh. Really?" she replied absently. She could barely speak as Max unveiled the finest chest it had ever been her privilege to see. It was lightly sprinkled with light brown hairs, trailing down his stomach to point directly into his pants. Dark brown nipples peeped out from the hair, tempting her into some very sinful thoughts.

"Yes, I was. And you know what?"

Emma didn't know her own name; Max was unbuttoning his jeans. "Um, nope."

"You live up to your voice," Max purred as he slipped his jeans down his legs.

"Urgh," Emma choked, "naked." She could feel her eyes bugging out of her head. Max went commando. A sinful buffet of man-flesh was laid out before her in one single sweep of his hands. She didn't know whether to sigh or to sob.

"Yes, I am." Max laughed huskily. "Now it's your turn."

Emma bit her lip, a sudden attack of shyness nearly paralyzing her. Max didn't know it yet, but he'd be her first, and from the look on his face she'd better tell him soon.

"Max?" Emma sat there, her hands clenched in her lap, her gaze riveted to his cock. The thing looked huge, all veined and red, and pointed straight at her. A small drop of liquid seeped from the slit. It twitched a salute to her rapt attention.

"Yes, Emma?"

Her gaze lifted to his; unknown to her, they'd turned pure, molten gold. "You remember the talk of other men?"

He growled low in his throat and crawled onto the bed.

"Eep," she whispered, lying down as he prowled up her body.

"You were saying?" he whispered huskily as he settled his naked body between her thighs. He brushed against her cheek with his lips, a caress so soft she barely felt it. It sent a shiver down her spine. Those same lips continued their incredible journey, trailing down the side of her neck to settle on the bite he'd given her outside the restaurant. Goose bumps raced up and down her arms as he moved his hips in a sinuous motion, brushing his naked cock against her mound.

"Um, there weren't," she squeaked, unconsciously arching up into his body as he scrapped his teeth along his mark.

"Weren't what?" he muttered, one hand moving up to start sliding her camisole up her stomach. He paused long enough to caress her there, trailing fire in his wake.

"Any other men."

His hand stopped.

His mouth stopped.

His hips stopped. She was really sad when his hips stopped.

"You're a virgin?" His voice sounded oddly strangled.

"It's not a crime to be one, you know. I'm not the Oldest Living Virgin, or anything. It's not like I'm in the Guinness Book of World Records," she babbled. "Besides, I've done other things...oh!" His hands had started moving again, with a swiftness that startled her. Her camisole was toast as he ripped it literally from her body, his claws barely scrapping her skin, sending shivers of need once again down her spine.

Claws?

Emma had barely registered the fact that Max had used his *claws* to ruin her favorite shirt when he started working on her jeans. "No! Bad kitty!" She slapped him on the top of his head, determined to save at least some of her wardrobe.

He lifted his head, his eyes golden and burning, a rumbling sound emanating from his throat as he pinned her hands above her head. Emma thought about struggling, but something about the way he looked had her lying passively. "You're a virgin."

Emma blinked, unsure how to respond. "Duh."

Max stared down at her, his eyes narrowing as he studied her features as if seeing her for the very first time. "No man has ever touched you."

She thought about telling him about the make-out sessions

her one and only boyfriend had talked her into, the oral sex they'd indulged in a few times, but decided that discretion was the better part of valor. Jimmy was a nice guy, and deserved to live. "Again. Duh."

"No man will ever touch you again."

Emma studied granite-like features above her. "Even you?" The growl deepened. She sighed, inexplicably happy to hear that sound. "Okay." She rolled her eyes. "Duh." She grinned. "By the way, Lion-O, that was my favorite shirt."

He looked down. "Damn, Emma."

"What?" She looked down, expecting to see something odd, like very dried alfredo sauce decorating one boob or something. Instead she saw the pale pink lace bra she'd put on that morning, the one that was completely see-through. It helped give her confidence to feel the sexy lingerie against her skin, so much so she'd replaced all of her old undies with the lacy stuff.

From the look, and feel, of things, Max definitely approved.

Max switched her wrists into one hand. The other trailed down her body to her jeans, undoing the snap and zipper with ease. "Lift your ass, Emma," he commanded. She obeyed without thinking, shifting so he could ease her jeans down her legs.

He hissed out a breath at the sight of the pale pink lace panties that matched the bra. Underneath, she was hairless. "A full Brazilian," he sighed.

"Uh-huh."

He moved his hand and began petting her over her panties, cupping her intimately. "Mine," he sighed. His golden eyes bored into hers, a silent command in them. "Keep your hands where they are."

"Why?" Emma complied as Max moved his hand slowly from her wrists, trailing down her arm to the side of her breast.

"Because I'm not ready for you to touch me yet. I want this first time to be yours."

"I'd rather it was ours." She gasped as his hand gently embraced her breast. His thumb strummed gently over her nipple, causing it to peak under the pink bra.

"Trust me, Curana. The pleasure will be ours." Slowly, oh so slowly, Max lowered his head. His tongue snaked out and licked over her nipple through the lace, watching her reactions as she gasped softly. "I'm going to get you naked now, Emma." He lifted his head from her breast. "Leave your hands where they are. Remember, Emma."

Max gently pulled the cups of her bra down, resting her breasts on the lowered cups until they looked like an offering laid out on pink lace. He bent and suckled one nipple into his mouth, stroking it with his tongue until she writhed against him, panting and moaning in need. He switched to the other nipple, suckling and nipping with such force it was nearly painful. Emma panted, damn near coming from the sensation.

He pulled away from her. "Uh-uh, little Emma," he purred. "No coming unless I'm in you, remember?"

She groaned as he moved down her body. His hands went to her lacy panties, thumbs hooking under the band. With slow deliberation he pulled them from her body, slowly exposing her to his hot gaze. "You were right, Emma, to stop me before." He looked up with a grin that made her moan. "I'd forgotten how much fun it is to play with my food."

And with that, Max began a sensuous torture that had her writhing with need.

He began by slowly nibbling his way up her left leg, starting at her ankle and ending at her inner thigh, right next to her pussy lips. He then switched sides, once again kissing and nibbling his way up her leg until she was practically begging him to eat her.

When she felt the first hot swipe of his tongue on her pussy she came, screaming his name. With a purring rumble, he continued to lap at her until her orgasm subsided, the vibrations making the orgasm that much more intense.

"Naughty, Emma. I wasn't inside you."

"Whoops." Emma looked down at him with a lopsided grin.

"I'm pleased you've left your hands in place, though. So maybe, this time, I'll forgo punishing you."

Emma blinked. "And once again, Captain Caveman rears his ugly head," she gasped. Max had started rubbing her clit in oh-so gentle circles, bringing her arousal back to near peak. "Max," she sighed, her hips moving in time to his hand.

"Do you want to come, Emma?" Max asked, the heat in his gaze damn near burning her.

"Yes," she sighed again, licking her lips as she stared down at him. "Please, Max."

He shivered slightly. Then his rough tongue was once again on her clit, licking and nibbling as she gasped and moaned beneath his mouth. His finger had moved to her opening, circling slowly until finally settling inside her. He stroked her gently, matching his rhythm there to the movements of her body. His finger curved slightly, and Emma saw stars.

"Come, Emma," he whispered, using his thumb to stroke her clit as his finger picked up speed. She didn't even mind when he inserted a second finger; she was too busy seeing stars as her climax hit her with the force of a freight train.

When she came down from it, Max was gently stroking her soaking wet pussy. She opened her eyes to find he'd moved so that he lay next to her. With a satisfied smile, she pulled him down, kissing him lovingly. She could taste herself on his lips, and it added an element of eroticism she'd never felt before.

"I'm going to take you now, Emma."

Emma shivered. She licked her lips, her body tensing slightly with nerves. "Okay."

"Shhh." He kissed her again, gentle and loving as he moved his body between her thighs. "I will never willingly hurt you, Emma."

"I know," she whispered, awed. This was Max, the only man

who'd ever held her heart, and he was claiming her for his own. She gently clasped his shoulders as he began to slowly invade her body, his cock stretching her open. The slight burning pain caused her to dig her nails in. She bit her lip and forced herself to relax as much as humanly possible while slowly being invaded by a red-hot iron bar.

"So tight," he gasped as he finally seated himself all the way inside her.

"Were your parents psychic?" Emma asked, gulping a little at the sting of his invasion.

Max frowned down at her confused. "No, why?"

"Are you sure? I mean, with a name like Max Cannon—"

"*Emma!*"

"Sorry, but from the feel of things that can't be a small caliber you've got shoved up there, boyo."

Max leaned down, resting his forehead against hers as he started to laugh shakily. "I love you, Emma."

"Oh boy," she breathed as he slowly began to move.

"Is that all you can say?" He was grinning down at her knowingly, as if he had no doubts as to what her answer would be.

Emma felt all her old insecurities come to the fore, even as his cock had her gasping in pleasure. "Are you sure?"

He stopped, leaning down to kiss her thoroughly. "I'm sure."

She stared into his face, reading the love there, the heat, the need. With deliberate slowness she raised her arms above her head and grasped the headboard. She lifted her head out and to the side in an instinctive show of submission, giving him her throat, accepting him fully. "Fuck me, Max."

Max lost control for the first time in his adult life. His teeth bit into his mark as he began pounding into her body with little finesse. He fucked her into the mattress, and she loved every minute of it. She wrapped her legs around his waist and held on for dear life as he once again sent her over the edge, her climax so strong she nearly passed out. The clenching of her body was enough to bring him off, his semen pouring into her in a tidal wave of wet heat. With a gasp that was almost a sob he collapsed on top of her, his breathing harsh and uneven, his heart pounding.

"I love you too," she whispered, cuddling him close as he began to purr.

Chapter Five

Max woke with the most incredible feeling of well-being he'd ever experienced in his life. Emma was curled up against him, his arms around her protectively as she slept. Her luscious backside was nestled firmly against his morning erection, a situation Max totally approved of. Her scent was all over him, as his was all over her. His hips bucked forward involuntarily and he moaned as her hot, slick flesh stroked the head of his penis. God, he hoped she liked morning sex. And afternoon sex. And evening sex...

"Morning, Max." Her voice was amused, rough from sleep and sexy as hell.

"For the love of God, please tell me you aren't sore," he whispered, practically begging.

Emma leaned up on one elbow, twisting around to stare at him. She wound up partially on her stomach, and Max's eyes immediately zeroed in on that incredible ass of hers. "Not much, but honestly, other...issues...need to be taken care of first." She blushed slightly.

Max looked at her uncomfortable face and grinned. "Bathroom's that way."

She was up and out of the bed before he'd finished pointing, sprinting naked across the room. Max leaned back and enjoyed the brief view he was given before the bathroom door shut behind her. He snickered when he heard her sigh of relief. He was grinning as he climbed out of bed and snagged his jeans.

"You want coffee?" he yelled through the bathroom door just as she flushed.

She opened the door, peeking around the edge. "You have tea?"

He thought for a moment, frowning, running a mental inventory of what his mother may have left behind on her last visit. "I have Darjeeling, Earl Grey and Spiced Chai."

"Spiced Chai, sweet, with cream?"

"Coming right up. Borrow my toothbrush; we'll pick up your stuff from your apartment later today." He ignored her sudden frown and walked out of the room. He slipped his jeans on once he was in the hall and made his way to the kitchen. He whistled cheerfully as he began making her tea and his coffee, setting both machines to working as he contemplated what to make his prickly little mate for breakfast. He pulled out the eggs, knowing he could at least make scrambled eggs and toast without looking like a total idiot in the kitchen.

"You owe me a shirt, Lion-O."

He turned, his cock hardening as he saw his shirt on her. It practically swallowed her whole, and she looked damn fine in it. It didn't hurt that she wasn't wearing anything beneath it. Her tousled hair and kiss-swollen lips completed the just-fucked look.

Then he looked into her eyes and nearly dropped the eggs.

Her eyes gleamed gold, full of heat and passion. He felt his own flare in response, his gaze raking her from head to toe as he prowled towards her, the eggs left behind on the counter. "Emma," he purred, wrapping his hands around her waist.

"Hmm?" She stroked his chest with her small hands, fingers tangling in the hairs on his chest.

He leaned down and lapped at his mark, groaning when she bared her throat. "You're changing."

"What?" she asked absently, her hands moving towards the

73

snap of his jeans. "You taste so good," she whispered, licking his neck with a tongue turned raspy.

Max shivered. "Emma," he groaned as her teeth nipped at his neck. Her canines had grown in. "You're changing, sweetheart."

"Thought you said I had two days," she muttered as her hand worked its way inside his pants. With a happy sigh she stroked his shaft, pulling it out of his jeans to run her thumb over the head.

Max moaned, ready to push her down on the table and take her swift and hard. That could be a problem if she shifted before they were done. "Emma, you have to stop."

"Who says?" She knelt in front of him and took his cock in her mouth, sucking lightly on the head, her tongue rasping along the slit. "Mmm, you do taste good." She licked her lips, teasing and seductive.

Max stared down at her, fighting his own instincts. He wanted to thrust between her lips, hold her head in place while he fucked her there, make sure she swallowed every last bit of him.

But she was changing. It was up to him to act responsibly He was Alpha, it was his job to protect her, and...

She'd wrapped her lips around his cock again, licking up and down the shaft, her head bobbing in a steady rhythm that would soon have him coming down her throat. With a snarl, the Puma took over as he grabbed the sides of her head and held her in place for his pleasure.

"That's it, baby, use your tongue," he growled, watching her pleasure him as his hips moved slowly, sliding his shaft between her lips. She curled that wicked tongue slightly, rasping it against the throbbing vein, catching the flared edge.

One of his hands moved to the back of her head, gently bunching her hair in his fist in a show of dominance as the Alpha in him took over. He could feel chills run up and down his spine as his climax neared, but he kept his rhythm steady, trying not to choke her while forcing her to take everything she could. He crooned to her, telling her how wonderful her hot mouth felt against him, how beautiful she was to him.

He moved the hand not holding her hair to just under her chin as he felt her incisors turn sharp. "Suck, Emma," he commanded, his power flowing free as he lost control, his climax almost on him.

She gave him a teasing flick of her tongue before she obeyed, her cheeks hollowing out as she sucked on the head of his cock, pulling the orgasm out of him as she increased her purr at the same time. He erupted into her mouth, back arched, head thrown back as his cry of completion came out more like the primal snarl of his Puma. His mate took everything he gave her, swallowing him down as he held her head in place.

With a final, rumbling purr, she licked him clean then stood. She gently tucked his softening cock back into his jeans, zipping and snapping them shut before she gently patted his chest.

"You still owe me a shirt, Lion-O." With a wicked grin, she sauntered off to the bedroom, her ass swaying beneath his shirt. Max grinned, eggs forgotten, and followed her into the bedroom.

Emma felt edgy all day. She'd had yet another fight with Max, insisting on going to work that afternoon and giving Becky her allotted evening off. She could feel the Puma crawling under her skin, trying to break free; Max had warned her what could happen if she allowed the change to occur without him present. Like she wanted to change into a mountain lion in the middle of her store! He'd grumbled all the way to her apartment, the entire time she changed clothes, and all the way to Wallflowers. By the time he dropped her off, she was ready to bite him, and not in a good way. She felt caged, pacing the storeroom when she wasn't waiting on customers. She'd managed to keep her eyes from changing, a trick Max had taught her quickly when he realized she wouldn't give in. He'd also told her he would be picking her up after work. She agreed with him that she was in no condition to drive.

She barely made it through the day, closing an hour early and leaving the receipts for Becky. She needed more room to pace, more room to...run.

Emma walked the six blocks to Max's office. Both Adrian and Max were there, as was the receptionist, Lisa Pryce. Emma waved hello to a puzzled Lisa before sitting in the waiting area, tapping her foot impatiently.

Adrian Giordano walked out of one of the examination rooms, talking quietly to Livia Patterson. She looked thoroughly disgusted, completely ignoring the hunky doctor as he tried his best to get her to pay attention. Adrian spoke to the receptionist as Livia, without even a glance at Emma, flounced out of the office.

"Emma?"

"Hi, Adrian." Emma smiled tightly. "Was Livia upset she got you instead of Max?"

Adrian grinned. "So Max told you about her attempts to get to him?"

Emma had a hard time not baring her teeth. She wanted to rip Livia's heart out. It took all of the self-control she had to keep her eyes brown instead of gold. "Yup."

Adrian coughed, turning away abruptly. "Max? Emma's here."

"Emma?" She could hear his muffled voice from behind one of the examination room doors. It opened abruptly and a frowning Max stepped out, followed by the elderly Mrs. Roman. "Why didn't you wait at your shop for me?"

Emma grinned at him, her expression tight, her body strung out. Her foot jiggled impatiently. It felt like the worst caffeine high she'd ever been on. Her skin itched and crawled, her gums ached, and her eyes hurt with the effort to keep them brown.

"Oh." Max sighed and turned to Mrs. Roman. "Here's your prescription, and a copy for your records, Lena. Why don't you have Lisa help you pick out a pair of frames? We can see to it that they're sent off to the lab first thing in the morning."

Mrs. Roman grinned wickedly. "Hot date, Max?" She waggled her eyebrows at him when he merely smiled smugly. "Taking Emma out, eh?"

"Yes, ma'am." Max smiled and winked at Emma, who had to bite her lip to keep from snarling.

"Well, you take good care of her, you hear? From what Jimmy said, she's a keeper." Max's grin froze on his face. "You mark my words, if you haven't snapped her up by the time he gets back this way, he'll steal her back out from under you."

"Who's Jimmy?" Max asked. His tone was pleasant, his expression wasn't.

"Jimmy was Emma's boyfriend until about four months ago when he had to leave town to deal with some family issues. Rumor has it he's headed back this way any day now. Who knows? He might give you some competition!"

Emma groaned and put her head in her hands as Max's attention swung back towards her. "We broke up two months before he left town, Mrs. Roman."

"Not to hear Jimmy tell it, you didn't," Mrs. Roman replied with a laugh.

"I'll just have to make sure Jimmy knows Emma's taken." Max's hands went to his hips as he took in Emma's red cheeks and guilty eyes.

Mrs. Roman cackled with glee; she was the biggest gossip in town, and Max had just handed her a prime piece to chew on.

"Can you do me a favor, Mrs. Roman? Can you wait to tell anyone that Emma and I are together until the masquerade party on Saturday? We want to surprise a few people." Max smiled down at the elderly woman, using all of his not inconsiderable charm.

"Those few people being Olivia Patterson and Belinda Campbell?" When Max merely shrugged, Mrs. Roman grinned. "Max, anything that will make Livia and Belinda squirm is okay by me. But..." she wagged her finger under his nose, ignoring his little boy grin, "...you have only until Saturday!"

She was so happy she forgot to wait around and pick out the frames for her new glasses, heading straight out the door with an absent wave good-bye. Emma knew the story of Max's declaration would be all over town by mid-afternoon Saturday. She stared right at a smug Max, torn between laughing and screaming. "Happy, Captain Caveman?"

Adrian's choked laugh and Lisa's snort of amusement broke the tie. Emma laughed up at Max, who was still grinning like a schoolboy.

"You okay to close up, Adrian?"

"Can you give me just five minutes before you head out? I have a question about Mr. Davis."

Max looked over at Emma, who was practically dancing in her seat, and back at Adrian. He nodded, clearly torn. "Hey, Emma? Can you wait in here for me? I'll just be a few minutes, okay?"

Emma huffed and followed him into an examination room. He kissed her quickly and closed the door behind him. The room was typical of eye exam rooms everywhere, with a black examination chair and all of the equipment surrounding it. A desk sat in one corner of the room off to the side of the chair. A mirror on one wall showed the letter "E" when she turned the lights off.

Emma paced, her skin twitching. She rubbed her arms briskly, trying not to scratch. She felt like she could peel her own skin off. Sure enough, when she looked down at her hands she saw claws where her nails should be.

"Ah, hell." She ran to the mirror and looked in it. Gold eyes stared back at her. She licked her lips, feeling the edges of fangs as her tongue went back in her mouth. Scenes from *Teen*

Wolf were going through her mind as she desperately tried to stay human.

She gave up when the fur started sprouting.

Max entered the examination room, not terribly surprised to see the Puma in his examination chair. The cat was sitting in a pair of blue jeans and a red lightweight sweater, the same clothes Emma had been wearing when she entered the office. It looked adorably pissed.

Max leaned against the doorjamb and sighed, desperately trying not to laugh. "I told you not to go into work today."

She snarled at him. She kept snarling at him as he untangled her from her clothes. She quietly snarled at him as he led her to his SUV, which he pulled in behind the office so he could sneak her into it. She snarled the whole way out of town.

She was still snarling at him when he led her into the woods. She stopped snarling when he got naked. When he changed, she began purring.

With a playful flick of her tail she invited him to chase her.

She purred loudest of all when he caught her.

Chapter Six

"You expect me to wear that?" Emma looked at the picture on the bag of the most incredibly X-rated (okay, maybe high-R) pirate outfit she'd ever seen. All the model needed was a half-naked pirate next to her to make the picture complete. The frilly, lacy cream skirt hit the girl just before full exposure; God forbid if the poor thing tried to sit, she'd be showing her assets to everyone in the room! The girl's breasts spilled out of the matching top, helped along by a burgundy waist cinch with an attached overskirt. The cinch and skirt combo was embroidered in an elaborate design done in gold. Lace bell sleeves allowed her hands freedom while promising to drip into everything. The feathered hat matched the cinch, with the edges decorated in creamy lace. No less than four feathers peeked around the rim of the hat. Tall black boots with three-inch heels and a remarkably lifelike saber completed the outfit. If Max thought she'd wear the lacy thigh-high stockings he'd bought, he was in for a rude awakening. The stockings definitely took the outfit into X-land.

Max's innocent expression didn't fool her for a moment. There was simply no way he could hide the heat in his eyes. "It matches my costume. Besides, the model in that thing has to be taller than you. The skirt should hit you mid-thigh."

"Oh, yes, that makes it *so* much better."

They were sitting in Max's breakfast nook, finishing the last of their coffee. Emma needed to open the store that day; Becky would close at five. Emma planned on handing Becky her costume just before she left for the day, leaving Becky no option but to wear what Max had provided since the masquerade was that night. Although, looking at the costume he'd chosen for her, she was a little leery about the costume he'd gotten for her friend. "Who picked out Becky's costume?"

"Simon."

"Oh boy. Can I see the costume she's probably going to throw at my head?"

Max grinned and reached into the bag he'd brought to the table that morning. He pulled out an off-the-shoulder black lacy top with long sleeves that were tight at the arms and flared out at the wrists. Next he pulled out a black skirt. It was short and flaring, the kind that would fly up if you spun in place. On top of the skirt he laid out a leather belt with a silver belt buckle, a swordsman's belt meant for a real rapier. Tall black boots almost identical to Emma's, a black bandito hat, black cape and black mask completed the outfit. Where Emma's outfit was blatantly sexy, Becky's was sexy in an understated way. Her skirt would probably hit her mid-thigh as well, but in all other respects she was almost modestly covered, especially since it was obvious the cape would hit her at her knees, thus covering her dignity in back. Unlike Emma's outfit, which took dignity and kicked its ass to the curb with a cheery wave and a fond farewell.

"Wow. I'm impressed. I should have let Simon pick my outfit, too."

Emma grinned at the sound of Max's low-pitched, possessive growl.

"Okay, so..." Emma folded her hands on top of Becky's costume, "...where's my outfit for the party? I mean, I have to assume this outfit is for, like, role-playing at home or something."

"I am going to show the entire world exactly how sexy I find you." His hands covered hers, both soothing her and locking her into place. Gold flecks danced in the blue of his eyes and Emma shivered. "No one will doubt how much I want you. I plan on having every single male there drooling with envy that I'm the one who has you. I want every female there to hate you on sight."

"Just being with you will do that," Emma muttered.

Max grinned. It wasn't pleasant. "I want Livia to grind her teeth into powder when she sees you on my arm. And then I want us both to smile at her and wish her well after she bows down to you."

"Damn, Max, you should have been a girl. That's totally bitchy."

He picked up one of her hands and kissed the palm, sending more shivers of heat through her. "And then tomorrow we finish moving the rest of your stuff in."

Emma had given in on moving in with him just the night before. She hadn't been to her apartment since the night Max bit her, other than to pick up a few changes of clothing, her toiletrics, her full-length mirror that she refused to live without, and her makeup. Her red PT Cruiser had finally made its way to his garage last night, too, and was now nestled next to Max's Durango. He'd frowned darkly over the fact that it was a convertible, muttering something about knives and maniacs, but he'd just have to learn to live with it. Emma loved her car, and her car loved her.

"I'll make you a deal." He'd never go for it, and then she'd get to change costumes. A win-win situation, as far as she was concerned.

"Shoot."

"I'll wear the costume if we take my car to the party."

"Done." Emma's jaw dropped. He hated her car. He'd made it clear he absolutely hated it, but he hadn't even hesitated. He stood, reached out with a finger and shut her mouth. "You're going to be late for work, sweetheart."

"Oh shit!" Emma looked at her watch and bolted for the

garage, leaving the costumes behind.

"Emma!"

She turned in the doorway, grabbed the bag he held out with Becky's costume in it and raced out, doing her best to ignore his chuckles. She shoved the bag in the car, opened the garage door and darted back inside.

Max turned, confused as she barreled back into the house at Mach speed. He managed to catch her as she threw herself at him, wrapping her legs around his waist. She pulled his startled face close and kissed him soundly. "Bye!" she yelled as she dropped out of his hold and ran back out the door again, the picture of his stunned, happy face and silly grin staying with her the entire way to work.

"You expect me to wear that?" Becky stared at the costume Emma had laid out on the Victorian sofa in Wallflowers with something akin to horror. "Emma, I thought Max was Zorro. Are you sure you want me to match his costume?"

Emma grinned; Becky was one of the few people who knew about her hook-up with Max. "Max isn't going as Zorro. That was a smokescreen he threw up to keep Livia at bay. Trust me, you won't match Max tonight."

Becky paled as Emma's slight emphasis on Max's name registered. "Tell me Simon isn't going as Zorro."

"Simon isn't going as Zorro," Emma deadpanned, already inching her way towards the door.

"Emma!" Becky shrieked, totally horrified.

Emma stopped. "Becky, you've been dancing around your attraction for Simon for months, probably years! And you know what? I think he's just as attracted to you as you are to him! So, why don't you go for it?"

"You know the type of women Simon goes for! Hell, I know for a fact where he's been. You think I want to boldly go where everyone else has gone before?"

"Simon hasn't dated in months, Becks."

"That's a lie, Emma. He went out with Belinda just last week!"

"Nope, he didn't. You have got to stop listening to what those two say, Becky! Trust me, I have inside information. The night Simon was supposed to be with Belinda he was with Max!" Becky looked unconvinced. "Look, let's try and figure this out logically, okay?"

"Okay," Becky drawled reluctantly. She seated herself gingerly on the sofa next to the sprawled out Zorro outfit and watched Emma pace.

"Fact one: Livia Patterson is a class-A bitch. Yes or no?"

"Yes."

"Fact two: Belinda Campbell is also a class-A bitch. Yes or no?"

"Yes." Becky sighed impatiently.

"Fact three: Livia and Belinda hate our guts for some obscure reason, possibly to do with the fact that cherry punch is a bitch to get out of white satin. Yes or no?"

"Yes."

"Fact four: Livia and Belinda are both interested in making sure no other woman gets either Max or Simon. Yes or no?"

Becky looked uncomfortable. She bit her lip, suddenly uncertain. "Yes?"

Emma snorted. "Trust me, when Livia finds out I've hooked up with Max she's going to shit a brick." Emma waved off Becky's sputtering, startled laugh with a small frown. "Belinda is just as bad, but she wants Simon."

"So?"

"So, from what I've heard, and seen, I should add, Simon seems to want you."

Becky blinked. "You know, I've heard they've got some pretty good outreach programs for drug abusers. You should look into them."

Emma sighed. "Becky, the man made his Madonna look just like you. Only smiling and happy instead of grouchy. So maybe it doesn't look *exactly* like you."

"Har-de-har-har. Seriously, Emma, Simon's never shown a lick of interest. And, frankly, knowing where his tongue has been I'm not certain I *want* him licking me."

Emma eyed Becky with disgust. "Quit making excuses, Becky. Wear the costume and see how Simon reacts. If he's interested, he'll let you know."

"And if he isn't interested?"

Emma grinned. "Somehow I don't think you need to worry about that." Ignoring Becky's sudden blush, Emma headed out the door. She'd made an appointment to have her hair done for the masquerade and she had no intention of missing it.

The gossip in the salon was running fast and furious. None of the women there knew about her hooking up with Max yet, so a lot of the gossip fluttered around who the town's hottest hunks were taking to the masquerade. Some believed Max was taking Livia, a rumor Livia herself skillfully confirmed without actually confirming anything. Emma had a hard time keeping her snorts of amusement to herself. Max wanted no one to get wind of their relationship until the masquerade when she would enter on his arm; otherwise she would have taken great delight in setting Livia straight. Everyone agreed Simon was the wildcard; no one had any clue who he'd be taking, although Livia tried to make it sound like he'd be taking Belinda. Since Emma knew for a fact that Simon was flying solo, she kept her mouth shut.

Adrian Giordano was also rumored to be flying solo, something Emma could have confirmed but didn't. There were a few other men the women were interested in, but she didn't know those men personally so she just closed her eyes, relaxed into the stylist's chair and let the rumors fly over her head.

"And, of course, we all know Becky will be taking Emma."

Emma popped one eye open to see Livia smirking at her. She did the one thing she knew would piss the woman off the most. She smiled serenely and closed her eyes, ignoring her for the rest of her appointment.

Max walked into the house a half an hour late. He had very little time to get showered and dressed before the masquerade, and the quickie he'd been hoping to indulge in wasn't going to happen. The Pride Alpha couldn't be late, especially when he planned on introducing his Curana to the rest of the Pride for the first time.

"Max?"

"Hey, sweetheart." Max put his briefcase down next to the sofa and headed for the bedroom, pulling his tie off as he went. "How'd your...day...go..."

Emma stood in the middle of the bedroom in the pirate outfit he'd picked out for her. The skirt hit her mid-thigh, just as he'd predicted. The boots hit her just below her knee, showing off an awful lot of skin. The thigh-high stockings were nowhere in evidence, not that she needed them. She'd had her hair styled in a half up, half down thing, with curls and twists she normally didn't have, framing her face beautifully. The frilly captain's hat was the icing on the cake.

Her makeup was a little darker and richer than she normally wore. The pale rose lip gloss she preferred had been exchanged for a darker shade, closer to wine. Her eyes were dark and smoky. Thick gold hoops adorned her ears and around her neck was a stylized golden cat. She stood with her hands behind her, an uncertain look on her face, the toe of one boot digging into the carpet as she looked at herself in the full-length mirror she'd moved from her apartment. She looked like a confection just waiting to be eaten. "Max?"

"Huh?" God, he hoped she didn't want him to actually talk, since he was pretty sure he couldn't form complete words, let alone sentences.

She looked at him out of the corner of her eye and bit her lip, and Max nearly swallowed his tongue. "Are you sure this skirt isn't too short?"

Max gulped as he took her in from her incredible face to her edible legs. "Is that a trick question?"

Emma rolled her eyes, some of the uncertainty leeching out of her face as she turned back towards the mirror. "Why don't you go take your shower and get dressed? We have to be at the Friedelinde's in an hour." She reached up to adjust her breasts in her bra and Max nearly fell on the floor. When she shimmied everything back into place, he practically ran for the bathroom. It was either an ice cold shower or throw her to the ground and mount her, to hell with Jonathon Friedelinde and the masquerade.

He showered quickly, since ice bathing wasn't his favorite sport. He dressed in record time as he listened to Emma putter around the great room muttering to herself. At the last minute he remembered to grab the signet ring before going to gather up Emma.

When he stepped out of the bedroom, he was gratified to see Emma just as spellbound as he'd been when he'd seen her costume. His long jacket was burgundy, with the same gold embroidery that was on her waist cinch and overskirt. Black lace peeked out at his wrists. He wore a black shirt with a black lace jabot underneath, skin-tight black pants and black boots cuffed just below his knees. He carried his saber since he couldn't wear it while driving. His tricorn hat was black with gold trim. Three black feathers in the hat polished off the look.

"Oh boy. If we don't get out of here now, we are so going to be late." Emma's voice was husky with desire and her eyes had turned gold. Max had to struggle not to push her up against the wall, free his aching cock and give them both what they wanted.

Max clenched his hand around the signet ring and stopped, the ring reminding him of something important he had to do before they left. "Wait, give me your hand." Emma held out her right hand. Max took it and gently slipped the signet ring of the Curana onto her middle finger. The Curana's ring was identical to his own, but smaller and daintier. Two stylized pumas surrounded a gold oval, paws to tails. In the center of the oval, the face of a puma had been engraved with two yellow diamonds for eyes. When she looked confused Max held up his own right hand, displaying his ring on his middle finger. "You are my Curana. Now everyone will know it."

Emma stared at the ring on her finger, a slow, utterly content smile stealing across her face.

"Livia is seriously going to shit a brick."

"*Emma!*"

Laughing, she rose up on her toes and kissed him with all the love in her heart, knocking both their hats to the floor in the process.

Chapter Seven

Emma had never seen so many versions of pirate wench and pirate captain in all her life. The wenches ranged from modest, immodest, to downright erotic. One woman actually bragged that her pirate costume was by Playboy! Considering how little there was of it, Emma didn't doubt the woman; compared to her Emma felt as covered as a nun. Then there was the usual assortment of ghosts, vampires, witches and ghouls, with a rare werewolf thrown in for fun. Jamie and Marie Howard had both come as gunslingers in matching black outfits and cowboy hats, both looking happy and proud enough to burst over the success of their party. They were the first to notice the ring on Emma's hand, and, with warm smiles and friendly hugs, they congratulated her and Max on their mating.

As Max and Emma moved through the crowd, other people came to congratulate them. Jonathon Friedelinde was polite, if somewhat cool. It irritated Max, but Emma understood on some level that Mr. Friedelinde was taking a "wait and see" attitude. In fact, Jonathon's attitude was the one that prevailed among the men as more and more people became aware of Max's mating. Everyone had expected him to pick someone as strong as he was, and none of them truly believed Emma was strong enough. The women, on the other hand, were, well, cattier. By the time they found Adrian, Max was trembling with the need to force his will on all of his Pride and *make* them accept his mate, something that would diminish Emma further in their eyes.

"Hey, Adrian." Emma smiled wearily. By the end of the first hour, she'd become so busy holding Max back that she didn't have time to worry about her outfit.

"Hey, Emma. Congratulations." Adrian dipped his head to her with a warm smile, shocking her. She'd had no idea Adrian was one of them.

Max nodded back, and Emma followed suit. "Thanks, Adrian. Have you seen Simon yet?"

"Oh, you mean Zorro?" Adrian grinned, gesturing with his hand. "He's over there, trying to chase down this cute little bandita."

"Becky's here?" Emma craned her neck and went on tiptoes, but it was no use; she was just too damn short to see over anybody. With a huff, she settled back down and glared at Max, waiting.

"Would you like to go see Becky now?" Max asked, smirking. He was staring off to his left, tracking someone through the crowd.

"Frigging tall people," she muttered, trying to see past the crowd of bodies to where Max was looking.

She squealed with surprise when Max bent down and picked her up, practically sitting her on his shoulder. She daintily crossed her ankles and held on for dear life as she scanned the crowd. "There! She's heading into the garden. Aw, son of a bitch."

"What?" Max asked, holding her steady with little effort.

"Simon's just been waylaid by Belinda. By the way, she *so* picked the right costume."

"Witch?"

"Catwoman. From the movie."

"Ah, sexy yet lame." Max winced when Emma tweaked his ear. "I'll rescue Simon, you find Becky." He set her down gently, careful to make sure her skirt didn't fly up, up and away. With a quick kiss and a nod at Adrian, Max went after Simon.

Emma found moving through the crowd without Max at her side more difficult. It seemed like people went out of their way to get in her way. "Excuse me, pardon me, excuse me." Emma tried to be polite as she shimmied around more than one person. When she reached a particularly large knot of people, she tried the polite route, though by this time she was becoming seriously irritated. She tapped the broad shoulder of a vampire standing in front of her. "Excuse me, let me pass, please."

The vampire ignored her, laughing with his companions.

"Excuse me, please, I need to get into the garden."

The vampire continued to ignore her.

"Will you please excuse me?" Emma practically shouted.

The vampire turned, frowned down at her, and turned back to his companions with a shrug and a laugh.

Emma lost it. Her temper, frayed by the tension in Max and the subtle snubs to herself, snapped. Emma could feel a strange power flowing through her, tied to yet separate from the Puma, and without thought she used it.

Her eyes narrowed on the group in front of her. The tone of command was the same one Max had used on her several times, the same one she was able to (almost) ignore. Power flowed out of her, surrounding her till she nearly glowed with it.

"Move out of my way."

The crowd behind them grew quiet as the men stopped laughing. The men in front of her visibly cringed and got out of her way, their heads bowing down, their shoulders hunching against Emma's anger. Using her power like the prow of a ship, Emma forged her way through the rest of the crowd, her head held high as she stepped into the garden.

With a deep breath, Emma sucked that power back into her body. It settled in, warm and cozy, purring but ready to pounce. The Puma, she sensed, was pleased with her display of dominance.

The garden was well lit, except in strategically placed spots where pools of darkness prevailed. Emma was pretty sure what went on in those spots, and hoped her nose would help her keep out of other people's business. Sniffing cautiously, she tried to scent Becky.

The sharp tang of coppery blood filled her senses, mixed with Becky's earthy scent. Emma stepped into the garden and made a beeline for the smell. Halfway there, she heard Becky scream.

Emma began to run.

Max finally pried Belinda off Simon by ordering her off. With a coy shrug, the woman finally let go, but not before giving both men a peek at what they were walking away from.

"Ugh." Simon shuddered. "You'd think she'd get the hint. 'Get off me, get off me, what the hell are you doing, get off me' just didn't seem to get through to her."

Max snickered. Simon was brushing at his shirt as if he could brush Belinda's scent off of him. "Becky seems to have headed into the garden. Emma went to find her."

"In this crowd?" Simon stopped brushing himself and straightened his hat. "I heard a couple of the young bloods claim they were going to 'test' Emma."

Max growled. "How?"

"The usual. Forcing her to use her powers. She's small enough that simply not getting out of her way will do it."

Max's smile was feral. "In that case, they're in for a surprise."

"Never doubted it."

The two men waited until they felt the burst of power flowing from a point not far from the garden doors. It was strong enough to nearly have Max bowing down before it. Simon actually grimaced before pulling himself upright by force of will alone. Emma had finally gotten fed up and was forcing her way through the crowd, her strength clearly a match for, if not slightly greater than, Max's. Max and Simon managed to find spots where they could watch her regal exit from the ballroom. Her head moved neither left nor right; her eyes were pure molten gold. She flowed towards the garden doors, her stride sleek and sultry, commanding the attention of all around her. There was more than one shocked face in the crowd as Emma, her power swirling around her like a cape, stepped out of the double doors and into the Friedelinde's garden, every inch the Curana Max had claimed her to be.

"My God, she is so fucking hot." Max grinned as he watched his pissed-off mate saunter out into the night, the sexy sway of her hips riveting to more than one pair of male eyes. He was unsurprised at how the Pumas around her practically scraped the floor in her wake.

"Yeah. Good for you. Go home soon, fuck like bunnies, make little Alphas for Uncle Simon and Aunt Becky to play with. Speaking of which, can we go get *my* woman now?" Simon grumbled, already beginning to push through the crowd.

Max merely grinned, too pleased with and proud of Emma to call Simon to task. He moved through the crowd on Simon's heels, almost barreling into him when the man stopped. "Simon?"

Simon looked over his shoulder at Max, confusion and fear mingling in his expression. "I smell blood."

Max sniffed. There, on the evening breeze, was the tang of blood mixed with Becky, Emma...and Livia?

Simon's eyes went gold as his claws ripped through the leather swordsman's gloves. "Becky's bleeding." He took off into the night, following the blood trail of his mate.

"Fuck." Max chased after his friend, knowing that if Livia had hurt Becky it would take a miracle to keep Simon from killing her.

Emma took in the scene before her, trying not to shudder. Livia had Becky pinned beneath her, her claws going for

Becky's soft stomach, her teeth at Becky's throat. Becky stared at Emma, obviously terrified, bleeding from numerous small cuts inflicted by Livia's claws, and one bad-looking bite wound on her left shoulder. Her unsheathed sword was just beyond her reach, probably knocked out of her hand when Livia pounced. Her hat had fallen off during the scuffle as well, landing brim up next to a rosebush. Livia had cuts on her arms and a slash in her right cheek, showing Becky had fought back.

Livia snarled, the warning of one cat to another over prey, and Becky froze.

Emma cocked her hip, hands going to her waist as she tried to still the frantic beating of her heart. She had to hit Livia where she lived, get her to turn on *her* and get the hell off of Becky before someone died. "Okay, some of the peroxide must have leaked into your brains to make *this* seem like a good idea. What will killing Becky accomplish, other than to piss off Simon and Max *and* ruin your manicure?" Livia snarled again, but she didn't tighten her hold on Becky's throat. Her claws remained poised above Becky's stomach. Emma racked her brains, trying to think of ways to get Livia's undivided attention. "Did you run out of Liversnaps or something? Oh wait, that's dogs."

Livia dug her claws into Becky's stomach, making her gasp. Red beads of blood, black in the night, dribbled down Becky's sides as Livia released her throat and sat up slowly. Her hand flexed, driving her claws in deeper. "I want the Curana's ring."

Emma stared at her, stunned. "A ring does not make you Curana, Livia."

Livia sneered. "It does to them!" She tossed her head towards the house, indicating all the other Pumas inside. "If they see I took the ring from you, they'll never acknowledge you as Curana." She smiled, her fangs glistening in the moonlight. "They'll see you for the weak, pathetic wallflower you've always been. Max will be mine, like he always should have been; he won't have a choice. He and I will run the Pride the way it was meant to be run, and you'll be seen as nothing but the Alpha's whore."

94

Emma nodded thoughtfully. It took everything she had to stay focused on Livia and not her friend. "Yeah, all of that is true. Except for one thing. Well, two, really."

"What's that?"

"One, Max doesn't want your double-processed skanky ass."

"Hey! I'm a natural blonde!"

The woman is obviously a few tacos short of a fiesta platter. Emma mentally rolled her eyes. She was so done dealing with Livia. "Two, even without the ring, I *am* the Curana." Emma's power punched out, reaching for the woman in front of her. "Let Becky go. Now."

Livia whimpered as Emma forced her to do her bidding. Her hand trembled with the force of Emma's command, her claws slowly, reluctantly withdrawing from Becky's stomach. She crawled on all fours off of Becky, her shoulders hunched. Emma's will compelled her away from the bleeding woman.

"Kneel."

Emma's command punched out, forcing Livia to her knees. She shook with the need to break free, her breath panting in and out of laboring lungs, but Emma kept her tied to her will.

Out of the corner of her eye, Emma saw Max helping Becky, which left her free to deal with Livia. Or so she thought.

The sound she heard behind her caused the hair on the back of her neck to stand on end. She now knew why pumas had earned the nickname mountain screamer as Simon's Puma let loose a high-pitched yowl at the sight of his injured mate. Before Emma could stop him, Simon pounced on Livia, claws extended, and bore her to the ground.

"I should kill you where you lay," he snarled over her, digging his claws into her stomach in the same exact spot she'd wounded Becky. The scent of blood and fear were thick in the air as Simon leaned down, his canines extending. "I could rip your throat out right now."

Emma glanced over at Becky and saw her shuddering in

fear, held in place only by Max's arms. "Uh, Simon?" Golden eyes blinded by rage met hers. "You're scaring the crap out of Becky."

She watched as he looked over at Becky. The sight of her seemed to calm him somewhat, though his claws never left Livia's flesh.

"Becky." Becky jumped at the sound of his voice, moaning as her wounds bled some more. "What would you have me do to her?"

Max's gasp was audible; in essence, Simon was giving Becky the kill.

"Simon?" It was more of a plea than a question, but for what Emma didn't know.

"Tell me, Becky. What should Livia's punishment be for injuring you?"

Becky blinked back tears and stared at Livia. "What is she? What are you?"

"Pumas. Werecats. I'll explain more later. Right now, you need to decide her punishment."

Becky looked at Emma, who cringed to see the confusion and hurt on her best friend's face. "I didn't know until Max bit me, then I didn't know if you would believe me or not. But I planned on telling you tomorrow, if Simon didn't do it first."

"You're a..." Becky swallowed hard at Emma's slow nod. "And they're..." Emma watched as Becky absorbed the information. When she blew out a hard breath, Emma relaxed. "This is going to cost you a fortune in Tidy Cat." Becky's laugh was shaky but Emma knew everything would be all right.

Emma grinned. "What would you like Simon to do with Livia?"

"What can he do with Livia?" Becky asked, staring down at Livia.

"Well, let's see: she was willing to kill you to get the Curana's ring, so Simon is well within his rights to rip out her throat." Emma shrugged. "Wouldn't be all that big a loss as far as I'm concerned."

"What the hell is the Curana's ring?"

"It's the ring Emma now wears that proclaims she's my mate and queen," Max replied, gentling his grip on Becky's arms as he realized she was reacting to the news far better than he'd expected.

"Whoa. Wait, so I was bait for Emma?"

"Becky, the longer Simon smells the blood, the harder it will be for him to not kill Livia. Decide her fate quickly."

Becky looked at Livia one last time before staring straight into Simon's golden eyes. "What is the lowest status a Puma can hold? If Max is king and Emma is queen, is there a lowest of the low?"

"No!" Livia moaned, trying to break free of Simon's hold. Simon merely dug his claws in deeper while his other hand held her down by her throat.

"Outcast," he answered. "Someone who's been made Prideless. She'll hold no privileges, no responsibilities. She will no longer be welcome at Pride functions or homes. Kits will be taught to avoid her. If she wished for status again she would have to leave, find a Pride willing to take her in and earn it."

Becky nodded. "Since the whole damn thing was about status, I think that would do nicely."

Simon nodded with a slow smile of approval. He bowed his head formally to Max. "My mate requests a casting out of the one named Olivia Patterson." He ignored Becky's startled gasp and Livia's moaned denial.

Max eased Becky gently to the ground before stepping up beside Emma. He positioned himself so that Becky could see everything that was happening between them. His right hand, the one with the Alpha's ring, came to rest on Emma's hip as he stared down at Livia. "The Beta of this Pride has requested a formal casting out. My Curana witnessed the unprovoked attack of our Beta's mate, Rebecca Yaeger." Emma saw Becky shoot Simon a narrow-eyed glare. "The attack was motivated by greed rather than self-defense. In light of these allegations I ask you, Olivia Patterson: how do you plead?"

"Fuck you." Livia tryed once more to buck off Simon, but he didn't budge an inch. Emma hoped she was having trouble breathing with the massive artist sitting on her chest.

Max's expression turned icy cold as he stared at the woman who'd tried to hurt Becky and steal his mate's power. "I'll take that as a guilty." Max's power whispered forth, like a slow moving mist, creeping out onto the grounds and into the house. As that fog of power touched the Pumas, they became aware of what was happening in the garden, if not exactly why. "As Alpha of this Pride, for the unprovoked attack against the Beta's mate, I hereby declare Olivia Patterson outcast. You are no longer one of us. You may no longer run with us, or hunt with us. You are no longer welcome in our homes. You may no longer approach our kits without risk to your life."

Livia began to sob quietly as Max formally kicked her out of the Pride. "Any attack on you will go unpunished within the Pride; we leave you to human laws. If you attack a mate of one of ours, you will be dealt with as an outsider, and your life will be forfeit. Any further contact with Rebecca Yaeger will be considered an attack, and will be dealt with as such. Again, your life will be forfeit. Any Pride member giving you succor will suffer the same fate as you." With a gentle nudge, Max turned so that he and Emma had their backs to Livia, effectively dismissing her. Simon pulled his claws from her flesh, his eyes returning to their normal dark brown, his fangs receding as he approached Becky.

"Um, down, kitty? Good kitty?" Becky smiled weakly as Simon reached for her. Simon gently picked Becky up, careful of her wounds, and walked out of the garden, undoubtedly headed for the cars parked in front of the Friedelinde's mansion. A long overdue conversation was about to take place, and if Emma wasn't wrong some more biting was also going to take place.

"Will Simon's bite heal Becky's wounds?" Emma asked as they slowly walked away from the weeping woman huddled on the ground behind them.

"For the most part. She'll bear some scars, most likely on her neck where Livia bit her, but otherwise she'll be fine. I'm pretty sure Simon will take care of that quickly."

"Hmm. What do you think Livia will do?" Emma tucked her hand in the crook of Max's arm and leaned on him. Her feet were beginning to hurt in the damn boots he'd bought her.

"Move, preferably far, far away." Max picked up Emma's hand and kissed the back of her knuckles. "You, by the way, were magnificent, my Curana."

Emma grinned up at him. "You think so?"

"I saw your performance in the house, and part of it out here." Max stopped and pulled her into his arms, his mouth brushing against his mark on her neck. "Watching you put all those assholes in their place really got me hot."

Emma giggled and wriggled her hips against him. "I thought I rocked."

Max purred slightly as he nipped the mark on her neck. "Simon told me I should take you home and start making kits. What do you think?" Max looked down at her, love and lust glowing equally in his brilliant smile.

She leaned into him as they began walking back to the house, Livia forgotten behind them. Her hand rubbed his chest absently, her ring gleaming in the moonlight. "Max?"

"What?" His tone was wary; he'd come to expect the unexpected when she used that particular tone of voice.

"Will I give birth to a baby or a litter?"

"Emma," he groaned.

"I mean, will we be feeding them baby formula or Kitten Chow?"

"Emma!"

"If they get stuck in a tree, who do we call? Does the fire

department *do* kitten rescues anymore? This is important stuff to know, Lion-O!"

"God save me." She could tell from the way his chest rumbled under her hand that he was holding back a laugh.

"Too late. Oh, and we're not naming any kids Richard. I mean, Dick Cannon? Almost as bad as Max Cannon. Has anyone ever mentioned you have a name like a porn star? I mean, not that you don't have the equipment to live up to it."

"Emma!"

Emma giggled.

Life was good.

Sweet Dreams

Dedication

To my mom and dad, who are still trying to figure out what happened to, "I want to be Isaac Asimov when I grow up."

To Memom, who's willing to discuss ménage a trois stories with her granddaughter with surprising enthusiasm. Yet another thing that has Mom shaking her head in wonder.

To my beta readers, Beth, Stephanie, RC and Alice: you guys rock! I love getting stuff back from you. ("Wait. I really wrote that? Are you sure? Because I don't think eggplants go there.")

To my editor, Angie, who takes the rough diamonds I dig up and send to her and polishes them until they gleam.

And to Dusty, who mutters about maniac, knife-wielding car-jackers/killers every time I mention buying a convertible, or how cute I'd look in one. I love you too, sweetheart. Even if you won't let me get that sweet cherry red one I've always wanted.

Chapter One

Oh, yeah. Come to the masquerade party, she says. Simon will be there and he wants you, she says. You'll have a blast, she says.

I am so gonna kick Emma's ass over this.

A low, inhuman growl rumbled from Livia Patterson's throat. Becky inched back, startled at the sound coming from the blonde. The hairs on the back of her neck stood up as Livia slowly paced forward, her lips curling in a feral smile. Her teeth were way too sharp. Her eyes were weird, too. They gleamed like a cat's in the dim light provided by the paper lanterns.

If I live long enough.

Becky took another step back, her heart pounding with fright. The woman's nails had turned into claws. "Wow. Neat special effects." She laughed nervously. "It doesn't really go with the genteel *senorita* costume though. You might want to rethink it."

Livia's answer was a hissing growl that revealed a mouth full of razor-sharp teeth.

"Okay, *not* special effects." Never had she been more grateful that she'd decided to wear live steel rather than a plastic toy with her *bandita* costume. She drew her rapier and pointed it at Livia. *Thank God for those fencing lessons I took in college.* "Damn, I always knew you were a bitch, but this is ridiculous."

Livia lunged at her. Those sharp black claws swiped along

her sword arm, shredding the lace and nearly causing Becky to drop her sword. "Ow!"

Becky gasped at the transformed Livia. The next time Livia lunged Becky parried, slicing Livia's arm. This time it was Livia who bled.

The weirdest sounds came out of Livia. They were scary as hell. She snarled, then growled, then finally screamed. It sounded like one of the big cats at the zoo. If Becky wasn't so focused on keeping those claws off of her she would be seriously freaked.

"More of a pussy than a bitch, huh?" She grinned when the woman snarled, riding that adrenaline high that always kicked in during a fencing match. Everything came into sharp focus as she began fighting, parrying Livia's lunges, making a few of her own. She knew the woman would rip her apart if she got her claws into her. They danced around each other, circling, lunging, parrying till both women were panting. She had the advantage of reach, but the blonde moved faster, coming in under her guard and going for her stomach.

The good news was the tight red *senorita* dress Livia wore hampered her movements, while Becky's flowing *bandita* outfit was almost perfect for fencing. The bad news was Livia was incredibly fast and agile, a fact that nearly made up for her hampered movements.

You know, I have better things to do on a Saturday night than get my ass kicked by Senorita *Psychopath.* Becky knew she was outmatched. She got a few good hits in, drawing blood along Livia's stomach and a deep slash along her cheek, but unless something happened, and soon, she would lose. She was covered in small bleeding cuts, far more than she'd managed to inflict on the other woman. The rapier hilt was becoming slippery with blood. She made sure she kept a death grip on it. From the look of raw hatred on Livia's face dropping it would end in her death.

Livia whirled away after a missed blow and Becky took the

opportunity to thrust in low, slashing into her stomach and earning herself another growl.

The two women slowly danced around each other, looking for an opening. Livia snarled again, fur rippling along her arms as she lunged for Becky. With a startled cry Becky backed up a step, ready to parry the blow but stumbled over a bush and landed flat on her ass. Her hat rolled away and came to rest against another bush. Her rapier was knocked from her hand as Livia landed on top of her.

Becky screamed in pain as Livia bit down on her shoulder. Her claws raked along Becky's sides, drawing even more blood.

Livia sat up slowly, one clawed hand wrapped around Becky's throat. "Emma's coming," she purred, tilting her head to the side as she listened to something only she could hear. "So happy she could join our little party."

"Swell," Becky coughed, digging her fingers into Livia's forearm. She *had* to get the Bride of Satan off of her!

Livia hissed at her and arched down. Her teeth were pinching at Becky's neck when Emma appeared. Becky looked over Livia's shoulder at Emma and saw the horror in Emma's expression before it was quickly shuttered away.

Emma cocked one hand on her hip and stared at Livia like the blonde had lost her mind. "Okay, some of the peroxide must have leaked into your brains to make *this* seem like a good idea. What will killing Becky accomplish, other than to piss off Simon and Max *and* ruin your manicure?"

The bitch snarled again, but she didn't tighten her hold on Becky's throat. Those wicked black claws remained poised above Becky's stomach.

"Did you run out of Liversnaps or something? Oh wait, that's dogs."

Livia dug her claws into Becky's stomach, making her gasp. She really wished Emma would shut the hell up before Livia gutted her like a fish.

Beads of blood, black in the night, dribbled down her sides

as Livia released Becky's throat and lifted her head. Her hand flexed, driving her claws deeper into Becky's stomach. "I want the Curana's ring."

Ring? What ring? Becky glared at Livia, but neither woman was paying any attention to her.

"A ring does not make you Curana, Livia."

Livia sneered. "It does to them!" She tossed her head towards the house, her hand flexing and sending shafts of pain rippling through Becky. She held still and quiet through sheer stubbornness alone; no way was Livia getting another sound out of her. "If they see I took the ring from you, they'll never acknowledge you as Curana." She smiled, her fangs glistening in the moonlight. "They'll see you for the weak, pathetic wallflower you've always been. Max will be mine, like he always should have been; he won't have a choice. He and I will run the Pride the way it was meant to be run, and you'll be seen as nothing but the Alpha's whore."

Curana? Alpha? What the fuck is going on?

Emma nodded thoughtfully. "Yeah, all of that is true. Except for one thing. Well, two, really."

"What's that?"

"One, Max doesn't want your double processed skanky ass."

"Hey! I'm a natural blonde!"

And I'm the next Powerball winner. Looking past Emma, Becky thought she saw a flash of gold, and frowned.

"Two, even without the ring, I *am* the Curana." Emma's expression turned fierce. "Let Becky go. *Now.*"

There was a weird quality to Emma's voice she'd never heard before, the command running through her like an electric shock. She felt Livia stiffen above her, a small, almost unnoticeable shudder wracking her body. She watched wide-eyed as Livia whimpered, her claws slowly, reluctantly withdrawing from Becky's stomach. She crawled on all fours off her, her shoulders hunched as Emma's command somehow pulled the shaking blonde to her. "Kneel."

How the hell are you doing that? And can you teach me?

Livia knelt, trembling, at Emma's feet. She tried to sit up, wincing, when a pair of hands reached around her and gave her a helping hand. *Max, thank God.* She looked up to say thanks and gasped. His normally sunny blue eyes were gold and they glittered like...a cat's. "Oh, hell, not another one."

The angry scream of another big cat rent the night. Three of them? *What did I do, stumble into some freaky werewolf convention?*

Out of the corner of her eye she saw a streak of black land on Livia, knocking her to the ground. "I should kill you where you lay," Simon growled over her, digging his claws into her stomach in the same exact spot she'd wounded Becky. Simon leaned down, his canines extending. Becky felt her jaw drop open as his black Zorro cape partially obscured Livia's body. "I could rip your throat out right now."

Oh. Oh, shit. Simon? Hot, hunky Simon, the man she'd secretly been in love with for years, was like *Livia?*

"Uh, Simon?" Golden eyes blinded by rage met Emma's. "You're scaring the crap out of Becky."

His head swiveled towards her; whatever he saw seemed to calm him down a bit. "Becky." Becky jumped at the sound of his voice, moaning as her stomach protested sharply. "What would you have me do to her?"

Max's gasp was audible; his hands tightened on her arms. She'd have to ask what that was about some other time.

"Simon?" She *knew* she sounded pathetic, but the thought that he was like Livia was just way too much to deal with.

"Tell me, Becky. What should Livia's punishment be for injuring you?" Simon's voice was rough and growly, hitching slightly on the word *injuring*. He sounded supremely pissed off.

Becky blinked back sudden tears (damn, her stomach *hurt)* and stared at Livia. "What is she? What are *you?*"

"Pumas. Werecats. I'll explain more later. Right now, you need to decide her punishment."

Becky looked at Emma, who flinched with guilt. "I didn't know until Max bit me, then I didn't know if you would believe me or not. But I planned on telling you tomorrow, if Simon didn't do it first."

"You're a..." Becky swallowed hard at Emma's slow nod. "And they're..." Emma watched her, her expression pleading for understanding, which Becky gave. Emma was, after all, her BFF. *Although Lucy still has a lot of esplainin' to do.* When she blew out a hard breath, Emma visibly relaxed. "This is going to cost you a fortune in Tidy Cat." She laughed shakily, still trying to absorb everything that had happened.

Emma grinned, obviously relieved. "What would you like Simon to do with Livia?"

"What *can* he do with Livia?" Becky asked, glaring down at Livia's terrified face.

"Well, let's see: she was willing to kill you to get the Curana's ring, so Simon is well within his rights to rip out her throat." Emma shrugged. "Wouldn't be all that big a loss as far as I'm concerned."

She turned back to Emma, her patience just about at an end. She was bleeding all over herself, her stomach and shoulder hurt, and she *still* had no idea what the fuck was going on. "What the hell is the Curana's ring?"

"It's the ring Emma now wears that proclaims she's my mate and queen," Max replied, gentling his grip on Becky's arms.

"Whoa. Wait, so I was bait for Emma?" *That bitch is so dead.*

"Becky, the longer Simon smells the blood the harder it will be for him to not kill Livia. Decide her fate quickly." Max's voice cut through the mental fog surrounding her, focusing her again on the woman on the ground.

She looked at Livia one last time before staring straight at

Simon. Something she saw in his face let her know that he would do whatever she asked of him, up to and including murder. The patient way he waited for her to pronounce sentence reassured her. Somehow she knew Simon would sit there all night if she needed him to. "What is the lowest status a Puma can hold? If Max is king and Emma is queen, is there a lowest of the low?"

"No!" Livia moaned, trying to break free of Simon's hold. Simon merely dug his claws in deeper while his other hand held her down by her throat.

"Outcast, someone who's been made Prideless. She'll hold no privileges, no responsibilities. She will no longer be welcome at Pride functions or homes. Kits will be taught to avoid her. If she wished for status again she would have to leave, find a Pride willing to take her in and earn it."

Becky nodded. *Bye-bye,* Senorita *Psychopath. Have a nice fucking life somewhere far, far away from here.* "Since the whole damn thing was about status, I think that would do nicely."

Simon nodded with a slow smile of approval. He bowed his head formally to Max. "My mate requests a casting out of the one named Olivia Patterson."

Max eased Becky gently back down to the ground before stepping up beside Emma. He positioned himself so Becky could see everything happening between them. "The Beta of this Pride has requested a formal casting out. My Curana witnessed the unprovoked attack on our Beta's mate, Rebecca Yaeger."

Becky shot Simon a narrow-eyed glare. *Mate?* She'd read enough werewolf romances to know what *that* meant. So if she was his mate, why was Belinda all over him like white on rice?

"The attack was motivated by greed rather than self-defense. In light of these allegations I ask you, Olivia Patterson: how do you plead?"

"Fuck you," Livia growled, trying once more to buck off Simon, who didn't budge an inch. Becky smiled, hoping she was digging Simon's claws in just a little bit deeper.

"I'll take that as a guilty."

Becky watched from her place on the ground as Max's stare turned icy cold. A strange, barely there mist seeped from the ground he stood on. Something about that mist seemed alive. His right arm rested around Emma's waist, unconsciously snuggling her close to him, the gesture sweetly protective. "As Alpha of this Pride, for the unprovoked attack against the Beta's mate, I hereby declare Olivia Patterson outcast."

There was that mate thing again. *What the hell is Simon thinking?*

"You are no longer one of us. You may no longer run with us, or hunt with us. You are no longer welcome in our homes. You may no longer approach our kits without risk to your life."

Livia began to sob quietly as Max formally kicked her out of the "Pride", another thing Becky was going to have words with Emma about. Curana? Queen werepuma? Hello! This was a bit bigger than "I'm screwing Doctor Hubba-Hubba"!

Not to mention that, thanks to Livia, it looked like she'd be joining the ranks of the perpetually fuzzy soon. Would she have to bow down to Emma? Kiss her ring? *Sniff her butt?*

Ew.

"Any attack on you will go unpunished within the Pride; we leave you to human laws. If you attack a mate of one of ours you will be dealt with as an outsider, and your life will be forfeit. Any further contact with Rebecca Yaeger will be considered an attack, and will be dealt with as such. Again, your life will be forfeit. Any Pride member giving you succor will suffer the same fate as you." With a gentle nudge, Max turned so that he and Emma had their backs to Livia, effectively dismissing her.

Simon pulled his claws from Livia's flesh. His eyes returned to their normal dark brown and his fangs receded as he approached Becky with a wicked smile and a purposeful stride.

"Um, down, kitty? Good kitty?" Becky grinned weakly as Simon reached for her. Simon gently picked Becky up and walked out of the garden. He headed straight for the cars parked in front of the Friedelinde's mansion. And unless Becky missed her guess, they weren't headed to Halle General.

Her hands went to his shoulders, his dark brown hair brushing over the back of her hands. She suppressed a shiver at the feel of that dark silk sliding over her skin. "Let me go, Simon." Becky frowned, struggling slightly as she tested his hold on her.

"Not happening. Stay still, baby."

Becky flopped back in his arms, wincing when her neck and stomach protested. The big lug barely noticed, just tightened his hold slightly. "Great. Just great. I get to trade in my GP for a vet."

"GP?"

"General practitioner. As in my human doc. Geez, if you have to explain the joke it just isn't funny anymore."

Simon rolled his eyes. "No, you won't have to trade in your GP for a vet. Where do you come up with stuff like that?"

Becky's disbelieving stare merely caused his shit-eating grin to blossom. "I got bit by a werecat, Brainiac. Traditionally that now means I get to wear a flea collar and pee in a sandbox."

Simon was shaking his head before she'd even finished speaking. "Nope. We have to deliberately change someone. I'd be able to smell it if she'd done it, and she didn't. You're not going to change."

Becky sighed in relief.

"Yet."

That single word held a dark promise Becky did her best to ignore. He was scanning the large driveway like he expected an ambush. When Belinda stepped out from between two of the parked cars, Becky smiled cynically.

"Oh, look, it's Bondage Barbie." She ignored his snort of laughter as she remembered the way the blonde had been all over him during the masquerade. "Simon, your date's here, you can put me down now."

His only answer was to tighten his arms around her.

"Not now, Belinda. Becky's hurt."

Belinda's horrified gaze fastened on Becky's stomach. "Livia did that?"

Simon turned on the other woman with a low, warning growl. "If I find out that you had a hand in helping Livia hurt my mate I will kick your ass so hard you'll shit out of your mouth *after* I have you cast out of the Pride. You understand me?"

Becky groaned, "She's one too?" just as Belinda gasped, "Mate? *Her?*"

"I said, do you understand me?" He drawled out the syllables as if Belinda were an idiot.

"She *can't* be your mate." Belinda looked horrified.

"Damn straight."

Becky jumped when Simon pressed a quick kiss on her forehead. "You shut up." His voice was oddly affectionate as he looked down at her. His gaze, when he turned back to Belinda, was sharp. "I expect my mate to be welcomed by the Pride. *Do you understand me?*"

Belinda sniffed. "She's not even one of us."

"She will be."

"Will not!" Becky tried to straighten up and glare at him but the pain made her gasp and settle right back down. *Note to self: stomach wounds and sit-ups don't mix. Ow.*

"Will too. Now shush." His gaze never left the woman in front of him, but Becky knew he was well aware of her glare.

"Ass wipe." She folded her arms across her chest with a sniff.

He looked down at her and frowned. "What did you just call me?"

"You heard me. You have been, and always shall be, an ass wipe."

"But... I thought we would mate." Belinda's voice was shaky with unshed tears.

"What on earth would make you think that?" Simon looked totally confused.

Becky saw a shudder pass through Belinda, and wondered just how much the other woman loved Simon. If she did, she felt sorry for her. Simon had never been the type to settle down. *Although he did call me his mate... Better not go there. That way leads to heartache a la Belinda.* "Put me down, Simon. I'm bleeding and I need to go to the hospital."

"Good point. Good night, Belinda." He strode away, Becky still held firmly in his arms.

Over Simon's shoulder she saw the other woman lower her head into her hands. An unexpected wave of pity went through her. Belinda was a pain, but she'd never been as bad as Livia. The fact that Simon had dated her off and on for years had probably contributed to the other woman's belief that he was meant to be hers.

They reached Simon's truck. "C'mon, put me down. Seriously. I can go to the emergency room. It's just chock full of people docs."

His eyebrows rose in disbelief. "And how will you explain your wounds?" Simon put one foot on the running board and propped her butt on his leg, thus freeing a hand to dig out his keys. "Hello, I got bit by a werepuma, can I have some stitches and a rabies shot? Or will you send the county on a cougar hunt?"

"Considering who bit me, maybe a rabies shot isn't a bad idea." She winced when he had to shift her slightly.

He stared down at her, waiting patiently for her reply. She rolled her eyes and gusted out a sigh. Simon took that for the surrender it was. He opened the truck door and gently placed her in the passenger seat, putting her seat belt on with infinite care. He removed her bandit mask and put it in his pocket. He got behind the wheel, put on his own seat belt and removed his

Zorro mask. He started the truck and drove carefully out of the mansion's driveway.

She didn't even realize where they were going until he pulled into his own driveway, and by then it was too late.

Chapter Two

The dark green wooden siding and gray slate of Simon's craftsman home was topped by a dark gray A-line roof supported by the traditional pillar and post design so common to the architecture. His favorite part of the house was his open, extended front porch. It ran half the length of the house and well into the front yard, making it more like a small deck than a porch. He'd installed a wooden porch swing off to one side where he could sit, beer in hand, and think after a long, hard day. The glass insert in his front door was his own design, a stylized cat's head with jade green eyes just like Becky's. The house was deeper than it was wide, with the two-car garage towards the back of the house.

Simon pulled up into his driveway, content for the moment to have his mate beside him despite the scent of her blood. He pressed the button to open the garage doors, pulling the truck in and killing the engine. He pressed the button again, closing the garage door and sealing Becky in his home. The Puma in him purred, knowing their mate was now in their den, even if it was only temporary.

Her bleeding had slowed; if it hadn't, he would have bitten her before they left and to hell with who saw what. Her well-being was the most important thing in the world to him. Seeing Livia crouched over her, Becky's blood smearing her lips, had driven that fact home forcibly. If he'd had any doubts that Becky was his mate that little scene in the Friedelinde's garden had set them to rest permanently.

The bitch was lucky Becky hadn't asked for her life, even jokingly. Simon would have killed her without a second's hesitation for spilling his mate's blood. And with the Alpha present he would have been well within his rights. Jonathon Friedelinde wouldn't have batted an eye. As the old Alpha he'd seen his fair share of bloodshed.

The only thing that had stopped him had been seeing the fear on Becky's pretty face. Fear of him.

He was going to have to work on that.

He took a moment to study her as he got out of the truck. She was too thin and jittery, something else he planned on doing something about.

Her wildly curling light brown hair floated around her face as she watched him move around the hood of the truck. She was smart enough to stay put when he opened her door, allowing him to carry her into their home. He carried her through the mudroom and straight through the kitchen into the great room. He was pretty sure his feisty mate would kick him in the nuts if he tried to carry her straight to the bedroom. He set her gently down on his sage green couch, enjoying the way the color lit up her pale skin. He hadn't consciously chosen the colors of his home with her in mind. It wasn't until he set her down on the couch and he saw the way her skin came alive that he realized he'd done his entire home in colors suited to her. The result was light, warm golden walls and bright, fun fabrics that brought her coloring to life. The fabrics were soft to the touch, almost like velvet. He'd gone with the lighter wood tones, opting for maple wherever possible, with little touches of black here and there to bring the whole thing back to earth. Yet another way his Puma had tried to get his attention, and he'd ignored it.

If a man could kick his own ass, Simon's would be bruised all to hell and gone. If he'd mated her months ago when he first realized what was happening she would have been able to kick

Livia's ass. In short, it was his fault that she'd been hurt.

"Whoa." Becky looked around, taking everything in, much to his amusement. This was the first time she'd been in his home. He hoped she liked it, because if he had his way she wasn't leaving it. The sofa he'd put her down on was a sectional with an attached chaise; the coffee table and entertainment center were contemporary in design. The glass in the center of the maple coffee table was Simon's work, depicting a puma with jewel-bright eyes stalking through the woods. "It's not what I expected."

"What *did* you expect?"

Her expression was pleasantly surprised. "Something a little more 'bachelor slob' and a little less 'comfy contemporary'."

He grinned. "Do you like it?"

"Yeah." She winced as she tried to sit up and take everything in. He leaned over her and helped her, wincing along with her until he had her in a comfortable position. Her look of gratitude was all the thanks he needed.

Simon walked away but quickly came back with a bowl of warm water and a washcloth. "Okay, shirt off."

Becky raised her brows in challenge.

Simon sighed. "I have to see how bad the cuts are. And the bite mark." He glared at the side of her neck, his lips tight, hands clenched around the bowl. Even with the enzyme changing her that scar would more than likely remain. *Damn, he should have just gone ahead and killed the bitch.* The fact that Livia had left a permanent mark on his mate had his Puma snarling again.

"I'm not taking my shirt off." She almost crossed her arms over her chest but winced as the pain in her stomach stopped her.

"Oh yes you are, baby." Simon put the bowl down on the table and perched on the edge of the chaise. "Those wounds need to be cleaned."

"That's what doctors are for, Oh Artiste."

117

Simon grinned. With one swift move, he ripped her shirt open from neck to waist. "All duh...you didn't wear a bra." His tongue tripped all over the place. Becky's beautiful breasts were bared to his delighted gaze. They were small, the nipples rosy pink. They perked up slightly in the cool air. He could feel his IQ drop by ten points just from staring at those beautiful nipples. He literally felt his thought processes grind to a halt as all of the blood rushed out of his head and pooled in his dick. If it wasn't for the blood all over her stomach and shoulder he'd be having a much harder time not fucking her on the spot, and he was having a *really* hard time of that already.

Becky crossed her arms over her chest with an outraged squawk followed by a squeak of pain. "My shirt!"

"*My* shirt." He gently tried to pry her arms off her chest, but she wasn't letting him. He almost pouted over the fact that she'd covered her entirely edible breasts. Damn, he wanted a taste so badly his mouth watered. He realized they'd fit perfectly in his mouth and had to hold back a groan. His dick was beginning to press insistently against his black pants, the thin material doing nothing to hide it.

"Huh?"

He stared at her, scrambling to remember what they were talking about. *Oh yeah. The shirt.* "I paid for it."

"What?"

He looked up from her breasts and frowned absently. "I picked out this outfit and paid for it, therefore it's my shirt and I can rip it any time I want." With a gentle hand Simon began cleaning the blood from her stomach, paying special attention to where Livia's claws had dug in.

"I am *so* killing Emma, vows of eternal friendship or not." Becky fumed, struggling briefly when Simon tried to move her arms out of his way again.

"I just want to see if she scratched you there."

From the way she glared at him he was pretty sure she wasn't buying his act. "Trust me, I didn't get scratched there."

"What about here?" He rubbed his fingertips gently over the top slope of her left breast.

Becky slapped his hand away. "Bad kitty!" When he reached for her again, she smacked him upside the head.

Simon grinned at her, loving her fire. "I can't help it. It's been so long since I've had a beautiful, half-naked woman on my couch."

"Yeah, sure, that's such a rare occurrence." She rolled her eyes and scooted back from him with a groan. "This particular half-naked woman is off limits, buster."

Simon's frown was ferocious. "You did it again."

"Did what again?" Becky inched a little further away from him on the chaise, but unless she wanted to do a back-flip over the armrest she really wasn't going anywhere.

"Pulled away. Backed off." He sighed and dropped the washcloth into the warm, now pink water. "Becky, I..."

"Your phone's ringing." Becky looked towards the kitchen with an amused grin.

"What? No it isn't."

The phone rang. Becky smirked. Simon looked at her strangely and got up to answer the phone. "Hello?"

"Hey, Simon."

"Oh, hi, Adrian."

"How's Becky?" He could hear the sounds of the masquerade in the distance. Adrian must have called on his cell after stepping outside the mansion.

"You heard, huh?"

"Rumor flies fast, especially where the Alpha and his new Curana are concerned. Is she okay?"

He sighed. "Yeah, she's fine."

"And she's your mate?" Adrian's grin could be clearly heard.

"Yes." He stared, puzzled, at the woman lounging on his chaise. *How the hell did she know the phone was going to ring?*

119

"Mind if I keep Belinda…occupied? Seems she's a little upset right now."

"Belinda? Hell no, go for it. Just remember she's on the prowl for a mate."

Adrian laughed. "Don't worry; I'm not planning on sleeping with her, just keeping her from rushing over to your place. Is Becky still bleeding? That must be driving you nuts."

He looked back at Becky and frowned at her smug smile. "Yeah, she's bleeding on my couch as we speak."

"Have you cleaned the wounds and begun dressing them?"

"Gee, Doctor Dufus, what the hell do you think I was doing before you called?"

"Asshole." Adrian's amusement was once again loud and clear. "We still on for next Saturday?"

"Yeah, we are. Anything you need me to bring?"

"Nah, I got it all covered. I remembered to pick up everything we forgot when we did *your* floors."

Simon and Max were helping Adrian install new hardwood floors in his living room. Remembering all of the screw ups that had happened when they'd installed *his* floors, Simon couldn't help but grin. "All right. See you then."

"I'll have donuts and coffee ready to go. And tell Becky I said get better, and welcome to the Pride. Bye."

Simon hung up and turned towards her, finger raised, mouth open.

"Phone's ringing."

Simon tilted his head, listening. The phone rang a second later. Becky snickered.

"How the hell do you *do* that? It's freaking spooky." He shook his head as he picked up the receiver. "Hello?"

Becky listened in as half the Pride called to check up on her, laughing silently over Simon's frustration. She'd always known when the phone was going to ring, even as a child. It had freaked people out back then, and still freaked most of them out now. Except for Emma, who didn't really freak over much.

She was surprisingly touched; she didn't think that many people cared about her. Or was it because Simon was the Pride's Beta and had declared her his mate? It was possible all this "hail-fellow" stuff was pure political bullshit. Sniffing the Beta cat's butt, as it were.

"That's it, the answering machine is going on." Simon ended yet another phone call with a gruff laugh.

"Phone's—"

"*Don't* say it!" Simon pointed a commanding finger at her, but his tone didn't fool her. She could tell he was fighting a grin. He turned on the answering machine just as the phone rang. He left the machine to take the call as he stalked back towards her with a fresh bowl of water. "That must drive Emma nuts." He sat on the edge of the chaise once again, leaning one hand against the back of the sofa.

Becky bit her lip to keep from giggling at the look on his face. "Nah, she's used to it. She just makes me answer it." She hissed out a breath as he began cleaning her wounds once again. "Oh, ow."

"I know it hurts, baby." His hands were gentle; his expression was anything but. "I'll hunt her down and kill her if you want." She stared at him, seeing the dark rage in him again. It was the same rage that had scared her spitless as he hovered over Livia, his claws dug deep into the blonde's stomach. "I'm very good at stalking my prey."

"Yeah, well, guess what, Garfield, there are laws against stalking."

He chuckled, some of the darkness receding from his face. He began gently cleaning the bite wound on her neck. She could feel his breath against her shoulder and she shivered. The feel of his hands on her skin was distracting despite the pain.

"I'll cover you up in a nice warm blanket as soon as I'm

done, baby," he crooned in her ear. Which only made her shiver again, much to her disgust. A smug, self-satisfied smile crossed his face as he leaned towards the wound in her shoulder.

She gritted her teeth and rolled her eyes. *Arrogant jerk.* "Bite me, Simon."

He struck with a swiftness she couldn't evade. The sharp, stinging feel of his teeth piercing her skin made her gasp in pain.

But then pleasure hit, so intense she writhed, moaning in pure ecstasy. It raced from where his fangs were imbedded in her neck all the way down to her toes. She felt his big hand cover her pussy and stroke her gently through the fabric of her skirt and panties. It couldn't have felt better if he'd touched bare skin. She felt as if her entire body was having an orgasm. Even her toenails felt good.

He groaned against her neck, his body arching above hers as he settled himself between her thighs. His hands moved to her breasts, plucking at her nipples as his hips came in contact with hers. He carefully ground his hard cock against her and she moaned again.

She whimpered as his teeth left her skin. She could feel the roughness of his tongue as he licked at the mark he'd left behind. She ran her hands up and down his back and felt a strange rumbling under his skin.

Simon was purring. She ran her hands soothingly up and down his back, making him purr even louder. She bit her lip to keep from giggling.

This has got to be the weirdest freaking night of my life.

Simon purred as Becky stroked his back. He just couldn't help himself. The feel of her hands running up and down his body felt so right.

Finally she's mine. He couldn't believe how incredible it felt to mark Becky as his own. The feel of her moving under him as she came nearly triggered his own orgasm. He'd moved between her thighs without even thinking, his dick aching with the need to sink into her body. He wanted to taste every single inch of her, fuck her until they were both raw, and then do it all over again. The urge to complete the mating had been so strong that, if her blood hadn't still scented the air, he'd have had her naked and mounted within minutes.

"Ow," she whispered. He felt her flinch as she tried to move under him and damned himself for an impatient fool. She would heal faster as a result of the bite, most of the wounds closing in a matter of hours thanks to the enzyme he'd injected into her, but she was still in pain now. He carefully climbed off of her, any urge to purr gone as he scented her blood over their lust.

"Sorry, baby." He stroked those wild curls away from her cheek. Her skin was so soft he wanted to nuzzle her. "I lost my head." He placed a gentle kiss on her forehead before he stood and went to his hall closet, pulling out a colorful afghan his mother had knitted. He went to his bedroom and pulled one of his T-shirts out of a drawer. It was large enough that it could act as a short nightgown for her. He had no intention of taking her back to her miniscule apartment over Wallflowers. Tonight, and every night from now on, his mate was sleeping in *his* bed.

He stepped back into the great room and handed her the T-shirt. "Put that on." He ignored her raised brow at his order, crossing his arms over his chest and waiting. She pulled off the torn lace shirt and replaced it with the white tee. He covered her up gently with the afghan and perched on the edge of the sofa next to her.

Picking up one of her hands he gently caressed her fingers, his possessive gaze never leaving her face. He took her hand to his mouth and gently nibbled at her fingers. "You're mine now."

Chapter Three

She was having the best dream of her entire life. Hard, calloused hands kneaded her breasts, bringing her nipples to stinging life. A warm tongue lapped at her clit. She moved slightly, sighing as it found just the right spot. A rumbling, vibrating purr moved along the tongue and she gasped at the added sensations. She came with a low moan, riding the tongue as it slithered and slid against her moist pussy.

"Mmm. Tasty."

A deep, rumbling voice was coming from between her legs. *Simon.* She opened her eyes to see his dark hair spread across her legs as he lapped one last time at her clit. She jumped. *Not a dream.* She stared around the bedroom, wondering how the hell she'd gotten there. She remembered staring sleepily into the fire he'd started while he sketched a new design for a stained glass window. He must have carried her to bed when she fell asleep. She had no clue what had happened to her skirt, panties, or...her hands flew to her breasts...yup, her T-shirt. "Damn it, Simon, what are you doing?"

"Having breakfast," he replied, looking up at her with a sexy grin.

He was naked. All that glorious male flesh rose above her as he kissed her softly. "Good morning, baby."

She licked her lips and tasted them both. "Good morning, Simon."

She was still warm and sleepy, the remnants of her orgasm

fogging her brain. He leaned down for a more thorough kiss, his tongue gently trying to stroke into her mouth. She bit down on it gently as she felt his cock nudge her opening.

"Ow. Cah I haf ma thongue bach?"

She giggled and released him.

"What was that for?" He sat up, a cute little boy pout on his face. His cock bobbed above her mound.

"A, I have morning breath, b, I have to pee, and c, *you* have morning breath."

He sighed with exaggerated impatience as she shuddered. "Fine. Bathroom's this way." He crawled off her and helped her get up. The small smile on his face faded away to concern. "Any pain today?"

"My shoulder, a bit. My stomach feels fine."

The relief that touched his face made her heart melt. She smiled up at him, startled when his eyes turned gold.

He put his hand at her waist. "Morning breath and pee break. Right." He steered her into the master bath. He picked up a toothbrush and started putting toothpaste on it while she stared at him.

"Simon?"

"Hmm?"

She thought about crossing her legs and hopping but didn't think he'd take the hint. "I have to pee. *Badly.*"

He looked at her, confused. He pointed with the toothbrush. "Toilet's right there, baby."

"I can't do it while you're in the room!"

"Why not?"

"We haven't even done the nasty yet and you want to share space while I pee?"

"I just licked you to orgasm and you're worried about me being in the same room while you relieve yourself?"

"Yes! Duh!"

He rested one hip against the countertop, the adorable

125

confusion morphing into a smug male look that made her want to bop him on the head with the toilet brush. "This is a girl thing, isn't it?"

"Out!"

"Okay, okay!" He left laughing, toothbrush stuck in one corner of his mouth. She tried not to stare at his ass as he went, but apparently her willpower just wasn't up to the task. She nearly ran to the door to watch that ass flex its way out of the bedroom and down the hall. She would have if the memo from Mother Nature hadn't been marked *Urgent.*

It was only after she was done that she realized she was so comfortable being naked in front of him that she'd completely forgotten about it.

"Here."

Okay, I haven't forgotten the fact that he's *naked. Yum.* She bit back a sigh and stared at whatever it was he was waggling under her nose. She frowned at the toothbrush in his hand. It was hers. "How did you get that?"

"I went by your place and picked up a few things after you fell asleep." He put a finger over her mouth, stalling her immediate reaction. "I thought you'd be more comfortable with them."

That's so sweet. "Thank you, Simon."

"You're welcome. Now brush your teeth." He grinned and gently tweaked one of her nipples. "I haven't finished my breakfast yet."

This time, when that fine ass left the bathroom she *did* peek out the door. She stared as he walked back out of the bedroom, his butt cheeks flexing in the most mouth-watering way. The sexy grin he tossed over his shoulder as he chuckled on the way out let her know he was well aware of what she was doing.

She collapsed against the doorjamb and sighed. *Okay. Obviously I'm in a coma brought about by an accident or something. I'm actually lying in a hospital bed covered in tubes*

126

while some husky nurse bends my legs so my muscles won't atrophy. Because hell if I'm not having the best God damn dream of my life.

She picked up her toothbrush and began brushing her teeth. Not even his dream self was going to taste the early morning funk in her mouth.

Simon stood in his kitchen and waited for the coffee machine to finish working its magic. He could hear the sounds of water splashing in his bathroom, bringing a sense of peace he'd never experienced before. His mate was naked in his bathroom, coffee was brewing and donuts rested on the table ready to be eaten. All was right in his world.

He heard the water cut off and pulled out two mugs. He'd barely begun pouring when he heard her behind him.

"Coffee?"

"Mm-hmm." He held out a mug. "Come give me a kiss and I'll give you some."

Her lips curled in a snarl. "*Cooffeee.*"

He bit his lip to keep from laughing. "Down, girl." He handed her the mug, groaning at the look of sheer bliss that crossed her face. She'd had that same look on her face the first time his tongue had brushed against her clit. He gently lifted her onto the countertop, careful not to spill a drop of the mug she cradled protectively against her chest. No way in hell was he going to allow her to be hurt again, even by her favorite beverage.

She didn't fight him as he spread her knees apart. He wasn't even certain she noticed him at first. She was so wrapped up in her caffeine intake she could be sitting on a purple elephant and not notice. He made sure he had one hand wrapped around her mug when he touched her pussy.

"Simon?"

"I told you I wasn't done eating breakfast."

She shuddered as he circled her clit slowly. *The coffee look isn't the same. This one is much better.*

"Drink up, sweetheart."

She gulped and finished her mug in record time. Lifting it out of her hands he wrapped her legs around his waist and carried her back to the bedroom.

Donuts be damned. He had something much sweeter in mind to nibble on.

Simon practically threw her down on the bed. The fierce hunger on his face would have been frightening if she hadn't seen the glint of the humor peeking through. He tweaked one of her nipples, watching intently as it budded beneath his fingers. "What are you thinking about, baby?"

She grinned. She just couldn't resist. "Mmm. Donuts."

His big body stilled. His face went slack in shock before he began sputtering. "*Donuts?*"

She bit her lip to keep from laughing in his face. The look on his face was absolutely priceless. She only wished she had a camera so she could capture it for posterity.

"Donuts, eh?" She shrieked as he began tickling her. She squirmed under him, giggling as they began to tussle. She managed to roll onto her stomach and tried to get away but he pounced on her, holding her down under his big body. Becky was at a serious disadvantage, since Simon refused to allow her to roll back over.

All that squirming had a big, predictable result, one Becky could feel digging into her backside. Simon's erection pressed down against her, and suddenly she realized there were a lot more caresses than tickles in the way Simon was touching her. She looked at him, not surprised his eyes had gone completely gold.

Simon stilled above her, panting from the tickle fight. His expression slowly changed from playful to possessive. He lowered his mouth to hers, kissing her with a ravenous hunger that left her breathless. She barely felt it when he pulled her over on to her side, curling around her like a vine, taking her lips and claiming them as his own.

She could feel his hand trembling as he cupped her breast. He groaned into her mouth, his hands roamed over her skin, sensitizing each and every inch of her body. His tongue thrust in and out in a promise of lovemaking, coaxing hers out to play.

She allowed herself to be persuaded, and got her first real taste of Simon Holt. Her fingers curled into his dark chest hair, pulling slightly as he tried to practically crawl inside her. When his mouth descended on her breast she gasped, pulling his head in tighter to her body. Her fingers buried themselves in his hair in a fierce hold. She took a deep breath, ready to invite him into her body, when she realized she could *smell* his arousal. His scent, that musky, dark scent, entered her bloodstream, increasing her own arousal a thousand-fold. When he lifted from her breast and bit her neck Becky shuddered and came with a keening cry, shocked and aroused beyond belief, riding the thigh Simon suddenly shoved between her legs with a desperation bordering on insanity.

Oh, yeah. She could get used to this Puma stuff.

"God, yes, more." He groaned and went wild above her.

His mouth was sucking and licking and biting her all over. She rolled onto her back and spread her legs, eager for more of the oral loving he'd given her that morning. But apparently he had something different in mind.

"Don't move." Simon stood next to the bed, stroking his cock.

"Duh." Her gaze fastened on the most luscious piece of man-meat it had ever been her privilege to see. It was a thing of beauty, and according to Simon it was all hers.

He pulled her up by her arms, sitting her on the edge of the bed. He pushed her head towards his groin with a gravelly command. "Suck."

She shuddered as those talented fingers delved into her wet

pussy, his thumb circling her clit just the way she liked it. *He must have been paying serious attention this morning.*

She sucked on him for all she was worth, hollowing her cheeks out to provide even more suction. "God, yes, baby." His moans intensified when she started moving her tongue along the underside of his shaft. He started chanting softly, "Good, so good," as he moved his hips, fucking her mouth, his gold eyes staring down at her with a desperate hunger that urged her on and inflamed her own.

His fingers set up a strumming rhythm, and before she knew it they were both coming. Becky swallowed, the salty sweet taste filling her senses, making her hungry for more. From the look on his face, she was going to get it, too.

Simon pulled out of her mouth with a happy sigh. "You have no idea how long it's been since I came with someone else doing the honors. My wrist was beginning to develop carpal tunnel syndrome." He sighed as he flopped down next to her.

"Poor baby."

Turning with a grin he curled up around her, gently caressing her breasts. "Yup." Leaning down he gently rasped his tongue over one engorged nipple. "Ready for round two?"

"Round three for me, actually." She grinned, pulling on his semi-hard cock with long, smooth strokes. She buried her head against his neck and licked him in the same area he'd bitten her. His groan as he rolled her over onto her back again told her how much he liked that.

She shivered when Simon began lapping at his mark on her neck. It was strangely sensitive, almost as much as her nipples, and sent the same tingles down to her clit. He began to purr, sending that vibration down his tongue, making her think wicked, wicked thoughts. She was about to beg him to bite her again when he lifted his head.

"Wanna feel that against your pussy, baby?"

She nodded, damn close to whimpering.

He arched above her body, his legs thrust between her own.

His grin was feral. "Better than donuts." He lapped and sucked his way down her body, leaving love bites all over her fair skin. "Sweet, sweet Becky breakfast. I could eat this every day." His rough, purring tongue lapping at her nipples had her practically coming from just that alone. From the wicked grin on his face he knew *exactly* what he was doing to her.

She experienced a moment's jealousy as she wondered who else he'd done that to before he took all capacity for rational thought away. He blew gently on her mound, causing goose bumps to rise along her skin. One hand began petting her soft brown curls as his tongue reached out and barely touched her clit. Slowly he lapped at her, never varying his pace, never failing to nail her clit in exactly the right spot. He had to hold her hips down with one big, brawny arm or she would have been dancing across the bed.

The vibrations from his purring had her screaming an orgasm to the ceiling so fast it startled her. Simon groaned as she came, lapping her juices while she shuddered and squirmed.

"Simon," she panted, both hands gripping the sides of his head. She tugged, *hard*, hardly noticing his laugh as she put that tongue right where she wanted it. The man licked, nipped, sucked and lapped at her pussy as if he had all the time in the world until she'd screamed out two more orgasms.

With a wild groan he pulled free of her hold and thrust into her with a fierceness that ripped through her. He began a bruising pounding that was sure to send the oak headboard right through the wall. Simon sat up on his heels and grasped both of her thighs, pulling her into his body as he fucked her hard.

The orgasm that rolled through her was so intense she felt her lungs seize. Simon roared above her, head thrown back in ecstasy as he pumped his seed into her welcoming body over and over again.

He collapsed on top of her, sweaty and gasping for air, his

body still buried in hers. His arms came around her and cradled her close; his face buried itself in the side of her neck, right next to his mark.

"Holy Mother of God." She was having a hard time catching her breath. Every part of her body tingled. "I'm not in a coma. I'm dead, and this is my reward for living a good life." She looked over at the naked, sweaty, very happy man lying in a boneless puddle next to her. "A *very* good life." His shoulders started to shake. Her hand languidly stroked one muscular butt cheek. "Hell, I must have been a fucking saint."

She giggled as his purr tickled her neck.

Chapter Four

Max and Emma were due any minute. Between the fight with Livia and the night (and morning...good Lord, the *morning*) with Simon, she was looking forward to a nice, quiet meal with friends. She smoothed her unruly hair back, studying the curls with a frown. They were the bane of her existence. No matter what she did her hair looked frizzy. Although she had to admit it looked a lot better than it had in high school when she'd tried wearing her hair in a bob. She shuddered at the memory.

She slicked on pale lip gloss just as Simon walked into the bedroom.

"Damn, baby. Never mind dinner, let's skip to dessert."

She rolled her eyes and ignored his ultra-hot grin as he slowly took in her violet halter dress. She'd gone shopping with Emma that afternoon, intent on making an impression. From the look on Simon's face she'd done a good job. The halter dress enhanced what few curves she had, and the fact that it hit an inch or two above her knee didn't hurt. Becky knew her legs were her best asset, and tonight she'd decided to play that up.

She stared at him in the mirror. Damn, the man looked good. The hunter green button-down shirt and black slacks he'd chosen were a far cry from the jeans and T-shirt he normally wore. And he hadn't tied his hair back, either. It brushed his shoulders, making her fingers itch with the need to touch it.

He moved closer, sliding his hands around her waist. His

teeth sank gently into the side of her neck just above his mark. "Are you sure you want to go out tonight?"

The doorbell rang. She laughed as he groaned. "You're the one who invited Max and Emma, remember?"

"Don't remind me."

He'd made the invitation when Emma had shown up on his doorstep, practically bouncing, and announcing she was kidnapping Becky for the day. She'd agreed quickly and dragged Becky out of the house, Simon's hearty laugh following them all the way to Max's car. Emma had taken Max's car because she'd decided they were going shopping.

Becky had laughed. Knowing Emma, she'd known they'd need the extra room Max's Durango provided. She'd been right. She just hoped Max hadn't been *too* horrified when Emma got home, bags and boxes piled in the back seat.

She followed him to the front door. "Hi, Emma, Max."

"Hi, Becks. Hi, Simon." Emma looked gorgeous in a caramel colored turtleneck sweater and heather gray slacks that complemented her golden skin tone. She wore her favorite black pea coat.

"Rebecca."

If anyone could beat Simon in a Hottest Man in Halle contest it would be Max Cannon. Golden blond hair framed the face of a wicked angel, the only flaw being a small scar on the side of his nose. She could see a sapphire blue shirt under the bomber jacket he was wearing, and his long legs were encased in black slacks. His sunny blue eyes and easygoing grin hid the fact that he was one of the most powerful men in town. Without even thinking about it she bowed her head slightly in respect to the Pride Alpha and his mate; the smile was for her friends.

Max poked his head in the door and stared around at the floor, a puzzled expression on his face.

"What the hell are you doing?" Simon asked, frowning.

"Wondering where you stashed the piles and piles and *piles* of bags Becky must have brought home."

Simon's brows rose up. "You did know they were going shopping today, right?"

"By shopping, I thought they would pick up a dress, maybe get some shoes or a purse. Instead I could probably open a boutique in my living room."

"You know, all Becky brought home was one itty bitty bag." Simon smirked as Max growled good-naturedly. "She took the *Durango* shopping, Max. That should have been your first clue."

"Yeah, especially when she folded the seats down right before leaving." Max dodged the blow Emma aimed at his arm with a chuckle. He turned to Becky, still chuckling. "How are you feeling, Becky?" Max's gaze zeroed in on Simon's bite mark, visible through the straps of her halter dress. With a pure male grin he high-fived Simon, who grinned right back.

Becky shook her head. "Are they always like this?" she asked Emma.

Emma sighed. "Yup. Except when you throw Adrian into the mix. Then they get downright third-gradeish." She grinned up at her mate. "Rumor has it that it's amazing they ever got Simon's place fixed up. There should be glue and nails and other stuff just sticking out of everything, with the three of them buried under the wallpaper. I can almost see Wile E. Coyote holding up the 'HELP!' sign."

"We got it done because we're very good with our hands," Max purred, leaning in to place a quick kiss on his mate's neck.

Becky wrinkled her nose. "Ew."

Max laughed, obviously tickling Emma's neck, judging by the way she shivered and giggled.

"Where are we going to dinner?" Becky picked up her jacket and was surprised when Simon took it out of her hands and held it out for her. "Thanks." She blushed, putting it on. He pulled her hair gently out of the back of the jacket, caressing her curls with a soft, gentle touch. The fact that Simon wanted to touch her almost all of the time still had her head spinning. He'd barely let her out of his sight the entire time she'd been in his home.

His arm settled around her shoulders and guided her out of the house. "Noah's. It's Max and Emma's favorite place, and I always bow to the wishes of my Alpha." He locked the front door. She could tell from his expression he was doing his best to keep a straight face.

Max choked. "I wish." Simon's barked laugh was loud as Max led them to his Durango. "Like Noah's isn't your favorite place to go when you've made a big sale, right, Simon?"

"Nope, not at all."

Max helped Emma into the front passenger side as Simon helped Becky into the back. "Let me guess; his favorite food is lasagna."

Max looked at her, surprised. "How did you know?"

Becky grinned at Simon as he stuck his tongue out at her. "Lucky guess." She put on her seat belt and relaxed back into the butter soft leather. "Oh, Emma, thanks for going with me to get my baby back from the mansion."

"No problem. Besides, I enjoyed the shopping trip."

Emma grinned as Max and Simon shared a look in the rear view mirror. "You do know she drives a convertible, right?"

"So do I." Emma crossed her arms over her chest. She tried to glare fiercely at him and failed miserably as her lips kept trying to curve up in a smile.

"*I know.*" The glare Max sent Emma had Becky stifling a laugh again. The two of them were just too cute for words. "At least Becky's isn't candy apple red."

"Hey! I love my Cruiser, especially the candy apple red convertible part."

Becky turned to laugh with Simon and realized he was giving her the evil eye. "What?"

"Since when do you drive a convertible?"

"Since three weeks ago, Garfield." She ignored the twin snorts of laughter from the front seat and focused her attention on the big goob next to her. "You got a problem with that?"

"Hell, yes! Those things aren't safe!"

"My point exactly." Max nodded righteously and ignored the poke Emma gave him.

"How are they not safe?" Becky stared at Simon, one brow rising in challenge.

"Red lights. Maniacs with knives. Need I say more?"

"In Halle?"

"Didn't Emma get mugged right outside of Wallflowers?"

"Your point?"

"Crime happens even in Halle!"

"A mugging by a drunken college kid is a lot different from maniac, knife-wielding convertible killers."

Simon gave her an evil grin. "Fine. Let's see if it's strong enough to stand up to a full grown male Puma jumping up and down on the roof, shall we?"

"You are *not* breaking my brand new VW Bug, Simon!"

"Oh, even better. Cats love to play with bugs."

"*Simon!*" She reared back in surprise. His green shirt had turned an interesting shade of brown. She frowned and poked a finger at his chest, wondering what the hell was going on. She looked and caught a glimpse of her face in the rear view mirror. Her eyes had turned gold.

Oh. So that's what things looked like through the Puma's eyes. She turned her head and looked out the window, wondering what else looked different.

"She's changing." Max exchanged a look with Simon she couldn't interpret.

"I bit her last night, and she's pretty strong willed. I'm not surprised she's taking to it so fast." Simon was watching her with an expression of mingled worry and pride. "She should be fully changed within a day or two."

She looked at Simon and noticed his shirt once again looked green. "Great. I get to join the Fuzzy Club and buy stock in Nair. Can we eat now? I'm starving."

"You're always starving," Emma muttered.

Simon laughed. Becky grinned.

Max pulled up outside of Noah's with a groan. "Don't feel bad, I'm starving too."

Emma laughed as she climbed out of the SUV, much to Max's obvious disgust. Becky tried to follow her friend, only to find herself pulled out of Simon's door instead. He looked down at her and winked. She made a face at him and allowed him to tow her along behind their friends, the heels of her violet pumps clacking on the sidewalk.

Oh, thank you, God. Belinda's not working. The redheaded hostess smiled warmly and led them immediately to their seats. Simon held out her chair and helped her sit before taking his own seat next to her.

Things were fairly quiet as the four of them stared at their menus. Becky thought about getting the chicken marsala, but the lasagna the waiter carried past their table smelled so good she had a hard time deciding between the two.

"Stop biting your lip."

Becky looked at Simon over the top of her menu to find him grinning at her, and let her lip go.

"What's the problem, baby?"

"I can't decide between the chicken marsala and the lasagna."

"Share?"

"Sure!" Becky's stomach rumbled.

"Share what?" Emma looked between them, confused.

"Our dinner."

Emma looked at both of them and pursed her lips. "Oh."

"Actually, that sounds good." Max looked over at Emma. "Emma, you want the seafood alfredo?"

"No, I think I'll go with the shrimp primavera. You?"

"Chicken parmesan."

"Yum."

They placed their orders with the waiter, all four of them deciding on wine with their dinners.

"So, why did Simon's shirt turn brown, anyway? I thought cats were color-blind. Shouldn't it have turned gray?"

She watched while Max smiled. "Cats *are* color-blind. They're just not *completely* color-blind. They're protanopic."

"Proto-*what*-ic?"

"They lose the red-green spectrum. Everything either red or green looks kind of brown to us. Dogs lose blue-yellow. Grass to us is the color of spicy mustard. To a dog, it's shades of blue."

"Huh." She looked at Simon with delight. "So on your front door, the cat's head has green eyes."

"Which look golden brown when my eyes change."

"Clever."

"I thought so."

The topic turned to work as their food was delivered. "Simon, you have to have that sun catcher for Jamie ready to go by Thursday." Emma waved her fork menacingly at Simon. The effect was somewhat ruined when a piece of shrimp fell off it to land on the table with a soft plop. She looked around furtively before picking it up and plopping it in her mouth, much to Max's obvious amusement.

"Geez, Emma, I'm working on it, okay?" Simon practically whined, but Becky could see the smile he was trying so hard to hold back.

"You'd better be, or Jamie's gonna have our heads. If it's not done in time for his anniversary, Marie is going to be hurt. Then Jamie will be seriously hurt in a full body cast sort of way."

Simon snorted. "It'll be done."

"Good."

Simon turned to Max, his expression turning serious. "Oh, hey, Max, I forgot to ask. Did you get the e-mail from Sheri?"

"No, I haven't checked it today. What did she want?"

Emma turned and stared at Max, one brow raised in demand. "Who the hell is Sheri?"

Max winced. "Remember I told you there were two women I'd changed over the years?"

"Yes," Emma drawled, arms crossed over her breasts.

"Sheridan Montgomery is the other one."

"The one whose story you couldn't tell me?"

"Right, because if I told you I'd have to kill you."

Emma frowned. "If you kill me you aren't getting any nookie." She wrinkled her nose. "And if you are that's *really* sick."

Simon snorted, nearly spitting wine across the table. Becky, giggling, pounded him on the back.

"*Emma!*" Max groaned, laughing. He turned back to Simon. "So what was it she wanted?"

"She's petitioning to join the Pride."

"Did she say whether her problem was still a problem?"

"She hoped not, but I'm not as optimistic."

"What's the problem? And don't tell me you can't tell me, because you're the one who brought it up."

The two men looked at each other and grimaced. Simon shrugged. "Sheri was abused by a former boyfriend who's still chasing after her. She's seeking sanctuary with us. Max and I want to offer her a place in the Pride, instead."

Becky and Emma looked at each other, wide-eyed. "Why wasn't she already a part of the Pride?" Emma frowned.

"She refused. Said she didn't want to bring us her troubles, and since Jonathon was Alpha and agreed with her there wasn't much we could do about it."

"Oh. Well I for one say let's bring her in. As long as she's not another Livia things should work out fine."

"I agree. I'm pretty sure we can figure out a way to protect her if her ex shows up."

The two men began quietly discussing how to make Sheridan part of the Pride while minimizing the danger. Emma and Becky watched and listened quietly. Becky was a little alarmed to hear of some of the things the ex had done in the past to Sheri to try and get to her. He sounded really sick. She just hoped they'd be able to keep the poor girl safe.

Becky turned to Emma as the two men continued to discuss Sheri long after they'd completed their main course. "So I've been thinking about painting the walls in Simon's kitchen purple. What do you think, Em?"

"Go for pink." Emma grinned slyly and slanted Simon a sideways look.

"Pink? Really?" Becky saw Simon and Max grinning at one another. "I was thinking I might use the same wallpaper we used in the store. What do you think?"

"Please don't." Simon threw his hands up in surrender. "We'll be good. No more Pride business over dinner, I promise."

"Don't you like the wallpaper in the store, Simon?" Becky batted her lashes at Simon.

"Do the terms 'ick', 'yuck', 'ew' or 'gag' mean anything to you?"

It was Emma's turn to choke, and Max's to pound her back. Becky just crossed her arms over her breasts and raised her brows at Simon. "And just *what* is wrong with the wallpaper in the store?"

"Where to begin?" Simon began stroking his chin thoughtfully. "It's pink. And flowery. And frou-frou. And pink. Mostly pink. The flowers just up the blech factor by about ten."

Becky glared at him as Simon shuddered theatrically. "I picked that wallpaper out."

"In that case, thank you, God, my home is already decorated."

Becky gasped in amused outrage as Simon clasped his hands together in mock-prayer. "I'm putting a patch of that wallpaper above the bed."

"I'll never have a hard-on again," he muttered. "Couldn't you put Jessica Alba up there instead? Ow!" Simon's hearty laugh rang out when Becky smacked his arm.

"Ass wipe."

The waiter came back and took their plates. Emma and Max chose to share a cheesecake slice, while Becky went with the tiramisu and Simon just had coffee.

Becky tried to enjoy her dessert, but Simon was staring at her over his coffee cup. The heat in his gaze sent her pulse racing. She made a face at him, hoping he'd laugh and turn back to Max. Instead, he winked at her over the edge of the cup, his smile so happy she didn't have the heart to be snarky with him.

Chapter Five

Becky opened her apartment door and sighed. After being at Simon's for two nights and all day yesterday her tiny apartment above Wallflowers seemed even more cramped than usual. But she seriously needed some clothes and the rest of her makeup if she was going back to work today. He'd brought her the bare minimum to survive on at his place. Why he thought one pair of jeans and a pair of panties was enough clothing...no, wait. Male brain at work. He'd probably thought she'd run around his house naked all the time, or she'd wear one of his shirts or something. She practically swam in the damn things. No way could she work like that.

Simon had wanted her to take a few days off, just until after her change occurred. He'd been worried that what had happened to Emma would happen to her as well. Emma had also insisted on going to work and wound up changing in one of Max's examination rooms. Luckily for the Pride it had been after closing and no patients were in his practice at the time.

But she didn't feel the same itchy sensations Emma had warned her about during their shopping trip. No fur had sprouted on her arms. Claws hadn't appeared. True, her vision had changed in the car Sunday night, but so far that was the only sign of the change she'd experienced. She'd promised both Emma and Simon that if she felt any of the symptoms Emma had mentioned she would immediately call Emma to cover the store and she would go to Simon's house to wait for him.

In the meantime, she needed clothes, makeup and something to hold back her mane of hair.

She stepped into her tiny kitchenette and felt her heart melt. There on her counter was an eight-piece box of Godiva truffles with a note attached: *Think of me while you enjoy your treat.*

She had to swallow the lump in her throat as she picked up the note. *Damn, Emma, you go, girl.* The only way Simon could have known about her near obsession with Godiva truffles was if Emma told him. She popped one of the delicate confections into her mouth and moaned. *That is so good.* She picked up the box with a greedy grin. *And nobody is getting any of this but me.* If Emma knew Simon had picked her up a box of Godiva chocolate *anything,* she'd try and wheedle a piece out of her, but no way was Becky sharing. *Just call me the Godiva Grinch.* She snickered and put the box in her bedroom closet for safekeeping while she was at work.

Of course, she brought it back down and popped another piece in her mouth before forcing herself to put the box back. She changed clothes quickly, ran a brush through her hair and decided not to bother with makeup today. She was already running late, and her hands were shaking. She was feeling a little off. Everything around her was starting to swirl. "Damn. Should have eaten more than the chocolates." If Emma or Simon discovered that she'd gone to the doc about the dizzy spells she'd never hear the end of it, especially if they found out they occurred more frequently when she'd forgotten to eat. Sort of like this morning, when she'd dashed out of Simon's house. She'd planned on stopping at a fast food place for breakfast, but the accident on Twelfth had slowed everything to a crawl and she hadn't had the time. The last thing she needed was the two of them hovering over her while she waited for the test results to come in. It wasn't like she even knew for sure what was wrong, and until she did? She wasn't saying anything.

The dizzy spell was getting worse. *Better have a quick bite before I head downstairs.* She weaved her way into the kitchen and grabbed an apple off the counter.

A pair of bright green eyes peeked out of the apple and blinked up at her sleepily.

Becky screamed.

Simon was so proud of his mate he could burst. Last night she'd acted like a true Beta, helping make decisions that would ultimately affect the entire Pride. He didn't think she even realized she'd done it, it seemed so natural. And the fact that Emma and Becky already worked well together could only benefit the Pride as a whole, and Simon and Max's interactions as well.

He shrugged into his blue T-shirt and grabbed his wallet off the dresser. He shoved it and his cell phone in his pocket and stepped into his great room. He had a lot of work to do today and was eager to get to it.

He was putting on his sneakers when his cell phone rang. He put on his Bluetooth headset and answered.

It was Max. "I've contacted Sheri. It seems you were right. Her problem hasn't gone completely away."

"Shit." Simon finished tying his sneakers.

"Yeah. Parker found her again."

Simon stood with a sigh and grabbed his car keys. "So when does she arrive?"

Max snorted. "You know me so well."

He shrugged into his coat and headed out the door. "Dude. To quote Becky, 'Ew'. You make it sound like we're fucking married or something." Simon locked his door, grinning as Max made kissy noises over the phone. In the background he could hear Emma giggling. "Sorry, I'm just not into cocktail wieners."

"Asshole." Max laughed.

Simon climbed into his Ram and started it up, eager to get to his studio. "So?"

"She's already here."

"Cool."

"I want you and Becky to take her to dinner. Emma and I would do it, but we've got a meeting with the caterer after work."

"You popped the question?"

"Are you kidding me? She left post-it notes all over my office. What her favorite color is, what type of wedding ring she wants, even a build-your-own-engagement-ring URL with a detailed description of what to buy. She put a catering menu up as the backdrop on the computer, and wedding dress pictures as the screensaver. It was sheer self defense."

Simon put his head down on his steering wheel and howled in laughter. He could see the Little General Post-it bombing Max's office.

"And that was what she did at *work!*"

Simon couldn't breathe, he was laughing so hard.

"Go ahead, laugh. You should have heard Adrian when he got a look at it." Simon could practically hear Max roll his eyes. "She forgot Adrian and I share an office. I've never seen a grown man run so fast in my life." Max snickered. "I can't wait until he finds his mate."

"That should be fun." Simon wiped away the laugh tears. "Oh, man, I can't wait for that."

"Neither can Emma."

"I'll talk to Becky and make sure she's up for dinner tonight. We'll hold the formal intro Sunday?"

"My place; I'll send out the e-mails, let the Pride know. Oh, and bring Becky over to our place for dinner Friday so I can formally acknowledge her, too. She should have changed by then."

"Got it. Bye, Max."

Simon pulled out of his driveway. He pushed the number for Wallflowers and listened to the phone ring.

"Hello?"

"Becky?" He frowned. Something in her tone of voice seemed off.

"It's smiling at me."

"What's smiling at you, baby?" He stopped at a red light and listened to her panting.

"The apple."

"What?"

"I think it's mad because I wanted to eat it."

Her whisper was full of shaky fear. "Becky, where are you?"

"Behind the counter in the store."

"Where's the, um, apple?"

"In my kitchen. I can hear it hopping around up there."

He was starting to get seriously worried. He sped through the intersection as soon as the light turned. "I'm on my way, baby."

"Okay. Simon?"

"Yeah, baby?"

"Tell it I'm sorry and I promise not to eat it if it will go away. Okay?"

The thread of tears in her voice scared him to death. His Becky hadn't cried when the bitch-cat's claws had been imbedded in her stomach, but now she was crying over an apple? Something was seriously wrong here. "Hang on, baby, I'm almost there."

"Okay, Simon. Okay."

"Keep talking to me, sweetheart." Silence greeted him. "Becky?"

Nothing. Not a sound, not even a whisper.

He screeched to a halt in front of the store. Without bothering to switch the ignition off he ran inside, his heart pounding with fear.

"Becky! Where are you?"

Becky was slumped on the floor behind the counter, phone

in hand. She wasn't conscious.

"Hello?"

He turned at the hesitant, familiar voice in the doorway. "Belinda?"

"Simon? Is everything all right?" She stepped into Wallflowers. "Your truck is running and the front door was wide open...oh my God."

He picked Becky up in his arms and carried her to the front door, surprised when Belinda stepped behind the counter and picked up the phone. "What are you doing?"

"Calling Halle General to let them know you're on your way."

"What?"

She was dialing as she spoke. "I'll call Max's and ask Emma to come as quick as she can. I'll stay here until she gets here." She looked up at him. He could clearly hear the ringing of the phone on the other end of the line. "Go!"

He took a deep breath. "Thanks."

She nodded. "We're Pride." She turned back to the phone as Simon heard a voice on the other end say, "Halle General."

He raced out the door, his mate held securely in his arms.

Becky was floating. The colors were so beautiful, so peaceful. Simon had gotten there and everything was fine now. Everything was always fine when Simon was there.

"Any idea what may have caused it?"

He sounded worried. She frowned. Simon shouldn't worry. There was nothing to worry about. Couldn't he feel it?

She heard some papers rustling around. "Yup. She's hypoglycemic."

"Hypoglycemia doesn't cause hallucinations, does it? She was scared of an apple, for God's sake!"

"If it's severe enough, yes, it can. I gather she didn't tell you about this?"

148

Funny, that sounds like my doctor. Wonder what he's doing here?

"No, but you can bet I plan on bringing this up with her."

Oh, now he's getting growly. I wonder why he's growly?

"Simon?" She opened her eyes to see his worried face hovering over her own. She smiled dreamily. Damn, she felt *so* good. "You have beautiful eyes."

"Hey, baby. How are you feeling?"

She stretched. "Mmm, I feel wonderful. Don't you?"

He looked off to his left with a frown. "Doc?"

"Could be a side effect of the glucose we're pumping into her bloodstream."

She lifted one heavy hand and stroked Simon's cheek. "I'm okay."

His frown was fierce. "You scared the hell out of me. Why didn't you tell me you suffer from low blood sugar?"

"The tests hadn't come back yet, so I didn't know if it was hypoglycemia or my thyroid. I didn't want to worry anyone until I knew for sure." She shrugged. "Besides, I had the test on Friday and didn't, um, hook up with you until Saturday night."

"You could have told me any time this weekend."

She stared up at his fierce frown and blushed. "We were busy. *Remember?*"

She heard a laughing cough behind Simon and turned to look. There was Doctor Harrison, hiding a grin behind his hand. "Actually, Simon, you have Max to thank for talking her into getting checked out. He knew the dizzy spells weren't normal and asked her to come see me for blood work."

"So it's definitely hypoglycemia?"

Doc Harrison nodded. "Yup. This means we need to change a few things in your diet. Like making sure you eat regularly."

She winced and refused to look at either of them.

"Also we need to find out what the underlying cause is, make sure there's nothing more serious going on. The fact that you found her unconscious is cause for worry; however, her rapid response to the glucose is encouraging."

She felt Simon breathe a sigh of relief. "So you don't think it's serious?"

"Not enough to warrant an extended hospital stay. We'll monitor her for another hour or two, and then I suggest you take her home. Make sure she eats tonight, and under no circumstances is she to skip a meal. You'll want to get plenty of good carbs into her, along with reducing her sugar intake. But if she seems to be having another episode, by all means hand the woman a regular Coke or glass of juice."

Simon nodded and held out his hand. "Thanks, Doc."

"You're welcome."

"Thanks, Doc Harrison."

The doctor left, leaving them alone in the room. She peeked up at Simon from under her lashes, startled to see the fear in his normally sunny expression.

"You scared the hell out of me."

"I scared the hell out of me, too."

He pulled her into his arms, careful of the IV. "I just got you. I'm not ready to let you go yet."

He's trembling. She ran her hands down his back in an effort to soothe him. The fact that she could make him feel so much humbled her. "I don't plan on going anywhere." She grinned slowly. "After all, I never did get my donuts."

His amused snort was music to her ears.

She had to buy a glucose monitor. Simon wouldn't hear of taking her home without one, and the doctor agreed. Since her blood sugar was back up to normal and she was showing no further signs of problems they released her late afternoon. She'd insisted on returning to her apartment for toiletries and clean clothes and he'd grumbled the whole time. He refused to wait in the car for her, and tried his hardest to tie her to a chair so she wouldn't overexert herself. He was even talking about cancelling the dinner with Sheri just so she could get some rest, even though she felt perfectly fine.

"I'm okay, Simon, really." She watched as he went through her underwear drawer, discarding all of her comfy panties in favor of what she called her "dress-up" panties. She blushed when he pulled out a lacy, pale green thong. With a grin, he added it to the pile to be dumped into the suitcase on the bed.

"Well, I'm not, so indulge me."

The doorbell rang. "I'll get it." She practically flew off the bed, ignoring his growl to "Slow down, damn it!"

She threw open the door and was immediately enveloped by a pair of pale rose arms. "Hi, Emma."

"You scared me!"

"Can't. *Breathe.*"

Emma stepped back. "Oops."

Once Emma let go she sucked in a deep breath. "Damn, woman, you've been eating your Wheaties." She stepped back to let Emma through the door.

Emma blushed bright red. "Hi, Simon!"

"Damn it, Emma! Where's Max?"

"He's at his office, I think. Why?"

Simon stepped out of the bedroom holding a pair of black stockings and a matching garter belt. He had a fierce frown on his face. "Does he know you're not at the store?"

Becky eyed the underwear in his big hands and grinned. "Are you planning on going to see the *Rocky Horror Picture Show*? You'd make a lovely Dr. Frank-N-Furter."

Emma laughed so hard she turned purple. Becky could just see her friend picturing Simon in a corset and heels.

"What?" Simon looked down, rolled his eyes and threw the frilly underwear on the bed. "Well?"

Emma took a moment to catch her breath. "I'm shutting Wallflowers down early, and I'll meet him at home. We're going to the caterer's from there, remember? Why?"

"No reason. I just don't want my ass kicked because he can't find you."

A confused frown crossed Emma's face. "Why would he kick your ass?"

"Because he won't kick yours."

The two women exchanged a confused look and Simon sighed. "Just call the man, okay?"

Emma shrugged. "Okay, Simon, if it will make you happy."

"It will. I and my non-chewed-on ass will thank you."

Emma shook her head and sauntered into the kitchen to call Max. Becky grinned at Simon and shook her head. "I'm going to go pack my makeup and something to wear for tonight, okay?"

"Sure."

He was staring in the direction Emma had gone. He still looked a little growly so she stroked his chest. "Can you keep Emma company while I change clothes?"

Simon frowned, his attention back on her. "I'm still not sure we shouldn't just cancel the dinner with Sheri."

"I have to eat, right? So, why not eat with your old friend?"

His look said he still wasn't sure he shouldn't just wrap her up and put her to bed.

"The doc says I'm fine, Simon. He even told you since I reacted so well to the glucose that he was pretty sure it's *just* hypoglycemia. He also reassured you that I was fine to do everything I normally do tonight." She sighed at the stubborn set of his features. "Tell you what, tomorrow we'll order in some Chinese and you can feed me with chopsticks, okay? We'll stay in and cuddle in front of that wonderful fireplace you have."

He nodded reluctantly. "You're *sure* you feel okay?" He hissed when she started doing jumping jacks. He grabbed her arms and picked her up off the ground. "Don't *do* that!"

She kissed the tip of his nose. "See? I'm fine."

"I'm not!"

"Then let's pack and you can take me home, okay?"

They stared at one another, the shock of her calling his place home in both their faces. Becky could feel the tension slowly easing out of his big body as he lowered her to the ground. "Okay." His lips quirked up into a possessive smile. "Chinese or pizza?"

"Meat lovers?"

"Done."

Just then Emma ended her phone call and grinned at the big artist. "So, Max wants to know what size corset he should buy you. Just in case."

"Emma!"

"Just make sure you get it in pink." Becky was biting the inside of her cheek to keep from laughing, but when he blew a raspberry at them both women collapsed into giggles.

Chapter Six

She'd managed to sneak her truffles into her bag without Emma seeing them. Damn, that pretty brown box tempted her. And Emma was just as bad as she was when it came to Godiva.

"You ready, baby?"

She shoved the truffle in her mouth just as Simon walked through the bedroom door. "All set."

He smiled at her. "Man, I'm glad you wore another dress. You look incredible."

She twirled for him, causing her skirt to flare up around her hips. She heard him moan as the pale green thong flashed him. The black eyelet lace dress was lined in a pale jade silk that matched the panties. Long bell-like sleeves and a square neckline hugged her assets, while the above-the-knee skirt showcased her legs. The black boots she'd worn with the *bandita* costume and chunky gold hoops completed the outfit.

He held out her coat for her just like he had the night of their dinner with Max and Emma. He took her hand and led her into the garage, settling her in her seat first before climbing in himself.

He started the truck and opened the garage door. The soft strains of Loreena McKennitt filled the air, the haunting Celtic melodies flowing out of the speakers and soothing her. She looked at him with a slightly goofy grin. "You stole my CD, didn't you?"

He smiled. "Since most of your CD collection was this Celtic stuff I figured you wouldn't mind."

She stroked his cheek. "Thank you, Simon."

He took her hand and cupped it in his own. He kissed her palm and curled her fingers through his. "You're welcome."

She turned her head and stared out the window. She knew the goofy grin was still on her face.

Rain began to fall, coating the windows in running droplets. She watched the rainbows caused by the streetlamps dance in the drops. She traced one of the running drops with her finger as it slid down the window.

"Baby?"

"Hmm?"

"You okay?"

"Um-hmm." She leaned her head against the window and smiled. Everything felt so peaceful, so Zen. Rainbows danced all over the place. "So pretty."

"Becky!"

"Hmm?" She turned her head to see his worried frown. She patted his cheek, not wanting him to be sad. How could he be sad on such a beautiful night? "It's okay, Catman. Rainbows can't hurt you."

"*Shit*." He pulled into the parking lot of the motel Sheri was currently staying in. Reaching over her, he pulled a packet of cookies out of the glove compartment. "Eat one, baby."

She stared at the chocolate chip cookie he held out. It had rainbows playing across it. "Won't I hurt the rainbows?"

"No, baby. You'll take the rainbows inside, and they'll become a part of you, and that will make them happy."

"Really?"

"Yes, baby. Trust me."

She smiled at him. "Of course I trust you, silly." She took the cookie and began nibbling on it. Suddenly she giggled. "Does this mean I 'taste the rainbow'?"

"I'll be right back, okay? Can you stay in the car?"

She hummed softly to the music. The rainbows were dancing along with it. It was so beautiful she barely heard what he said.

With a sigh he climbed out of the truck. She barely felt his door slam shut, so caught up was she in the multicolored dance in front of her.

Simon was about to lose his mind. Twice in one day? What about that shit the doc told him about the glucose and how as long as she ate she'd be fine? Simon had seen to it personally that Becky ate lunch; hell, he'd stood there practically spoon-feeding her fast food he'd brought to her in the hospital. He'd refused to take a bite of his own until she'd downed at least the burger.

Now here she was, acting like she had that morning, although less scared. If he didn't know better he'd swear she was...

"Simon?"

He started. He had been so caught up in his worry over Becky he hadn't realized he'd stopped in front of Sheri's door. "Sheri, hi." He accepted the hug she gave him. Her pale blonde hair practically glowed against the darkness of his leather trench coat.

She must have felt his tension because she started pulling on his hand, trying to get him to come into her room. "What's wrong?"

"My mate is sick. She's in the car, and I have to get her out of here."

"Oh, no! Is there anything we can do to help?"

"We?"

"Jerry and I."

Simon smiled slightly. Jerry was Sheri's Seeing Eye dog, and usually he grinned whenever he thought of the name she'd given the golden retriever. Now, however, he just didn't have it in him. "No. Look, I'm sorry, but can we reschedule the dinner to tomorrow night? I need to get Becky to the hospital."

"Would you like a rainbow?" Simon turned to see Becky standing in the rain, holding out a cookie to Sheri. "If you eat a rainbow it will go inside you. The colors are so pretty."

He heard Sheri take a deep breath and could only imagine what she was thinking. "Becky, sweetheart, why don't you go sit in the truck, okay?"

She frowned. "I wanted to meet your friend." She looked over his shoulder at Sheri. "She needs a rainbow."

He felt a soft hand touch his arm. "It's okay, Simon." Sheri's pale blue eyes turned to Becky. "Would you like to come in my room and get out of the rain? I promise if you do I'll share the rainbow with you."

Becky's answering smile was beautiful. "Okay."

Sheri gently pulled Becky into her room. Simon was confused when Sheri leaned in close to Becky and sniffed her neck. He followed the two women into the room and watched as Sheri carefully broke the cookie in half. "Here you go. Becky, right?"

Becky nodded happily as she munched on the cookie and stared out the window.

"I'm Sheri."

Becky turned. "You're so pale. Where did your rainbows go?"

Sheri sighed. "I was born without rainbows."

Tears filled Becky's voice. "Here. Take mine." She handed the rest of her cookie to Sheri and turned back to the window. "Everyone should have rainbows."

Sheri sighed and tugged on Simon's arm. Worried sick, Simon allowed himself to be pulled to the other side of the cramped motel room. "I'm so sorry, Simon."

"I need to call her doctor. I *know* she ate today."

Sheri frowned, looking confused. "What does that have to

157

do with anything?"

"She's hypoglycemic. The doc said it can cause hallucinations if it gets bad enough."

"Simon?"

"Hmm?" He was already dialing the phone. He'd made sure to memorize Doc Harrison's number, just in case.

"I don't think it's hypoglycemia."

"Of course it is. She got tested and everything." He listened to the rings and waited for the doctor's answering service to pick up.

Sheri pressed the button to end his call. "Simon, I smell something on her skin."

His heart froze. "What are you talking about?"

Sheri bit her lip. "It smells chemical. I've smelled it before, once or twice, off of Rudy's friends."

At the mention of her ex-boyfriend Simon's Puma snarled. "What?"

"I think your mate's been drugged."

Simon watched as his mate batted at empty air, no doubt playing with the rainbows dancing in front of her, unseen by anyone but her.

I'm going to kill her. There was only one person he could think of who hated Becky enough to drug her, and he'd let the woman walk away. *I'm going to hunt her down and rip out her throat.*

Olivia Patterson was a dead woman.

Simon had been watching her like a hawk ever since their impromptu trip to the emergency room the night before. He'd refused to leave her side, even following her to work. It was driving him crazy that he couldn't figure out how someone had gotten to her. She'd finally talked him into taking a shower by promising she wouldn't eat or drink anything while he was gone. He'd tried to persuade her to join him, but she'd managed to convince him to go in alone.

He might not be sure how someone had gotten to her, but she was. Damn it.

She stared down at the pretty, more than likely toxic, brown box and sighed as the water turned off. "Simon?"

"Yeah, baby?"

"You didn't leave me a box of Godiva truffles, did you?"

"What?" He stepped out of the bathroom, looking yummy wrapped in nothing but a white towel. Droplets of water tripped down his muscled torso, distracting her for a moment. *Damn, he's fine.*

She lifted the box in her hands, the note she'd thought from him resting on top. "You didn't leave these in my apartment the night you went back for my toothbrush and stuff, did you?"

"No, I didn't." If she hadn't been sure before, she was now. The feral growl and ferocious frown were dead giveaways. "Are you telling me you took candy from a stranger?"

"I thought they were from you!" She held up the note. "See? Why would someone other than you write that note?"

"Gee, I don't know, Becky. Maybe because they wanted you to think of them while you were terrified of fruit?"

"Don't get mad at me, Simon. We both thought it was the hypoglycemia."

He ran a hand through his wet hair and sighed. "Damn it, Becky. Why didn't you just ask me? Or, hell, I don't know. Maybe say thank you? And when I asked you what for, you could have told me."

"We were a little busy dealing with the fact that I *am* hypoglycemic, remember?" She shrugged sheepishly. "But you're right, I should have said thank you."

He took the box from her and lifted it to his face. He took a good sniff and wrinkled his nose. "Damn, Sheri's good. I never would have smelled it if I hadn't been looking for it."

"Should we take these to the police?"

"Oh, hell no. The cops aren't really equipped to deal with a shifter, never mind what the outcasting says. That whole 'we leave you to human laws' crap is a holdover from the times when shifters were actively hunted and the Pride was necessary for survival."

"So who does deal with this kind of thing?"

Simon's frown eased as he put the box of chocolates on top of his dresser. "Usually, the Marshal is in charge of this sort of thing, but since you weren't actually hurt I guess he hasn't been alerted yet. Either that, or it has to do with the fact that Max hasn't formally acknowledged you as Pride since you haven't changed yet."

Becky shook her head. "Huh?"

He took her hand and sat with her on the edge of the bed. "Okay. Alpha and Beta run the Pride. The Marshal and his Second guard the Pride's well-being. They're sort of cops, but they only deal with issues that directly affect the physical well-being of the Pride. And the Omega is the heart. He or she keeps the pack emotionally stable, stops fights whenever possible, that sort of thing. Sort of the Pride's diplomat slash advice columnist. With the change in Alpha there's usually a change in the rest of the hierarchy as well. For instance, Adrian's dad used to be Marshal."

"Oh, wow. Wasn't his dad sheriff?"

"Yup. And now Gabe Anderson is sheriff."

"Does that make him Marshal?"

He shrugged. "I don't know. We've only been running the Pride for a few months, so we're not completely set up yet. Max knows instinctively who's supposed to fill what slots, and when the time comes, he'll clue them in. And, trust me, it will be obvious." He glared down at her. "In the meantime, we make sure you don't eat any more presents not handed to you by either myself or Max and Emma. Okay?"

"Okay." She stroked his cheek, knowing he was being so

grouchy because he was so upset. He relaxed visibly, nuzzling her hand. "Better get dressed and order in that pizza. I'm starving."

"You're always starving." He stood and dropped the towel, grinning over his shoulder at her when she wolf-whistled. He made a big production out of pulling on his underwear and jeans, wiggling his butt and waggling his eyebrows until she collapsed onto the bed with a fit of the giggles. With a big, smacking kiss on her lips he left the bedroom to order in dinner.

Becky heard the pizza guy before he rang the bell, and grinned. "Pizza's here."

Simon's stomach rumbled under her, making her laugh. He'd pulled her on top of him and cuddled her while they watched the cartoon DVDs she'd shoved into one of her bags.

With a groan he gently pushed her off him and went to answer the door. The sight and scent of the white boxes had her mouth watering. He carried the food into the kitchen, frowning slightly when she got up and followed him.

"One for you, one for me?" Becky was so hungry she could easily picture eating an entire pizza.

"Breadsticks."

Becky handed Simon the plates. He loaded them with pizza and breadsticks while she poured them both tall, frosty glasses of soda. They headed back to the couch to eat. Simon popped another DVD into the player.

"Man, I'm starving." Hot, cheesy goodness melted in her mouth, causing her to moan in appreciation. "God, that's good." She sighed in bliss just before taking another bite.

The opening strains of the WB's *Animaniacs* filled the small space. She grinned as Simon dropped next to her onto the sofa with a contented sigh. They sat and ate pizza, laughing at the antics of the Warner Brothers and their sister, Dot, until all of the pizza and breadsticks were gone. When Becky stood to get rid of their empty plates and glasses Simon turned the TV off.

"Bedtime."

Simon's husky purr sent a shiver down her spine. "Think I'm up for games tonight, big guy?"

"Considering the amount of food you just ate you should be fine."

She glared up at him as his arms came around her waist. "Are you saying I made a pig of myself?"

He tried to look innocent and failed miserably. "Not at all. I'm just saying I've seen high school linebackers eat less."

He laughed when she punched him in the arm. She shook her stinging hand. "Ow!"

"Poor baby. Did you hurt your hand?"

"Shut up, Simon."

"Want me to kiss it and make it better?"

"How about you kiss my ass instead?" Becky screeched, giggling madly as Simon picked her up, took her over to the couch and put her face down. Her face flamed as Simon kissed her butt with a loud smacking sound. "Simon!"

"Hey, you told me too." Laughter threaded through his voice.

She looked over her shoulder. "Jerk."

She felt him undo the snap on her jeans. "Go ahead. Tell me to kiss your ass again." He lowered the zipper, his grin heating. Gold danced in his eyes. "I dare you."

She shivered as one of his hands slipped under the waistband of her jeans and caressed her ass. "Simon?"

"Yeah, baby?"

"Your phone is ringing."

He paused and, sure enough, the phone rang. He waited to see who was calling. When the caller hung up he shrugged. "Thank God for answering machines." He pulled her jeans down her legs, sighing happily at the sight of the pale blue thong separating the globes of her ass. "Damn, woman. I love your ass."

"Yeah, sure."

He nipped one of the soft globes, suckling until he'd left a mark. "That's better."

She started to laugh. "Damn it, that tickles!"

"Oh, really?" He gasped in mock surprise. "Look! Another one!" He bent down and nipped and sucked until he'd added his mark. "There. That's better."

The male satisfaction in his tone only made her laugh harder. "Simon!"

"What?"

"Knock it off!"

"What will I get if I do?"

"Chocolate?"

He petted her ass again, then smacked it. Hard.

"Ow!" She sat up, glaring at him. "What the hell was that for?"

"A reminder." He stripped off his shirt, his eyes turning completely gold.

"Of what?"

"Not to take candy from strangers, little girl."

"Ass wipe."

"Want me to kiss it and make it better?" He stripped off his jeans, leaving them where they fell. He stood there only in his briefs, his erection twitching behind the white cotton.

Becky couldn't tear her gaze away from his cock. There was a damp spot on the front of the briefs, letting her know exactly how turned on he was. "What?"

He laughed, the sound low and rough. He pulled her jeans the rest of the way off her body, then began to crawl up her.

She backed up until she hit the backrest. "Simon?"

He licked her belly.

"Simon?"

His hands slowly began to push her shirt up, the calluses rough against her skin.

"Oh, boy. Simon?"

When his hands touched her naked breasts they both moaned. "No bra. Damn, baby." He thumbed her nipples under her shirt. He pushed it up impatiently, leaning over her to suck a nipple into his mouth.

"Mmm." She clutched his head, her fingers tangling in his hair. The pleasure his mouth was giving her shot through her body. She spread her legs wider, enjoying his groan when she pushed her hips up against his. She could feel his erection pulse through the thin material of their underwear.

"Bed. Now." Simon stood, picking her up and carrying her into his bedroom.

She started nibbling on his neck, loving the small shivers that wracked his frame as he carted her to the bedroom. He tumbled them both onto the bed, careful to catch himself on his hands.

"Now, where were we?"

She grinned, grabbed his head and pulled his mouth back to her chest.

The shirt disappeared as Simon suddenly seemed to become all hands, lips and teeth. She barely had time to whimper as his mouth descended once again on her breast, practically sucking the entire thing into his mouth.

Her hand shook as she reached down to caress him through his briefs. He ground against her hand, his hiss of pleasure spurring her on. She slipped her fingers into the waistband of his underwear, slicking her fingertips in the pre-come leaking from the tip of his cock.

"Fuck." He pulled away from her and shoved off his briefs. "Do you love these panties?"

"No, why?"

His answer was to claw them from her body. Long, shallow

scratches appeared on her hips. Surprisingly, instead of pissing her off the slight sting only turned her on.

Simon descended on her body, feasting his way down to her pussy with hungry slurps and purring licks until she was gasping for breath. He clasped her thighs roughly, fingers digging in as he pried her legs apart and fell on her like a starving man.

He took her clit into his mouth and sucked on it, stroking it with his tongue until she thought she would scream. It was almost too much, bordering on the painful, but she didn't care, she was coming into his mouth with an agonized groan.

Simon licked her juices from his lips. "Again."

She gasped at his rough growl. He slid a finger inside her, roughly fucking her with it as his lips once again fastened onto her clit. He purred again, vibrating his tongue as another orgasm raced through her shaking body.

"More."

"No, no more, Simon." She started pushing his head away, afraid her heart couldn't take another one of the mind-blowing orgasms he'd pulled from her.

He held fast, adding another finger to her already sensitized flesh.

"God, Simon, get up here and fuck me already!"

He growled and sucked one last time at her clit before sliding up her body. He slid into her easily. She was still soaking wet from her two previous orgasms. He leaned over her and nipped at her neck, right on his mark, and incredibly she could feel herself building to yet another orgasm.

"Move, move, move." She wrapped her legs around his waist and her arms around his neck as he nibbled at his mark.

He started to fuck her hard, his cock dragging in and out of her body in a steady rhythm as his teeth sank in. The spike towards orgasm shifted sharply. She could feel his muscles tensing, her pussy pulsing around him.

Her gaze fell on his neck, and she had the sudden, undeniable urge to bite him back. Without thinking about it she shifted her head slightly and bit down.

She tasted his blood as her fangs sank deep.

Simon stilled, releasing his bite. *"Fuck!"* He pounded into her body, the headboard banging into the wall so hard she heard something crack.

She came mere seconds before he did, pulling his seed from his body as she screamed around his flesh. She could feel him shuddering above her as he came, the *"Mine!"* he gasped no longer a surprise.

He collapsed next to her, his breathing labored, his face buried in his pillow. Sweat gleamed on his body. Her mark glowed red against his skin.

"Love you, baby."

She felt him relax with a soft sigh and realized with a start that he was already asleep. She had to hold back the urge to giggle. *Damn, I fucked him unconscious! I rock!*

She eased away carefully, pulled the sheets and comforter over them both, and curled up into him, her head resting below his chin. She dragged his arm around her waist. "Love you too."

Simon listened to his mate's even breathing and smiled. Now all he had to do was figure out how to get his stubborn mate to say those three little words when she knew he was awake.

Chapter Seven

"Mmm, coffee." Becky stared at the pot like it was liquid nirvana. "I love that you make me coffee." She looked up at Simon with what he privately thought of as Bambi eyes. "Marry me and bear my young?"

"Yes, and I'd be happy to if I had the equipment." He grinned and held out the mug of steaming coffee, not surprised when she shuddered in what looked like a mini-orgasm. "But I'll be happy to help you in all the stages. Especially the conception part."

He wasn't entirely certain she heard him. Her face contorted in bliss, the mug never far from her lips. *So much for a good morning kiss,* he thought, amused. *Good thing she doesn't know that's half strength, or I'd be wearing my nuts as a necklace.*

When she groaned in sensual pleasure he nearly came in his jeans. "Stop that, woman, we have things to do today."

The amusement on her face told him she knew exactly what she was doing. She'd propped her butt against the kitchen counter, no doubt remembering last night's love tap.

"C'mere," he whispered, pulling her gently to him. He hugged her, rubbing his cheek along the top of her head. He smiled, pleasure tingling under his skin when he realized she was purring. He tilted that fey face of hers up for a gentle kiss that tasted of coffee and Becky. "Good morning, baby."

She sighed and actually put the coffee mug down to hug him back. "Good morning."

"Are you ready for today?"

"What's today?"

"You're changing, baby."

"Huh?" She picked up her mug and took another sip, her eyes nearly crossing in pleasure.

"Your eyes are changing, and last night you marked me."

She eyed the mark she'd left on his neck. It was clearly visible under the edge of his black T-shirt. "Um. You mean the teeth thing?"

"Yup. You had fangs, sweetheart." He had to suppress a shiver at the memory of her teeth sliding into his flesh. His dick jumped, letting him know his body was more than up for another bite.

"Oh, boy."

"So that means you're not going in to work today."

"What?" She frowned, obviously ready to argue with him.

"You can't go into work today. Not that I'm all that upset about it." He could feel his Puma growling in his chest. The memory of his mate drugged was going to be with him for quite a while. He was more than happy to have an excuse to keep her close for another day.

"Haven't we been over this? I'm fine, damn it! Why can't I go to work?"

"You're changing." *Okay, if she's not getting it maybe I should have made the coffee full strength.*

"So?"

"So, how would you feel about having a Puma roaming Wallflowers?"

Her expression was arrested. Just about everything in Wallflowers was delicate and fragile. Not exactly a place for a Puma to stretch out in.

Simon laughed softly. "I'll take you somewhere safe for your first transformation. I'll be there to help you. After this one you should be able to control it all on your own. Okay?"

Becky sighed. "Damn."

"I've got donuts."

She grinned. "Oh, well, then. Count me in."

He couldn't help it. He leaned down and kissed the grin off her mouth, happier than he'd ever thought possible.

He waited until he knew the change was definitely coming. It surprised him that it took most of the day. He'd have to talk to Jamie Howard to see if the drugs in her system could have slowed it down. There was still so much they didn't know about their Pumas, but Jamie was dedicated to finding out.

At dusk he drove her out to the Fricdclinde's, the starting point of the Pride lands. When she asked about the duffel bag he put in the car, he grinned and told her to wait and see.

He'd called ahead to let Jonathon know what was going on and wasn't surprised to see Marie standing in the doorway. He hopped out of the truck and pulled out the empty duffel bag, turning to see Becky had gotten out of the passenger side on her own. He waved a cheery hello to Marie, smiling when she bowed her head slightly in deference to his status. When she did the same to Becky he couldn't hold back his proud grin.

"What was that all about?"

He led her around the back of the house towards the gardens. Behind the gardens were the woods and hills the Pumas loved to run in. "Once you change, Max will formally introduce you to the Pride."

"So?"

"So, you'll be Beta along with me."

"You're kidding. Just because I mated you?"

"No, because you're strong enough." He shrugged. "Some of them might try to test you like they did Emma, but I don't think you'll have a problem."

She stopped dead. "Tested Emma?"

He chuckled at the growl in her voice. He took her arm and started her moving again. "At the masquerade she tried to get out into the garden. Some of the Pride members decided to just not get out of her way. She was forced to use her gifts to get through them."

She whistled softly. "She must have been pissed."

"She was magnificent. Everything a Curana should be."

She was staring at him suspiciously. "Really turned you on, huh?"

It was his turn to stop as he stared at her in horror. "That's like popping wood for your sister." He shuddered.

She snickered as he led her out of the garden and into the woods.

He removed her jacket, revealing the pale green T-shirt molded lovingly to her body. He'd convinced her she didn't need a bra, and now her nipples perked up cheerfully in the cold November air. "Okay, baby, get naked."

"Excuse me?"

He grinned, something he found himself doing a lot around her. She had both hands on her hips, one hip cocked in that classic "you gotta be kidding me" woman pose men everywhere recognized. It just drew Simon's attention to those incredibly tight black jeans she was wearing. "You heard me. Get naked."

"Sure, Garfield. Do I get a brass pole to swing from?" She edged back, grinning at him with bared teeth.

"Baby, as much as I'd love to play chase right now, your eyes have turned gold and your arms are getting furry." He nearly laughed when she looked down at her arms and squealed. He even held back when she turned on him with a bright gold glare, her normally short nails turning into claws as the change began to overtake her.

"Get naked now or I'm coming over there to help you."

Max had allowed Emma to dictate how her change would

go, and she'd wound up in one of Max's examination chairs, fully dressed. Simon had no intention of following the Pride Alpha's lead in *that* regard. Pulling jeans off a pissed off Puma was not how he wanted to spend his evening.

She growled at him but pulled off her shirt, revealing her B-cup breasts to his hot gaze. "Careful there, Garfield, I've always wanted a fur coat."

"Don't worry, you'll be wearing me soon enough," he purred, watching as she stripped off her jeans and panties.

"Now what?"

For an answer he began undressing, watching her every reaction. He nearly groaned when he pulled off his jeans and she licked her lips, her gaze glued to his erection. When he stood naked before her he grinned. "Ready to play pounce?"

Startled, she looked at him a second before she began changing. He followed her, timing his change to hers. He let her see each stage as it happened to him, hoping to keep any fear and confusion on her part at bay. The playful flick of her tail and the affectionate head rub to his shoulder made the whole thing worthwhile.

She made a gorgeous Puma, sleek and deadly looking. They ran for a few hours, listening to the rustling of the night creatures in the forest. They lazed by a stream, watching the moonlight on the water. He thought about mounting her in cat form, but decided that the she might not be ready yet for Puma sex. Besides, he was still worried about her health. He made sure they hunted down a nice, juicy rabbit early in their run, giving her the lion's share of the meat. She'd wrinkled her nose when presented with the rabbit, but her Puma had quickly taken over and she'd done fine.

The sheer joy in running and playing in the moonlight with his mate was almost overwhelming. He cat-grinned as he watched her roll around in a field of clover; laughed his ass off when she tried pouncing on a field mouse and missed, going tail over ears. The half-hearted swipe she aimed at him missed him by a mile.

They were heading back to the car when he saw the deer. It was stumbling, obviously wounded. His Puma snarled as they smelled the blood; his human half smelled a trap. It took all of his willpower to keep from going after the animal.

Becky, however, didn't have his experience. She went after the deer, gleefully taking it down before he could stop her. He bounded after her, snarled a warning to try and keep her from ripping into the deer's entrails, but she ignored him. Red blood dripped from her claws as she gutted the deer in one swipe.

He managed to get to her just before she sank her teeth into the deer's soft belly. He pounced on her, biting into the back of her neck and holding her down, forcing her to submit to him. With a snarl she went limp beneath him.

He didn't dare change back to explain himself. If he did, Becky's Puma would pounce on the dead meat now lying on the forest floor, feasting on it with abandon. But he couldn't talk to her in this form. Unlike fantasy, shifters didn't automatically get the ability to speak telepathically with one another. They communicated in gestures, or waited until they changed back to human. So he was stuck there, holding down a young, newly made Puma while blood scented the air. His own Puma fought and snarled and raged, eager to feast on the meat its mate had provided.

"Hmm. Now isn't that a pretty picture."

A growl rose in his throat at the sound of Livia's voice.

"Hello, Simon. Hello, Becky."

She looked like she'd been camping in the woods. Her hair was braided tightly, a plaid cap pulled low over her brow. She was in a hunter's jacket, jeans and hiking boots, and she reeked faintly of wood smoke and sweat.

He snarled at the sight of the rifle in her hand. The barrel was trained on Becky's head.

"I've been waiting all week for this night. Now get off of her or I'll blow her head off."

Slowly he backed up, never looking away from the blonde who'd tried to take his mate from him.

My mate! Mine! The snarl of his Puma filled the air. By approaching Becky again and threatening his mate's life, *again*, her own life was now forfeit.

All he had to do was play the game and wait for his chance.

Livia shook her head. "Uh-uh-uh." She smiled sweetly down at Becky. "Why don't you have some dinner, dear?"

Becky growled low in her throat. Simon couldn't tell if it was over the meat or the blonde threatening them both.

"Go ahead, kitty. Have some venison. Mm-mmm, wouldn't some meat taste really good right about now? I bet you're hungry." Livia smirked. "Did you enjoy the chocolates I left you?"

The growl died in Becky's throat. Her attention zeroed in on the woman in front of her, her body moving into a classic pouncing pose as she froze in front of Livia.

"Don't even think about it." Livia stared down the barrel of the gun, hatred suffusing her features and rendering her ugly. He knew if Becky so much as twitched wrong Livia would fire.

Suddenly, Becky relaxed. She sat on her haunches, ignoring the blood on her claws as she tilted her head to the side. She stared at Livia with all the amused disdain a cat was capable of showing. He wanted to yowl. *What the hell is she up to?*

"You little..."

Simon's heart nearly stopped as Livia's finger tightened on the trigger.

Livia's cell phone rang, the tinny sounds of Mozart's *Alla Turca* loud and startling. She glanced down briefly at her hip...

...And Simon pounced, taking her down before she could get a shot off. Without giving Becky a chance to stop him he ripped the blonde's throat out, sitting back to watch impassively as her life bled out onto the forest floor.

As the last of her choking gasps faded away, Simon screamed his triumph to the sky.

Chapter Eight

Saturday morning dawned bright and clear. Simon sat up in bed, surprised to see Becky was up before him. The bathroom was empty, meaning she'd been up for at least half an hour.

He got up, stretched and padded naked into the bathroom. He did his business, brushed his teeth and hair, and thought about a shower. He decided against it, knowing that putting in Adrian's hardwood floors would be a tiring, sweaty job. He'd do better to wait until he got home. He got dressed quickly, anxious to see his mate before he started his day. She'd probably already had her first cup of coffee, so she'd be relatively human.

"Morning, baby," he called out cheerfully as he stepped out of the bedroom.

She merely smiled at him over the edge of her mug. There were still shadows on her face from their night in the woods, but not once had she flinched away from him. He'd been terrified that he'd lose her after she'd seen him kill Livia. Instead she'd curled up around him, trying her best to soothe *him*.

It baffled him, but hey, he'd been able to hold her close, and that was all that mattered.

Jamie had taken both Livia and the dead deer back to the mansion. The deer had been poisoned. If either he or Becky had eaten any of the meat they'd be lying dead on the forest floor themselves. After a little searching they found three other deer in the forest, similarly poisoned, and Livia's campsite.

He had no idea what Jamie did with Livia's body or the dead animals. He knew Max had been called and consulted. It was quickly decided that Livia's death was to be a secret between the Pride's Alphas, Betas and their doctor, Jamie. If a Marshal was ever appointed, he assumed he or she would be told, but no one else.

Thursday had been spent quietly cleaning up the mess and talking with his mate. He was surprised to learn she wasn't upset over his killing Livia. As far as she was concerned he'd done what he had to in order to protect them both. And last night Max had formally acknowledged Becky as part of the Pride and confirmed the fact that she was, indeed, Beta female.

Simon gave Becky a casual kiss on the top of her head and sat in front of his cereal bowl. He needed to decompress after the stresses of the last week. A day of back-breaking, sweaty labor with his best buddies, followed by cold beer and pizza, should do the trick nicely.

He picked up his spoon, eager to start his day. Luckily the odor hit his nose before the spoon hit his mouth. He looked down, staring at the Cat Chow in his bowl. He blinked and gently set the spoon down. "Am I allowed to know *why* I'm in trouble or should I just start apologizing generically?"

"Adrian."

He looked up at her with raised brows. "Adrian pissed you off and I'm getting Cat Chow?"

"You didn't ask me to help."

He looked up at her, totally baffled. "What?"

She huffed out a sigh. "I'm really good with home improvements."

"You're opening and closing the store today."

"I know."

"You *can't*, literally *can not*, help."

"I know."

"Then why the Cat Chow?"

"It's the principle of the thing," she sniffed.

His mouth opened, but nothing came out. He just couldn't think of a single thing to say to that, other than, *"What?"*

She huffed out a sigh. "If you'd asked me, I could have said no instead of feeling left out."

Simon lowered his head in his hands. "At least my life will never be boring."

"I heard that."

He glared at her from between his hands. He couldn't decide whether or not he wanted to paddle her ass or laugh. "Can you and Emma afford an assistant?"

Becky tilted her head to the side, her expression turning inward. He could practically see the numbers dancing in her head. "Part time, definitely. I'm not sure about full-time."

"Hire Sheri, she could use a job. Then when things like this come up you have coverage."

It was her turn for her mouth to open and close like a fish. "Uh. Good idea."

He got up, poured the Cat Chow into the garbage and poured her another cup of coffee. "Here. Apparently your brain isn't on-line yet."

She blew him a raspberry.

He blew her a kiss.

They both grinned. He was delighted to see the shadows were gone from her eyes.

He quickly ate a bowl of cereal; if he didn't hurry he'd be late. Becky watched silently, nursing her coffee.

He snagged his jacket off the back of the sofa where he'd dumped it the night before. Tugging it on quickly, he leaned over and kissed the top of her head. "Love you," he muttered absently as he strode for the door.

"Love you too. Have a good day."

He stopped, hand on the doorknob. She hadn't said it to him yet, other than that one time in bed when she'd thought he was asleep. He could feel his heart pounding as her words washed over him. "Could...you repeat that?"

She smirked at him over the back of the sofa. "Have a good day."

He growled at her, challenging her to repeat it.

She smiled smugly and snuggled back on the chaise part of the sofa. "Bye."

"Oh, no you don't," he muttered. In two long strides he was in front of her. "Say it again."

She bit her lip, trying to look innocent. "Bye?"

He leaned down and kissed the tip of her nose. "Becky."

"Simon?"

He smiled, slow and sensuous. "I love you."

"Good."

He gently took the coffee mug out her hands and put it on the coffee table. "Say it."

"Nope."

"Becky."

"Can't make me, neither."

Simon crawled on top of her, holding her in place by sitting on her legs. He pulled out his cell phone and called Adrian as Becky giggled. "Hey, I'm going to be a little bit late, okay? See you in about an hour." He put his phone back in his pocket and pulled his jacket back off. "Say it again."

"Nope." She was laughing up at him now, her hands resting on top of his thighs.

He pulled off his shirt. "Again, Becky."

"Nuh-uh."

He pulled off her shirt while she grinned up at him. "Again."

"Or what, you'll fuck me silly? Explain to me how I lose

here."

He leaned in and licked his mark, dragging his tongue along it slowly while she shivered beneath him. When he blew raspberries against the mark she giggled again and tried to squirm away. "Tell me." He was trying desperately not to laugh. His whole body felt so full of joy he felt like he could fly.

"No!"

She was laughing outright now as he began to tickle her. "Tell me."

"Uncle! Uncle!"

He sat up, grinning down at her.

"Your phone's ringing," she sputtered.

He leaned down and kissed her as the phone in his pocket began to ring.

Cat of a Different Color

Dedication

To Mom, who taught me the important things in life, like "That black doesn't go with that black" and "Never let your children know you aren't psychic".

To Dad, who grins whenever he hears about my work, even though he refuses to read it. For which I am eternally grateful, because that would just be... wrong, on so many levels.

To Memom, who encourages my madness and likes to know what I'm working on next.

To Stephanie, for pointing out some mistakes I'd made with Jerry and his responses, and gave me more insight into what it's like to be legally blind.

And to my husband, Dusty. Happy tenth anniversary, sweetheart. *"Every step I took since the moment I could walk was a step toward finding you."*

—*Message in a Bottle*

Chapter One

"God, I hate winter. If it wasn't for the hurricanes I'd move to Florida."

Adrian knocked on the hotel room door and sighed, rolling his eyes at the sight of his breath in the air. He hoped the girl (Cheryl? Shelly? No, Sheri!) didn't keep him waiting too long. Adrian shivered and wished desperately he was back in his own warm home, with a roaring fire and a good book.

He'd been volunteered by Max to pick up the newest Pride member. Tonight was supposed to be her formal introduction, though she'd already been approved by both the Alphas and the Betas. Only Max could get Adrian to stand outside in the cold like this, but that was okay. He planned on exacting his own kind of revenge. He grinned, thinking of all the ways he could encourage Emma's pre-marital madness.

The Alpha's mate had gone completely insane, post-it bombing the office with little notes and to-do lists. She either kept forgetting that he shared desk space with Max or enjoyed tormenting him with wedding cake photos. It was enough to send a confirmed bachelor into sugar shock.

Adrian didn't want a mate. He smiled to himself. His best friends had both become pussy-whipped, all in the space of a couple of weeks. Emma said "Jump!" and the big strong Alpha asked not only how high but which direction. As for Simon, if Becky so much as sighed he panicked. Watching the two strongest members of the Pride buckle under the Breast

Brigade made him all the more determined to stay sanely single.

"Just a moment," a soft voice called from inside. It sounded shy and sweet, and Adrian's Puma raised its head curiously. He could feel his dick hardening slightly at the sound of her velvety voice.

"What the hell?" he muttered, frowning at the closed door. Shrugging, he tried to dismiss his body's reaction.

"Who is it?"

That soft voice sent a shaft of pure lust through his veins. He twitched his shoulders and tried to dismiss the low growling sound of his Puma. "Adrian Giordano. I'm the friend Max said would be picking you up tonight." Why the hell the woman couldn't drive herself was a mystery, but he'd been so busy he'd forgotten to ask.

He could hear the locks disengage and tensed. His Puma let loose a low growl he'd never heard from it before, and he had to clamp his lips shut to keep it from emerging from his human lips. His eyes flashed, the colors of the setting sun turning from red to gold as he lost the red/green color spectrum. He forced them to change back, closing his eyes just as the door to the room swung open.

"Hi, Dr. Giordano. I'm Sheri Montgomery."

He opened his eyes to find a snow princess staring back at him. She had the palest, softest-looking blonde hair he'd ever seen. The nearly white locks fell in delicate waves just past her shoulders. Pale, crystal blue eyes surrounded by equally pale lashes glowed in a face that could make the angels weep. She was small and dainty, the top of her head barely reaching his shoulder. Her breasts were perfect for her slight frame. He had the inexplicable urge to pick her up, toss her over his shoulder and carry her off to his den where no one else would ever see her. Would ever want her.

Mine.

Adrian's eyes widened as his Puma snarled in his mind. "Crap."

She tilted her head to the side and sort of off center. She lowered the hand he hadn't even realized she'd raised in greeting. "Excuse me? Is everything all right?"

"Uh, no, everything's fine." He hoped to God she couldn't see the erection straining against his trousers.

"Would you like to come in for a moment while I get my coat?"

Adrian gulped as she smiled, sweetly uncertain.

Can I come in for a year? Or two? How about I just come? He did his best to bludgeon the voice of lust to death, but it refused to die. He wanted to throw her down on the ugly green carpet and fuck her until neither one of them could walk for a week. Maybe a month. *Try years,* his Puma purred. "Sure, thanks."

It didn't even occur to him that he was already thinking of her as his.

She opened the door wide, standing aside and waving him in with another shy smile. He stepped in quickly, grateful when she swung the door shut behind him. He took a look around her hotel room, her suitcases, anything to keep from looking at her, because the moment he did he wanted to strip her bare and sink into her. When she turned to grab her coat he nearly groaned at the sight of her perfect, heart-shaped ass.

She swiftly thrust her arms in the sleeves. The coat swirled around her, the off-white color only emphasizing her pale loveliness. Then she moved to the side of the bed. Carnal thoughts raced through his head as she bent to pick up something off the ground, really showcasing her ass. He couldn't see what she was picking up because a) it was on the other side of the bed, b) the object of his sudden and total lust had just bent over near a bed, and c) that *ass*. Even hidden by the coat it had the power to make him hard. He tried not to picture her naked, but he wasn't really trying all that hard. Another moan tried to escape, and the ugly green carpet turned yellowish brown, letting him know his eyes had shifted again.

"There you go," her soft voice crooned. His cock twitched in response; the stupid thing thought she was talking to him. He was surprised to see what she was talking to, although with all of the visual clues he shouldn't have been. She stepped out from around the edge of the bed holding the harness of a Seeing Eye dog. She bit her lip nervously. "It's okay if I bring Jerry, right? I know how some people are about dogs in their cars."

"Yeah, it's fine," he said, staring at the woman in front of him. *OCA, probably type one.* The white-blonde hair, pale blue eyes, nearly white skin...why hadn't he put the clues together before? Most people with type one albinism were legally blind and required vision aids; as an optometrist he should have caught the signs, but he'd been so busy trying to ignore his dick (and her ass) that he'd missed the obvious. "Do you have your sunglasses?" Another commonality in albinism was sensitivity to light, but some chose wide-brimmed hats instead of sunglasses since sunglasses could impair what little vision they had.

She smiled again, this one sunny and warm with a tinge of relief. "Yes, they're on the dresser." She walked to the dresser, picked up a pair of black sunglasses with dark gray lenses and put them on. "There. All ready."

As she walked past him he inhaled as quietly as he could. *God, she smells good; all crisp and clean, like fresh snow, with an overlay of...coconut? Sunscreen, right.* With the sun still in the sky she'd need the extra protection for all that pale skin. He cleared his throat and adjusted his pants; if his cock got any harder he'd be able to hammer nails with the damn thing.

He followed her out of the hotel room and waited while she locked her door. Taking a firm grip on Jerry's lead she held out her free hand. Without thought he tucked it into his elbow, leading her to his car.

"So you share a practice with Max?"

He ignored the sudden surge of jealousy at the affection in her voice. "Yes, Max came home and partnered with me a little over three months ago."

She smiled, her head tilted to the side again. "Simon and Becky took me to dinner a few days ago. I liked her. She suits him."

Adrian shuddered. "Yes, I know."

Sheri grinned up at him. "Why the shudder?"

"Becky's...well, Simon once told me that he thought of her as 'noisy, spiky and opinionated.'"

"She seems to have him well in hand."

Adrian ignored the thread of humor running through her voice and chose to focus on her words. "Yes, she does."

Her brows rose in surprise as he reached his black Mustang. "You have a problem with that?"

He opened the rear door and Jerry hopped right in. "It's more a bachelor thing than a Becky thing." He helped her in and shut her door, then moved to the driver's side. He climbed in and started the car. "Becky and Emma are both great women, and Simon and Max love them, but that whole 'hop because I said so' just doesn't appeal."

"So I gather you aren't looking for a mate?"

Nope. Already found her. Once again that annoying little voice refused to stay silent. "Not really," he hedged.

"Good," she replied firmly. "Neither am I."

His Puma screamed its protest. Adrian did his best to ignore it, but it wasn't easy. The world changed color on him in that subtle way that let him know his eyes had changed. Damn. He forced them back to brown as he pulled onto the road and headed towards Max and Emma's. "Rumor has it Becky and Emma offered you a job?"

She nodded. "Part-time, but right now I'll take what I can get until I can get a place and get my other business up and running."

"What do you do?" he asked as he took the turn to Max's house.

"I'm a technical writer. I write documentation, specializing in voice recognition software for the blind."

He slowly grinned. "Really?"

"Don't sound so surprised. Technology has made things so much easier for those of us who have handicaps."

"I never said it didn't. I just think it's awesome." He paused, wondering if she'd be offended if he asked. "How bad is your vision?"

She tilted her head down and off to one side again; he knew enough about her condition to know that she was making the best of her limited vision. "I'm twenty/two hundred."

To see what one person could see from two hundred feet away, she had to be within twenty feet. That was the definition of legally blind. It explained why she didn't drive. Most states would grant a limited license only if the person's visual range was twenty/seventy with correction.

He did his best to ignore her stare as he parked in the street. Max's driveway was full up; they were almost the last ones to arrive. He got out of the car and walked around to her side, letting her out first before he opened the door for Jerry. He stared at the dog, who stared back. "By the way, I've been meaning to ask you something." He took her arm again and began walking.

"What?"

"Sheri and Jerry?"

"Shaddup." She grinned, totally relaxed with him. That small sign of trust warmed him down to his toes despite the chill November air. "Dork."

Chapter Two

Thank God for her dark glasses. She'd been told that with most Pumas their eyes flashed gold when upset (*or aroused*, her inner kitty purred). Hers flashed red. These poor people would think she was some sort of demon if they saw that. They'd flashed red when she caught Adrian's scent outside her motel room door. When she'd heard his voice for the first time her claws had damn near extended. She'd managed to wrestle her Puma into submission, but every time the delicious Dr. Giordano spoke she could feel her inner kitty purring as if he'd petted her.

Oh, pet me, Dr. Adrian!

The *mine* her Puma had snarled hadn't helped. Her declaration that she wasn't looking for a mate sounded fake even to herself.

Although technically speaking, it was true. It seemed she'd found her mate, whether she wanted to or not.

She was going to have to figure out a way to keep him safe from Rudy; somehow she doubted that would be as easy as it sounded.

The front door to Max's house opened. "Hi, Sheri!"

She braced herself as Simon's enthusiastic mate embraced her like a long lost friend. "Hi, Becky." She could see the Beta female's ultra-curly hair and the paleness of her face. Becky's features were clear because she was so close, the bright jade green of Becky's eyes twinkling merrily. "Where's Emma?" Sheri was dying to meet the Curana. She'd spoken to her on the phone and Becky had heaped praise upon the woman's head, but it didn't change the fact that she had to meet the Curana face to face and get her approval before the other members of the Pride would accept her.

"Right here," a husky female voice replied. Becky was pulled away and Sheri braced herself again. A small woman moved into her field of vision, and she tilted her head to see her better. She saw long dark hair and dark eyes in a golden-skinned face, but unless she came closer her features would remain a blur. "Max," that husky voice drawled.

"Yes?" Max's familiar voice drawled back.

"Are you sure you never slept with her?"

"Emma." Max laughed as he moved up behind the small woman. His familiar scent wafted over her.

"Blonde, gorgeous...explain to me how you didn't sleep with her. Hell, I'm straight and I'd do her."

"Emma!"

"We didn't want to," Sheri replied, somewhat startled by her welcome.

She could feel Emma's attention swirl back to her. *Damn, the Curana is strong.*

"Oh?"

"Being chased by a rabid boyfriend out to force me into a mating meant men weren't high on my priority list. Or women." She grinned, relieved when the Curana chuckled. She felt Adrian's arm stiffen under her hand. "Besides, Max was dating-"

"Emma, why don't you let them through the door? It's cold out there," Max interrupted.

She could almost feel Emma's amusement as the Curana stepped back. "Sure, Sheri, come on in." The Curana leaned in and whispered in her ear, "Remind me that we need to talk later, okay?"

"Emma, come on." Max laughed again. "Do you really want to know who I slept with in college?"

"Not really." Sheri could hear the grin in Emma's voice. "I just like making you squirm."

There was the sound of a soft kiss. "I'll make you squirm later," Max purred softly in Emma's ear. It was obvious he thought no one else would hear him, but her hearing was even more acute than a normal Puma's.

She could feel her cheeks redden at the banked heat in his voice. Emma's soft "Oh, boy" sounded too much like how she felt as Adrian slid an arm around her waist and pulled her closer to him. His hand landed possessively on her hip as they walked into the room.

"What was that about a rabid boyfriend?" Adrian asked. His voice sounded strained.

Strained or not, she loved listening to it. It was warm and rich like melted chocolate, running over her skin in a sexy slide that raised goose bumps on her arms. Her eyes flashed red behind their glasses. *Darn it.*

Melted chocolate described the good doctor perfectly. Rich chocolate brown eyes, dark brown hair and tanned skin over smooth muscle made the man a rich treat she was dying to eat up, especially since she was a devoted chocoholic.

Too bad it wouldn't work out. Rudy would take one look at the good doctor and eat him for lunch. Literally.

Max sighed. "Long story, buddy, and one we'll be telling the entire pack. C'mon in, take your coats off and have a seat. Hey, Jerry."

She gave Jerry the command that let him know he was off duty, so when Max bent down and petted him, he wagged his tail hard enough to nearly pull the harness out of her hand. She laughed, glad her dog and her Alpha liked one another. "He likes you."

"Good, because he'll be seeing a lot of me." He took her coat and handed it to Emma. Adrian casually guided her to a large burgundy leather sofa. She could see people moving around, but couldn't really make out faces. Scents, on the other hand...

There were several men and women in the group; thankfully none of them wore perfume or cologne, something Weres tended not to do anyway. Their sensitive noses wouldn't allow it. None of their scents were familiar except for Max, the Betas and Adrian. Children squealed and laughed upstairs. She could make out the sounds of a video game running somewhere and figured the majority of the children were there.

The enticing scent of the luscious Dr. Yum drifted towards her. "Rabid boyfriend?" Adrian whispered in her ear as he settled in next to her.

She sighed. "I only want to tell it once, okay?"

Silence.

"Please?" She didn't know why she was pleading with him, but the weight of his stare was beginning to make her uncomfortable. And uncomfortably hot, something she did *not* need to be in a room full of predators.

She could just make out his nod before she heard his "Okay." He leaned in to whisper in her ear. "But we *will* talk about this later."

The feel of his breath on her ear and neck sent a shiver down her spine even as his commanding tone got her hackles up.

She frowned at him and started to say something, only to be interrupted by Max. "Okay, people, listen up. We have a new Pride member to meet tonight. She's someone Simon and I knew in college, someone I changed when she needed help. Her name is Sheridan Montgomery. She's a good person who's had a hard time. She's come to us for help, so please listen up."

Sheri could hear the Alpha in Max's voice, felt his power reach into the room. All of the conversations died down immediately as she stood and stepped forward. She could smell Max and his mate standing next to the fireplace, with Simon and Becky on Max's right. She turned reluctantly to face the room. *The moment of truth. Will they help me, or not?*

"Hello," she began, her fingers tightening on Jerry's lead. He reacted by going back on duty, settling down next to her in an alert posture. "I'm Sheri."

Adrian sat back as casually as he could and tried to get his tense muscles to relax. His mate had been threatened, and from the way Max and Simon were acting she was still under threat. His Puma was practically vibrating. If he'd had a tail it would have been swishing rapidly back and forth. Hell, even as a human he had the urge to stand up and pace, but he forced himself to stay still and listen to what Sheri had to say.

"Back in college, I dated a man named Rudy Parker. I was in my third year of the Comp Sci program, he was in the graduate program. Mechanical Engineering. He wanted to work with robots." She smiled sadly as she said it. "He seemed like the answer to every dream I'd ever had."

Adrian nearly growled. The thought of her caring about someone else that much set his teeth on edge, and he'd only known the woman for about an hour. Every possessive instinct he had began stretching, like a cat waking in the morning light, all of its attention centered on the slender blonde in front of him.

"In my senior year little things started to happen that had me worried. He'd tell me to wear a skirt, because he loved me in skirts, then he'd get upset if I wore jeans. He'd buy me hot chocolate to drink and pout if I wasn't properly grateful. Things began escalating right before I graduated."

Her voice was strong, but her hands began to shake. He had the urge to get up and put his arms around her, to let her know she'd be safe with him. *Did this Parker guy hurt her?* If he'd laid a hand on her he was a dead man. Adrian would hunt him down and gut him personally.

He felt someone's eyes on him and turned. It was Simon. The man looked at him as if he knew *exactly* what he was

193

thinking. And if anyone in this room did, it would be the big artist. His mate had been attacked and badly injured by a Pride member before she'd been turned, and Adrian knew Simon still wished he'd killed the bitch. Becky leaned into Simon and stroked his arm soothingly, but her eyes were glued to Sheri.

Adrian turned his attention back to his snow princess.

"Rudy knew I couldn't see very well. I'm legally blind. I used a cane when I went places at college and at home. I knew my way around fairly well, so it wasn't difficult, and the cane came in most useful when doing things like crossing the street. He took my cane, told me it had been stolen by some kids playing a prank, and then offered to help me around campus. He started missing his own classes to get me to mine, which seemed really sweet at the time. But if I didn't go into the building, or if he checked on me and I wasn't there, he would freak.

"That year I met Max." Her smile wasn't sad anymore; it was mischievous. "He was dating a girl who was getting too clingy and he was trying to get out of the relationship without hurting her feelings. And, no, there wasn't another woman involved; he just felt pressured and wanted out. So we wound up comparing notes and some of the things I told him triggered alarm bells for him. He said he wanted to meet Rudy and I said sure."

Adrian could feel her tension. Everyone, with the exception of the children upstairs, was completely still.

"Needless to say, Rudy wasn't happy to meet Max. That night we went on a date and he took me out into the woods. I didn't think anything of it at the time because we'd gone there before. It was his favorite place to be, someplace where we could talk about our dreams, how we wanted our lives to go, that sort of thing."

She sighed, her head dipping down and off to one side. Adrian had the impression she was looking at him. He caught a flash of red from her eyes before she tilted her head back up, hiding her eyes behind those glasses. "He attacked me that night. I didn't believe in Werewolves or Werepumas before that night."

"Werewolves?" Belinda asked. She'd taken up a position near Becky, as was her habit since the attack on the female Beta. Becky's eyes narrowed; Emma looked thoughtful. The Pride leaders both looked cold and emotionless, putting Adrian on guard. He turned his attention once again to Sheri.

"Yes. Werewolves. Rudy transformed right in front of me and attacked me. He held me on the ground and tried to mount me. My injuries were...bad." She took a deep breath, obviously rattled by the memories, and Adrian couldn't hold himself back any longer. He stood and went to her, standing next to her, holding the hand that wasn't holding Jerry's harness. She seemed to steady at his touch, her voice calming and growing stronger, and his Puma purred in satisfaction. "I managed to get away from him but I was bleeding pretty badly. Sometimes I think he wanted me to get away, that he wanted the thrill of the hunt, but I don't think he expected me to get to the road." She smiled slightly. "My guardian angel finally woke up when I reached the road, because I was nearly hit by Simon, who was coming home from a party." Simon nodded grimly, confirming her story. "I begged him to take me to the hospital. He took me to Max instead. I don't remember much of what happened after that, but when I woke up I was completely healed, other than a bite mark." She pulled aside the edge of her white sweater to reveal a scar. Out of the corner of his eye Adrian saw Becky rub a similar mark. Simon's hand covered his mate's and he looked down at her with a fierce protectiveness that, for once, Adrian completely understood because he was battling the urge to look down at Sheri the same way.

Sheri let the edge of her shirt go and took his hand again. He wasn't certain she noticed she'd done it. "Max bit me and changed me. If he hadn't I would have died. When Rudy tried to hurt me again I was able to defend myself. I was forced to run when he tried to hurt me with his Pack backing him up."

Max took over before Adrian could ask some questions,

like, *why aren't you a Wolf?* "At this point I was pretty sure Parker was rogue. I contacted the local Pack, and they knew nothing about him or his small band of friends. They promised me they'd deal with him. When Parker tried to get back at me for changing Sheri, Simon and I managed to fight him and his 'Pack' off. He's been chasing Sheri ever since. She's been forced to move around a lot and not have anyone close, like a Pride, for fear Parker would use them against her. She's petitioned to join our Pride, which means she's no longer alone." Max's hard gaze swept the room. "*We* deal with this threat now."

The Alpha smiled when his Pride members murmured their consent. Adrian felt Sheri's hand tremble in his.

"Now, for those of you with kits, keep in mind that Parker is a sick man who won't stop at anything to get Sheri back. Keep them safe, know where they are at all times. I'll e-mail everyone with a photo of Parker so that if you see him you know what to do. Contact me or Simon—"

"Or me," Adrian piped up, squeezing Sheri's hand reassuringly. He let up immediately when he saw her wince, but refused to let go.

"Or Adrian." Max nodded. "Under no circumstances, other than threat to your kits, are you to approach Parker in any way. He runs with about three other wolves. That may or may not have changed. I'll contact the Pack in the Pocono's and see if they'll help. Last I heard the Pack leader was isolationist, so we may be on our own on this."

"I'll help," Belinda said. "There are places she may need to go to that a man can't go. I'll go with her."

"Well, she's not the Curana so she should be safe," one of the females muttered.

"Excuse me?"

Adrian shuddered at the ice in Emma's voice as the Pride's Curana took offense at the woman's tone. A thin mist surrounded her, a serious indication of just how pissed off she was. "Do you doubt my word that Belinda Campbell had nothing to do with the attack on Rebecca Yaeger?"

Uh-oh, them's fightin' words. If the woman knew what was good for her she'd back down and apologize immediately. Adrian watched as several of the women winced and drew away from the offending member of the Pride.

"No, Curana." The woman bowed her head in submission.

"Good." Emma looked around at the other members of the Pride. "I expect this nonsense to stop. Belinda has proven to both Rebecca and me that she had absolutely nothing to do with Olivia's attack on Rebecca. Punishing her for Olivia's actions is wrong, and I expect better of my Pridemates. Understood?"

Adrian watched as Max positioned himself squarely next to his mate, a cool warning in his eyes for anyone who would challenge her. To challenge Emma was to challenge Max, and not a single male in the room believed himself capable of defeating the Alpha. When the Betas ranged themselves right next to the Alphas and added their glares the argument was pretty much over.

Murmurs of assent drifted through the room and the Alphas relaxed. "Sheri will be working part-time at Wallflowers, starting tomorrow," Emma added in a warmer tone of voice.

"She can move into Becky's apartment, it's right above the store," Simon said, his arm going once more around his mate.

Becky looked up at him. "She can? What about the person who's currently living there?"

"I thought she could move in with me. You don't mind, do you?" Simon grinned down at his mate, and Adrian had to hide a smile. The rest of the people in the room didn't even bother. A few went so far as to chuckle as Becky grunted in response.

"I like my apartment."

"It would be easier on Sheri and you'd be doing a very nice thing for a new friend."

Becky sighed. "That was a low blow, Simon."

"Plus my feet get cold at night."

"Oh, well, we can't have your feet getting cold, can we, Garfield?"

"I'll take that as a yes." Simon grinned as the room exploded into laughter.

That little bit of laughter helped ease the tensions in the room. People settled in comfortably to discuss how best to help Sheri while getting to know the newest Pride member. Adrian was never very far from her side, and surprisingly neither was Belinda. The two women seemed to hit it off. He sat back and watched as they laughed together over something, then made plans to go to lunch the following day after Sheri got off work. He felt some of his own tension ease; his mate would be safe with Belinda. He'd hit Max up for the full story tomorrow.

Chapter Three

"Go ahead. Ask." Sheri tried not to grin as Belinda put her sandwich down and leaned in on both elbows, looking both curious and guilty.

"What's it like being an albino?" Belinda asked quietly.

She sighed as she put her sandwich down. She wasn't offended. She'd gotten used to correcting people, but it still bothered her that people asked. "I really hate that word."

"Why?"

She'd been waiting for someone to ask her that question since yesterday at the Pride meeting, but Belinda was the first one to work up the courage. The two women were sitting in Kelly's Diner eating hamburgers and fries and totally blowing their diets. It was one of the nicest afternoons she'd had in a long time. It was nice to have a friend again. She hoped they weren't about to ruin that.

"I'm a person with albinism. Saying I'm an albino is like saying I have a communicable disease, like calling someone a leper. It's a condition I live with, not who I am."

"But it's no worse than calling me a blonde or blondie."

"I doubt that." She laughed. "Think about the stereotype of the 'albino'. We're always the evil one who's out to do some nasty stuff to some poor innocent who doesn't know that the albino is evil. And nobody stares at you just because you're blonde."

There was a moment of silence. "Okay," Belinda finally

drawled. "Tell me a blonde joke."

Sheri paused with the burger halfway to her mouth, her head tilted as she tried to catch the other woman's expression.

"How about this one? A redhead walks into the doctor's office and says, 'Doc, it hurts wherever I touch myself.' The doc has her touch everywhere on her body, and sure enough, she screams every time she does. The doc asks if she's a natural blonde; stop me if you know the punch line?"

She blushed; she *had* heard this one before, and had laughed as loudly as her friends had.

"The doc says, 'I thought so; your finger is broken.'"

Sheri could hear Belinda take a sip of her soda. "A blonde was playing Trivial Pursuit one night with some friends. When it was her turn, she rolled the dice and landed on Science and Nature. Her question was, 'If you're in a vacuum and someone calls your name, can you hear it?' The blonde thought for a moment and asked, 'Is it on or off?'"

Sheri bit her lip to keep from laughing, but she had the feeling the other woman saw it.

"Or my personal favorite, what do you call three blondes in a Volkswagen? Farfromthinken."

Sheri lost the battle against laughing, and was relieved when Belinda chuckled too.

"I have a Bachelor's degree in Management with a minor in Finance, but because I look like a Kewpie doll people who have known me all my life treat me like I'm an idiot."

Sheri could just make out the other woman's shrug. "Sometimes that's what life does to you, and sometimes it's what you do to yourself. So I know some blonde jokes, and I laugh at blonde jokes, and I try to make the best of things by not letting other people's opinions matter to me. It doesn't always work, but I try."

"Wow. Sorry."

"It's okay. I guess what I'm trying to say is, don't let the label bother you. If you do, you just wind up expending energy on something that doesn't really matter in the long run. If I got mad at every blonde joke I heard I'd be mad an awful lot of the time." Belinda leaned in close so Sheri could see her grin and whispered, "Or I'd be a redhead, worshiping at the shrine of Ms. Clairol."

They were quiet as each of them ate a little. "Do you own your own business?"

"No," Belinda answered with a sigh. "I worked at Noah's as the hostess, and I planned on applying for the manager's position...but that didn't pan out. I'm pretty sure I can afford to open my own place, but I wanted to be able to put down experience in a management position on my loan papers. I don't think I can qualify without it."

Sheri could hear the pain in the other woman's voice. "I'm sorry."

"It's okay. The market sucks right now for opening the kind of business I want to run anyway."

"What kind of business would that be?"

"Livia and I...we used to joke that we'd open up our own place. I wanted to open a bar and grill, and call it Blondie's or something; she wanted a day spa." Belinda shrugged. "It was one of the reasons I loved working at Noah's. I love the restaurant business."

"What happened with your job there?"

"I got fired."

"Why?"

"Because people thought I was in league with Livia. She attacked Becky, injuring her pretty badly, during this year's masquerade. Livia used the threat to Becky to try and get Emma to give her the Curana's ring."

"What?" Sheri couldn't believe her ears. "Someone tried to use Becky to get to Emma?"

"Yup. I didn't know anything about it until Simon carried

Becky off to heal her and change her."

"And claim her."

"And claim her." She could hear a different kind of pain in Belinda's voice and wondered if the other woman had feelings for Simon. If she did, it was too bad; Simon was obviously devoted to his mate.

"But the ring—"

"Doesn't make you the Curana, right? But if Emma handed it over—"

"She'd be seen as weak," Sheri finished thoughtfully.

"Exactly. She'd be cat chow."

Sheri laughed. She was going to like it here.

Adrian waited outside the diner and watched as the two women talked and laughed. Something in his heart eased as he watched her truly relax for the first time since he'd met her.

"Maybe if you stare hard enough her clothes will fall off by themselves." Simon stepped into view and stared at the two women.

Adrian rolled his eyes. "She's my mate."

Simon grinned. "And if anyone is going to use their amazing cloth-ripping stare powers on her it's going to be you?"

"Asshole."

Simon flipped him off, and Adrian grinned.

"She seems to be settling right in," Simon said, leaning against the brick wall of the diner.

"Yup."

"Becky trusts Belinda."

"And you don't?" Adrian kept his eyes on the two women but his attention was on Simon.

"To a point, yes."

"Do you trust Becky and Emma?"

Simon sighed. "Yes, damn it." It sounded like he'd had, and

lost, this argument already. Probably Becky had gotten to him and given him an earful. He decided to help reassure Simon. There were things he knew about Belinda that would shock Simon to his core.

Adrian nodded. "Have you ever been in Kelly's when Belle's in there?"

Simon looked at Adrian, one brow raised. "*Belle*?"

Adrian nodded. "That's what they call Belinda in there. Belle."

"No, I haven't been in there when *Belle's* been in there. Why?"

"She might surprise you."

Simon snorted. "I dated the woman off and on for years; nothing she does would surprise me, unless it was to grow a second brain cell."

"Really? Let's go in."

Adrian opened the door and pushed Simon in. Simon, surprisingly, allowed it.

"Hey, Belle!"

Simon's eyebrows rose into his hair as Frank Kelly called Belinda's name. Adrian grinned and waited. He already knew what was coming.

"Yes, Frank?"

"What do you do when a blonde throws a pin at you?"

"Run like hell, she's got a grenade in her mouth."

The entire diner laughed. "Hey, Belle," one of the patrons called out. "He ever throw one at you that you didn't know the punch line to?"

"Nope," Belle replied proudly.

"I'll get you one day, Belle!" Frank laughed.

"And my little dog, too?"

More laughter. Adrian could see Simon's shock as he pushed the man back out the door. "See?"

"The only time I ever saw her was with her upper-crust friends," Simon said. "She didn't act like that around them."

"Of course not, they would have kicked her out of the country club," Adrian replied. He set up against the wall again and stared into the diner, watching Sheri and Belle eat. "Besides, everyone knew why you went out with Belinda, and it wasn't for her conversation."

Simon winced. "She didn't act that way around me, either."

Adrian nodded. "She gave you what she thought you wanted."

"A blonde bimbo," Simon said thoughtfully.

"I hate to make you feel even worse, but as far as I can tell she never dated anyone *but* you."

Simon winced again. "Gee, thanks."

Adrian shrugged. "I don't know if she thought you were her mate or what, but when she finds him she'll know. Until then, I think Sheri's safe with Belle."

"Okay," Simon agreed with a sigh. "I'll trust her."

✧

"Spill." Adrian stared hard at his friend and partner, crossing his arms as he blocked the way out of the office. They'd just finished closing for the day and were the only ones left in the practice.

"Excuse me?" Max's blue eyes glittered gold for a moment, sensing Adrian's challenge.

Adrian sighed. "She's my mate, Max. How would you feel if Emma was threatened?" Max's low growl answered that question. "So tell me. What am I facing here?"

Max sighed and pushed his hand through his hair. "Rudy Parker is a sick fuck. He tried to mount her as a wolf. When that didn't work, he bit her. If she hadn't torn free she'd be Pack now instead of Pride."

"That kind of thing happens pretty fast, I thought. How did she get away before he managed it?"

Max shrugged. "I have no idea. All I remember is her shoulder was torn all to hell and gone, and a chunk was missing."

Adrian's growl slipped out. "He took a chunk of her shoulder?"

Max nodded. "It's why the scarring is pretty bad there. Even the Magic Puma Potion couldn't heal it."

Adrian snorted a laugh, his eyes returning to their normal dark brown. "Magic Puma Potion?"

"Becky's words, not mine."

"She would know." Adrian started to pace. "Okay, he tried to rape her, she managed to get away before he changed her, and he's been chasing her ever since. That about sum it up?"

Max nodded slowly.

"What are you leaving out?"

"She got away intact because she left before the abuse got too bad. She knows how dangerous he is now, though, and if he finds out the two of you are mates he'll do everything he can to take you down."

"I can handle him."

Max shook his head. "He won't come at you alone. He'll use his Pack, and Puma versus a Wolf Pack..."

"Puma loses." Adrian stopped pacing and stared blankly at the wall, his mind racing. "We need to keep the Pride around us, then."

"Sheri won't be alone; Simon's been detailed to watch over her when she's out and about. Belinda, Becky and Emma will stick with her whenever possible."

"And I'll be with her at night."

"If you can convince her of that."

"You doubt me?" Adrian grinned at Max, confident in his ability to seduce his mate.

"She'll try to push you away in order to protect you. To be honest, I was surprised when she finally contacted us again and asked to join our Pride. The invitation's been open since I bit her."

"Which means things are probably worse than she's telling," Adrian muttered, every protective instinct flaring to life. The urge to go to her, pick her pretty ass up and cart her home to his den where she'd be safe was nearly overwhelming.

"Yup."

"You okay with Emma doing guard duty?"

Max's grin was feral, and his eyes flashed to gold. "That son of a bitch touches my mate—hell, breathes on her wrong—I'll force-feed him his balls."

Adrian nodded, muscles tensed as Max's power rolled through the room. The need to protect was even stronger in the face of his Alpha's unconscious call. "If Emma doesn't do it first?"

Max's grin relaxed, and Adrian relaxed with him. "She broke a man's nose once."

"I know."

"You know?"

"Yeah, the whole town knew."

Max blinked. "So why didn't I know?"

Adrian shrugged. "Why would you? You weren't in town when it happened, and no one knew she'd turn out to be your mate."

Max blew out a breath. "The argument I had with that woman to get the story out of her... Okay. Never mind," he snarled as Adrian grinned. "You see if you can get Sheri to spill the rest of the story."

"No problem." Adrian turned to leave the office and saw one of the wedding gown pictures Emma had pinned to the bulletin board. He stopped with a grin. "By the way, can you pass on a message to Emma?"

"Sure, what is it?"

The curiosity in Max's voice nearly caused him to laugh. "Can you tell her that there aren't enough swimsuit pictures in here? If you guys are going to the Caribbean for your honeymoon, she'll need to pick out a bikini."

"Are you trying to get me maimed?"

"Can you get pictures of her modeling them? That would be cool."

"Out! Asshole."

Adrian left the office with a laugh. It was time to go claim his mate.

Chapter Four

Sheri very carefully lifted the sun-catcher out of the box Simon had packed it in. The big artist stood over her, watching her every move like a hawk. She made sure she was extra careful with the delicate piece.

She'd been working at Wallflowers for two days now, and she hadn't been left alone for a moment. If Becky and Emma were absent, some other member of the Pride "just stopped by to do some shopping". As if even a woman like Marie Howard could shop in one store for *three hours. Thank God for Belinda.* At least she made no pretense of why she was there, and the two women had become fast friends. And maybe if Rudy was gone from her life she'd be able to help Belinda get her dream off the ground.

"Please don't break it."

"I'm being careful," she replied, starting to get pissed off.

"No offense, but you're taking forever to do that."

"Would you like to do this?"

"Nah, looks like you've got it covered." He began to pace, moving restlessly around the delicate furniture like a caged...well, mountain lion. "Becky's officially moving in with me this week."

"I know. I'm helping her pack." She gently laid the sun-catcher in the white gift box bearing the store's name and logo printed in gold lettering. "She said I should be able to move in by the end of the week since she's not taking any of the furniture." Which was pretty fast work considering it was only Tuesday.

"So she's already taken you up and shown you around?"

"Yeah, I know the layout and everything."

"Cool. Not that you'll live there for very long if Adrian has anything to say about it."

"Simon?"

"Yeah?"

"Tell me about Adrian." She could have bitten off her tongue for letting the words slip out, but curiosity was eating away at her like mad.

"He's the same age as me, so a year younger than Max. He went to school locally, his parents still live here and have been happily mated for nearly thirty years. He's born, not made. He has a sister and a brother, both younger, both still in college, both out of town. He owns his own home and car, shares a practice with Max, and has never been in trouble with the law."

"Women?"

"None serious."

"As bad as you?"

Simon growled. "I wasn't that bad."

"No, of course not. Revolving doors belong in everyone's bedroom."

"Pain in my ass," he grumbled.

Sheri grinned. "So he's a player?"

"Not so much. He didn't date very seriously, but Sheri? He told me you're his mate, which means now he doesn't date at all."

"He's mistaken," she lied.

"So when he approaches you about it, you treat him right, okay? He's one of my best friends."

"I'll bang him on the head with a baseball bat if he tries," she replied calmly.

"He's a good man, and he'll take good care of you."

"I can take care of myself, thank you very much."

"His mother's going to love you."

"She's never going to meet me."

"She's Pride, she already has, and knock it the hell off."

"I don't know what you're talking about," she sniffed as she finished tying a pretty gold bow to the box.

Her hands were lifted away from the bow. She looked up into Simon's dark eyes. "You're mates. Trust me, there's no denying it. I fought my pull towards Becky for six months...hell, if I'm honest it was probably longer than that, and it was pure agony."

"So?"

"So if you fight it, the dreams will start. Hot, sweaty dreams. The kind that leave you aching. And it gets worse. You'll feel no desire for anyone else, because if your body can't have the real thing it'll take the dreams. There is *no denying your mate.*"

She pulled her dark glasses down and tried not to squint in the light. She allowed her eyes to flash red. "Rudy will kill him. If my denying him protects him—"

"Bullshit."

Sheri winced; she hadn't noticed the bell over the door jingling. She pushed her glasses back up her nose and pulled back into herself. "Hello, Dr. Giordano."

"Call Becky," Adrian said to Simon.

"Why?" Simon asked.

For an answer, Adrian vaulted over the glass countertop and slung Sheri over his shoulder in a fireman's hold. He ignored her squeak of protest, picked up Jerry's harness. Jerry, the traitor, immediately obeyed as Adrian carted them calmly out of the building. "Bye, Simon!"

Simon's laughter boomed out behind her. "Bye, guys."

"Put me down," Sheri growled.

"Nope."

"Put me down now, doofus!"

He huffed out a laugh. "You're not the first person to call me that."

She stilled, an unreasonable jealousy causing her to see red. "Who?"

"Simon and Max."

She relaxed. "Oh."

"You bite me and I'll paddle you. Just so you know."

His cheerful tone of voice was really beginning to grate on her nerves. That and her upside down position was beginning to give her a headache. "You and what army, bud?"

"You think I need help handling you, princess?"

She grunted as he put her in his car with a loud smacking kiss on the top of her head. She felt three years old. "You know, they have some pretty good drugs for people with your condition. Have you considered taking some?"

"Don't even think of getting out of the car."

"I wouldn't dream of it. You have my dog," she muttered and folded her arms over her chest as he shut the car door with a laugh. At least her sunglasses hadn't fallen off. Of course, Dr. Doofus hadn't bothered to grab her jacket, so she was sitting there freezing her ass off in her thin black blouse and pants. The dork.

He grinned, opened the driver's side door and put Jerry in the back. The traitor settled in happily, waving his tail as Adrian petted him. Then Adrian got in behind the wheel and started the car.

"Where are we going?"

She could hear the smile in his voice. "My place."

"No."

"No what?"

"No, I'm not going to your place."

"Oh. Sorry."

"Good. Take me back."

"Nope."

"Then what are you sorry for?"

"For disappointing you. You *are* going to my place."

"Dr. Giordano," she started to say.

He put his hand over her mouth. "My name is Adrian."

"Mph rr hmph."

"What?" Adrian took his hand off her mouth.

"Thank you."

"Uh, you're welcome?"

"Now take me back to the store." She folded her arms across her chest again and glared at him, trying desperately not to shiver with cold. He noticed it anyway and put the heater on.

"No."

"Now."

"No."

"I mean it!"

"No."

She growled. She freaking *growled* at him. "*Adrian.*"

"Sorry, mate, not happening, stop asking." They pulled into a driveway. Just as he hit the garage door remote she opened her car door and got out, intent on walking back to Wallflowers. She'd only gotten about ten steps before he picked her up and slung her over his shoulder.

He patted her butt soothingly as she growled at him.

"Oh, no you don't. I have your dog, remember?" The laughter in his voice merely caused her to snarl. She could feel her eyes turning red with aggravation.

"Good morning, Dr. Giordano."

"Good morning, Mrs. Anderson." She felt him lift a hand off her butt to wave at someone.

"Isn't that the newest Pride member?" the elderly lady asked in a scandalized whisper.

"Yes, and she's my mate," Adrian whispered back with wicked humor.

Sheri snarled again.

"Oh, good for you! Welcome to the neighborhood, young lady!"

"I'm being kidnapped against my will," she called out calmly. One of them needed to remain sane.

"That's nice, dear. Have a good day."

She could feel him chuckling under her stomach and punched his ass as hard as she could. *Double dork.*

"Ow." The slap he landed on her butt stung like hell. "Stop that."

"Put me down!"

"Just let me get the dog...there you go," he said as Jerry got out of his car and fell into step beside him. He slammed the car door shut with his foot and carried her into the garage.

She glared at her dog and considered making him cat chow. "I want to go back."

"Sorry, darlin'. No can do. Welcome home," he purred as the garage door shut.

"Your car is still outside," she pointed out, her teeth chattering a little in the cold air.

"But my mate is inside." He ran his hand over her bottom. "Hmm, a thong? I love thongs." He sighed happily.

"Pig," she muttered, amused despite herself.

"Where you're concerned? Oink oink."

She choked back an outraged laugh as he carried her into the house. He didn't put her down until they reached the living room. She could see dark brown hardwood floors, the burnt sienna walls and the beige furniture with chocolate and burnt sienna patterned cushions on it. The coffee table was a carved piece of dark wood, but she couldn't bring the carvings into focus. It looked so rich she longed to run her fingers over it and examine it more closely. She'd be able to see it if she got close enough, but she didn't want him to know she was interested in anything in his house. His furniture was modern and comfortable. She found out how comfortable when he unceremoniously dumped her on the sofa. The fabric had the soft feel of velvet under her fingertips, which meant it was probably microfiber. She damn near purred as her hand stroked over it once, then twice before she remembered she was pissed. She decided to go on the attack.

"You're not my mate."

"Yes I am. Soda or juice?"

She opened her mouth to reply *juice*, then shook her head in disgust. "I'm leaving now."

"Take one step towards that front door and you won't sit down for a week," he called back in the same cheerful tone of voice he'd used to ask her drink preferences.

"I'll call the cops and claim you kidnapped me!"

"Go ahead. The sheriff is one of us and Mrs. Anderson's grandson to boot."

"Ugh!"

"Yes, dear." He handed her the juice with a grin, and she stifled the urge to throw it in his smug face.

She tried a different tack. "You don't want a mate. You told me so."

"True, I told you that."

"I don't want one either," she growled.

"Too bad, so sad. You're stuck with me."

She bared her teeth at him as he sat down next to her, can of soda cradled in one big hand. "Not if I kill you first."

He reached out and took her juice out of her hand. "You know," he said, putting his can down next her juice, "I haven't marked you yet."

She jumped up just as he leaned in. "Don't even think about it!"

He sighed, lounging back against the cushions. "You're my

mate. I'm your mate. I'll bite you, you'll probably bite me-"

"But not where you'd want me to."

He glared at her, finally losing some of that cheer. "Is this because I said I didn't want a mate?"

She rolled her eyes. "Dork."

"Because if you say it's to protect me from Parker I'm *really* going to paddle your ass."

She shook her finger at him. "You've had as much touchy-feely on my butt as you're going to get. Eep!" He'd pounced up from the sofa and grabbed her, both hands landing on her ass and pulling her tightly into his body. He ground his hips against hers, letting her feel the erection under his slacks. "Oh, my," she gasped.

He took her sunglasses off, his dark eyes flaring gold as they caught the bright red of hers. "You are so fucking beautiful, you know that?"

"I'm not," she muttered.

His smile was slow and sensuous. He looked at her like she was a bowl of cream and he wanted to lap her up. "Oh yes, you are." One hand continued to hold her against him; the other dropped her glasses on the sofa and lifted to caress her hair. "Do you know what I thought when I first saw you?"

"Crap?"

He huffed a laugh. "No. I thought you looked like a snow princess."

"Snow princess. How original," she sneered, trying not to let his nearness (and his erection) distract her. It would have worked if her voice hadn't been trembling.

"I wanted to throw you down on the floor and fuck you until we both passed out."

Her knees wobbled.

"Then I wanted to mark you and hide you away so no one would ever see you again, want you again. Do you know why?"

"Pheromones?" she replied weakly. Her nipples were

beading beneath her bra, her breath coming in shallow gasps.

His hand began to caress her ass again. "Because you're mine."

She frowned. If it wasn't for his damn scent she'd be kicking him in the nuts for that one. "I belong to no one."

"It's okay. Because I'm yours," he whispered before he took her mouth in a kiss that nearly dropped her to the floor. This was no gentle persuasion, no first-date kiss. This was a warrior staking a claim to his woman, invading her mouth roughly, no quarter given, forcing her lips and teeth to part for him with all the finesse of a raging, hormonal bull. And she *loved* it. His hand on her ass tightened to the point of pain, and the one in her hair clenched and pulled until her mouth was exactly where he wanted it.

He plundered her, claimed her even without his bite, and she reveled in it. In the past lovers had treated her like spun glass, with delicate care, almost as if they were afraid they'd break her. They'd ignored her strength. Adrian not only acknowledged it, he savored it. She practically climbed his body, burying both hands in his short dark hair and placing his mouth where she wanted it. He helped by cradling her ass in both hands, pulling her in tighter against him. She wrapped both legs around his waist and moaned as they continued to orally assault one another.

When he reared back and bit her, marking her, she came so hard she saw stars. He hadn't even bothered to push the cloth of her shirt aside. He'd bitten her right through it, the savagery of the act heightening her arousal to a peak she hadn't even known was possible.

"Bed. Now," he muttered.

"Mm-hmm."

He laughed huskily at her weak, breathy reply, carrying her up the stairs. Everything was a blur of burnt sienna and dark wood as he moved at top speed, practically banging them both into the wall as he banked to make the turn into his bedroom.

"Naked. Naked's good."

"Um," she replied, biting down on his neck.

He stopped dead in the middle of the room and shivered all over. He arched his neck up to give her better access, which she greedily took advantage of as she marked her mate the way he'd marked her.

The sound of ripping cloth was her first indication that perhaps she'd pushed him just a bit too far with the bite. His claws raked her pants away from her body, their cool touch sending shivers down her spine as she felt them hook her panties and rip them off, too.

When his claws shredded his own pants she moaned; the good, respectable doctor went commando under his chinos. She barely felt him kick them off as he entered her still standing. It was the most wonderful thing she'd ever felt in her life. He filled her almost to the point of pain.

"Fuck," he muttered.

"Please do," she gasped.

Gold eyes gleamed at her. "Don't make me laugh, princess."

She rotated her hips slowly, the sensation making his eyes close on a pleasured groan. "Spoilsport."

He walked them to the bed, each step driving him further into her. With gentle strength he laid her down on the edge of the bed, his cock never leaving her body. "You ready for me?"

She stared up at him. "Nope. I thought I'd lay here and contemplate ceiling colors. Dork."

He pulled back and slammed into her hard, making her gasp. "You were saying?"

"If I repeat it will you do that again?" she asked, eyes wide.

He used his claws to shred her shirt and bra, pulling the tattered edges open and revealing her breasts to his hungry gaze. "I want to watch them move," he whispered. His fangs had extended, his eyes gleamed gold and his hands were tipped by claws that gently kneaded her soft flesh. The slight pain only heightened her awareness of him. He gripped her hips and began fucking her, hard, fast and furious, pumping in and out of her body, his eyes glued to her breasts.

"C'mere," she gasped, pulling at his arms. She needed to see his face clearly, wanted to watch as the orgasm took them both.

He allowed her to pull him down. She knew now that his Puma was stronger than hers. They were both too close to the surface as their humans made love, his strength obvious to her as he bent over her pale body. The knowledge that she could bring such a strong male to his knees heightened her arousal. Only when his forehead was flush with hers did he stop, staring directly into her bright red eyes as he pounded into her with all his strength. She knew she'd be bruised, sore from his rough handling, but damn it *nothing* had ever felt so good.

His hands glided along her arms until they reached her wrists, pulling with gentle strength until they were stretched out above her head. She was literally covered by him from head to toe. His eyes remained open, glued to hers, full of possessive passion, and she groaned, coming again.

"Mine," he growled, spilling inside her, his teeth clamping down on his mark once more. The sight and scent of his pleasure mixed with his bite triggered her own climax once more. Her hands clenched in his hair as her orgasm robbed her of breath, her back bowing off the bed, her mouth opening in a silent scream.

Chapter Five

Holy shit, Adrian thought, staring down at the woman sleeping on her stomach beside him. If he'd known sex with a mate would be like that he would have gone looking for her a hell of a lot sooner. He'd never come so hard in his entire. Fucking. Life. And there were so many more things he wanted to do to her luscious, creamy body. For instance, he still hadn't sucked those peach-colored nipples, or grazed her belly with his teeth. He hadn't lapped up her cream, something he planned to do as soon as she was conscious again. He wanted to leave the mark of his teeth on one of those perfect ass cheeks, or maybe on the inside of her thigh just before he ate her until she screamed his name. There was no way in hell she could deny the mating.

If she left him in some misguided attempt to protect him he'd either die or go insane.

No. He'd hunt her down and bring her back to his den where she belonged. Then he'd tie her down and fuck her until she couldn't move.

A thought that had some appeal even if she didn't try to leave him.

He'd left bruises on those pretty ass cheeks and scratches on her hips from his claws. He resisted the urge to kiss those marks better, knowing by the way she breathed that she was exhausted. That bastard who'd been chasing her would pay for making her so afraid she couldn't sleep. He'd pay double for hurting her, leaving a mark on that perfect skin.

He resisted the urge to throw up his head and snarl his challenge to the world as thoughts of Parker intruded on his lovely afterglow. He wondered if the bastard was in town yet, and what he'd try to do if he found out Sheri was mated.

He thought of his Mustang out in the driveway and decided it might not be a bad idea to move it into the garage. He got up carefully, not wanting to disturb Sheri. His princess needed the sleep. He had plans for her once she was awake again. Going to his closet he pulled out a worn pair of jeans and slipped them on, then threw on his oldest sneakers and his warmest flannel shirt. He picked up his shredded pants and carried them down to the living room, pulling his keys out as quietly as he could, then went to the closet and pulled down his father's old service revolver. He'd checked the gun carefully the day before, taking it out to the shooting range to make sure everything still worked properly. It did. He tucked it into the back of his jeans, covering it with his shirt. He went into the garage and opened the garage door.

Fuck. Looks like Parker's been here, he thought as he stared at the four flat, obviously shredded tires. He pulled out his gun and closed the garage door, eyes peeled to see if the bastard was still out there. When nothing happened he tucked the gun away and went back inside to call Gabriel Anderson, Max, and Simon.

He looked up just as he hung up with Simon to see Sheri wrapped in one of his shirts standing at the top of the stairs, her pretty blue eyes full of regret.

And that pissed him off.

"Don't even fucking think it," he growled, bounding up the stairs two at a time.

"Adrian..."

"No." He took her in his arms, her head resting in the cradle of his shoulder. Compared to him she was so small and delicate he felt like a caveman. The urge to protect his mate was so strong he trembled with it. "You're not going anywhere."

"I have no clothes," she said, smiling softly. "I have to go and at least get those."

He pulled back and looked down at her. "I think you look beautiful."

She rolled her eyes. "What happened to your car?"

"Someone decided to sharpen their claws on my tires."

Her jaw clenched, her eyes flashed red and her back stiffened in anger. He could feel her claws digging into his back.

"That is so fucking hot."

She frowned. "What is?"

"Watching you go all Xena on me. Makes me want to dress you in leather and bend you over a tree trunk."

She raised one brow, the regret gone from her eyes as she glared up at him. "Pig."

"Didn't we already have this discussion? Oink oink, baby."

Her lips twitched.

"Go on upstairs. I have a long robe you can wear. It's hanging inside the bathroom door. You'll have to come down and talk to Gabe and the others, but then we should be able to get some sleep."

"What about your car?"

"Max and Simon can help me replace the tires first thing in the morning. Belle can walk with you to work."

"I repeat: in what clothes?"

He frowned thoughtfully. "Good point. Let me call Max back. Emma can get some of your clothes from your hotel room."

"If Rudy knows I'm here, that might not be safe for Emma."

"Another good point." He pulled out his cell phone and dialed Max's number. "Hey, Max? I need you to bring Emma with you. Sheri needs some clothes from her hotel room."

"I'm not sure that's a good idea," Max replied. "If he's

already been to your place odds are he knows where she's staying. He might have the place staked out."

"Yeah, she mentioned that. I was going to ask you to go with her. If Parker can take on both of you we're in more trouble than I thought." He tried to ignore the nagging thought that he should be there, as well. His place was beside his mate, protecting her, not his Alpha. That was Gabe's job.

"I can pick out stuff for her. I think I know what to grab. Shirt, pants, underwear, right?"

"And makeup," Sheri said, knowing Max would hear her.

"Makeup?"

"And Jerry's dog food, and his bowls," she added.

"Anything else she needs?"

"Probably, that's why I said to take Emma." He put his hand over the receiver, knowing Max would hear him anyway. "Emma's the smart one in that relationship."

"Asshole," Max grumbled.

Adrian could hear Emma in the background. "Give me the phone, Lion-O. Hi, Adrian. Everyone okay over there?"

"Other than my poor Mustang, everyone's fine."

"Ouch. Did he scratch the paint?"

"If he did, it just ups the level of hurt he's gonna feel."

Emma snickered. "We're on our way. I'll find out what Sheri needs once I get there, okay?"

"Okay. Bye."

"Bye."

He hung up the phone and tugged her into his arms, then rubbed his hands soothingly down her back. "See? All taken care of." He pressed a quick kiss to her lips before stepping back. "Go grab that robe, sweetheart. Gabe should be here any minute, and he doesn't need to see you looking so damn sexy."

He could see the worry was back in her eyes just before she turned away and headed back into the bedroom.

Oh, yeah. Parker was in for a world of hurt.

"So are you and Adrian mated?" Belinda asked as they walked to Wallflowers the next morning.

Sheri tried not to grin smugly. Leaving him, denying the mating, no longer seemed to be an option. He'd made it clear, after everyone had gone the night before, that if she left he'd just follow her, muttering something about handcuffs and bedposts as he'd carried her back to bed. "He bit me right through my shirt."

Belinda whistled. "Rumor has it he carted you right out of the store, threw you in his car and took off into the sunset."

"Pretty much. The dork."

Belinda laughed. "What?"

"It's freezing out, and he left my coat and my purse behind."

"He left your purse?" She shook her head in disbelief. "Men are idiots."

"You said it."

"So whose coat are you wearing?" The laughing, knowing look on Belinda's face said she already knew the answer.

Sheri stroked the dark leather jacket Adrian had draped over her before kissing her goodbye, the smug smile she'd been fighting firmly fixed to her face. "His."

"It's his favorite."

"I know. He threatened me with severe bodily harm if I let anything happen to his jacket."

Belinda put her hand under her elbow as they approached the intersection. Just as the two women began crossing the street a black car screeched around the corner and barreled towards them at top speed. Belinda gasped, pushing Sheri back to the sidewalk just as Jerry began backing up, the signal for an oncoming car. She lost her balance and fell, banging her head on the pavement as the car clipped Belinda, throwing her a good ten feet.

Sheri's glasses flew off her face, blinding her in the harsh sunlight. Jerry was whining and licking her hand as the car, a dark sedan, hurtled down the street, narrowly missing another car before it turned another corner and was lost to sight.

"Belle?" she slurred. She was surprised at how hard it was to speak.

No answer. Or if there was one, she didn't hear it. The pain in her head blossomed as she tried to lift her head to find the other woman, and the world went black.

Adrian stared down at his mate and felt a depth of rage he'd never before experienced. He literally trembled with it. He had no doubt who was responsible for his mate's condition.

Rudy Parker was a dead man.

"Belinda's going to be okay. They've had to operate on her broken hip, and she has a broken arm and a concussion. The docs say she's lucky, it could have been a lot worse. But she'll be okay," Simon said quietly as he entered hospital room. He sounded both shaken and furious. "Gabe interviewed the eyewitnesses, and he'll be in to talk to Sheri as soon as she wakes up."

"I'm going to kill him." The lethal softness of his voice echoed oddly in the darkened room.

Simon looked at him strangely but nodded. "Max and I will be there."

Meaning that, if for some reason or another Adrian couldn't finish off Parker, one of them would do it for him. He already knew there wouldn't be a need for that.

Adrian could feel his Puma growling and pacing underneath his skin. He couldn't tear his eyes away from his mate. "I want protection here twenty-four seven until I get her home." The command in his voice was unmistakable.

Simon frowned. "Already taken care of, but you might want to watch your tone."

Adrian looked at his Beta and knew his eyes were gold with rage. He could feel himself straining against an unseen barrier as he and Simon stared each other down.

He'd never pushed the boundaries, never once tried to see which of them was the stronger Puma. He'd been perfectly happy with the status quo. He'd never felt the desire to lead, only to protect. But if the only way to ensure his mate's protection was to face down Simon, possibly losing his best friends in the process...

No contest.

"Stand down. Both of you." Max's voice was filled with quiet authority. Adrian and Simon both turned to find the Alpha standing in the doorway, the light from the hallway filtering through that strange mist that enveloped him whenever he needed to enforce his will.

Adrian felt strangely detached as that mist touched him. Simon flinched slightly and backed off.

"Sorry, man. I know you're worried about her. Christ, we all are."

Adrian nodded, his eyes glued to Max's. The strange smile the blonde man wore was beginning to grate on his nerves. "Protection?"

"That's for you to decide. What do you suggest?"

Max's tone was bland, the mist still surrounding him. It was clearly an order.

Adrian frowned, surprised, but answered anyway. "Twenty-four seven protection while she's in the hospital. Two Pumas on the door, two down the hall. Move her to an end room, have at least one of the Pumas keep an eye on the stairwell at all times. Males only, don't risk the females. No one enters this room without you, Simon or me approving it. One of the women stays in here with her while she's unconscious, in case of emergency. One we trust."

"I'd suggest putting the same precautions around Ms. Campbell," Gabe Anderson said from behind the Alpha. "If

Parker decides her interference cost him his shot at Ms. Montgomery he might decide to retaliate."

Adrian's frown tightened. "There's no one in the Pride I trust with Belle's safety right now."

"I'll deal with it."

Gabe's determined voice held a note similar to his own; he wondered briefly if the other man realized it.

Max nodded. "Good. Take care of it. Assign who you trust, both of you. Work together on it. Before they leave the hospital, I want suggestions for the protection of both women once they're back home. Simon, I need you and Becky to head up to the Poconos and talk to the new Alpha of the Pack there. His name's Richard Lowell. He's agreed to give us a hand with Parker. It'll take you about two hours to get there, barring changes in the weather. Emma's got the store covered; Marie agreed to fill in for a few days while Sheri and Belinda get back on their feet."

"I'm on it." Simon clapped Adrian on the shoulder, then did the same to Max in passing. He left without a backward glance.

"Maybe we can gather a hunting party, find this son of a bitch and end this." Gabe's low growl echoed the one Adrian could feel building inside of him.

"Do you have his scent?"

"I got a whiff, yeah, but not enough of one to track well. I've got partial plates and a description of the vehicle that I'm running through channels."

"Then we wait."

Gabe nodded, accepting Adrian's pronouncement without a fight.

Max's odd smile was still in place as he listened to the conversation between Gabe and Adrian. "Your mate's starting to wake up."

Adrian turned, all of his attention focused once again on Sheri. He bent low over her so that she'd get a clear look at him.

"Hey, princess."

She opened bleary blue eyes and stared up at him. "Sorry."

"For what? Nearly getting run over?" He forced his tone to be gentle when he felt anything but.

"Scratched your jacket."

A slow grin crossed his face. "Fine. I'll spank you for it later."

"Belle?"

Her pained whisper was driving him insane. It was intolerable to him that she felt any discomfort. "She'll be okay. Don't you worry about her."

"Alive?"

"Yeah, baby, she's alive. She has a broken hip and arm, and a concussion, but she's alive."

"Saved me."

"I know, baby. I know." And she'd earned his undying loyalty with that one act of self-sacrifice.

He couldn't resist touching her for one more second, brushing her platinum blonde hair back from her face as gently, as lovingly as he could. "Sleep, sweetheart. I'm here. I'll keep you safe."

When she nuzzled her cheek so trustingly into his hand and fell instantly asleep, two things happened. His heart broke in half, reforming with her as its core.

And his resolve to kill Parker before he could lay another finger on her blossomed into something more. The man hadn't just hurt his mate, he'd hurt his Pride. Looking into the dark blue eyes of the sheriff, Adrian finally understood what had driven his father to be a cop. Because the same fierce need to protect that haunted him burned in Gabe's eyes, too.

Chapter Six

Max had implemented every one of his safety suggestions. Surprisingly, Adrian had found he and Gabe made a good team, each one bouncing ideas off the other until they had working plans they both approved of. Gabe had managed to get the hospital's agreement on the guards, the room changes, everything they'd wanted.

And through it all Max had watched, silent, that odd smile on his face more often than not.

"Will you fucking tell me what you're smiling over?" Adrian finally demanded the next morning. It was just before they opened. Max had arrived at the practice with that damn smile on his face and it hadn't left. It was driving Adrian nuts.

For the first time ever Adrian felt Max's full power. The golden haired man drew up to his full height, his power whipping about him, filling Adrian's senses until he should have fallen to the ground, groveling. Why he didn't surprised him. He should have been down on the floor kissing cheap carpet. Instead he was standing upright, eyes locked on Max, every sense alert to some unknown threat. He didn't even realize he'd taken a battle stance until Max relented, the power withdrawing into him with a suddenness that sent Adrian stumbling, like he'd been leaning against a wall and that wall suddenly disappeared.

"Do you understand what's happening to you?"

Max's voice was gentle.

"No," Adrian said, horrified. *Did I nearly challenge the Alpha?*

Max grinned. "Knock it the hell off."

I nearly challenged the Alpha, and he's smiling about it? He bared throat in a submissive gesture that, despite his earlier posturing, felt perfectly natural.

"Don't bare your throat to me."

The command in Max's voice, the near anger there, surprised him. His head snapped up. "Why not? I nearly challenged you, for fuck's sake."

Max laughed. "Asshole."

Somehow, hearing his friend call him that made everything all right. "Fine, Lion-O, why don't you tell me what's going on with me?"

"Only Emma gets to call me that," Max groused, flopping down into an office chair. He stretched his long legs out before him, his feet crossed at the ankles, and folded his hands over his stomach. He was the picture of ease, and it didn't fool Adrian for a moment. Those sky blue eyes were too sharp for him to be truly relaxed.

"Fine. Oh Great and Exalted Leader, impart your wisdom unto me. And hurry it up, I've got a patient due in an hour."

Max rolled his eyes. "Do you remember the position your father held within the Pride?"

Adrian nodded; it was no secret. "Yeah. He was Marshal."

"And what does the Marshal do?"

Adrian frowned. Max was being a pain in the ass. "The Marshal protects the Alphas and the Pride from threats," he parroted. "Do I get a cookie now?"

"And when was the last time the Pride was threatened?" Max raised one brow and stared at him demandingly.

Adrian blew out a breath. "My father killed an Outcast who was hurting Pride members. Females, to be specific," he added with a little growl.

"Uh-huh. And that was, what? Twenty-five years ago?"

"Yeah. So?"

"So your dad is no longer Marshal."

Adrian shrugged. "I know. I figured Gabe was. That's why he came back to the area." Adrian gulped as his eyes went wide. "Are you telling me I'm Gabe's Second?"

Max rolled his eyes. "No. Idiot. Gabe is *your* Second. You're Marshal."

Adrian blinked. "No fucking way."

"Yes fucking way."

"I'm an eye doctor. I'm not a cop."

Max grinned. "So? Are you saying I can't kick ass with the best of them?"

Adrian's eyes widened. "No! Hell, no. Do I look stupid?"

"I'm not going to answer that."

"Asshole."

Max grinned. "What about Simon? Do you consider him a wimp?"

"No," Adrian agreed thoughtfully.

"Okay then. Didn't you notice how Gabe listened to you, followed your directions, added on only after he'd gotten your approval?"

Adrian blinked again, startled. The other man had done that, hadn't he?

"That's because he knew instinctively who you are, and who he is. And he's fine with it."

Hell, maybe Max was right. He blew out a breath as all the odd sensations he'd been feeling recently suddenly made sense. All males felt the need to protect their mate, it was bred into them. A male who wasn't willing to lay down his life in defense of his mate and kits didn't deserve either. But his reaction to Belle's pain had been almost as strong as his reaction to Sheri's. His need to ensure his Alpha's safety and the safety of his Pride had been eating at him for the past two days, ever since his tires had been slashed. Adrian was both horrified and fascinated. "Marshal?"

Max sighed. "You know how the hierarchy goes, Adrian. Why are you surprised you'd be right at the top? You're damn near as powerful as I am, and you are as powerful as Simon. And, hell, the three of us have been best friends for years. I just had to make sure you accepted it before confirming it."

Alpha, Beta, Marshal, Omega; that's the way the hierarchy went. Alpha was the ruler of the Pride, the Marshal was its paw, and the Omega was its heart. All were positions you were born to, not made into. The Alpha could tell you how the Pride was as a whole, but had trouble seeing the details, so the Marshal filled in the physical aspects for the Alpha while the Omega filled in the emotional ones. Without all three the Pride would falter and eventually die.

He looked into Max's eyes and saw the understanding there. Max had a similar burden, but his, as Alpha, was even greater. There was no sympathy in his gaze. Like him, Adrian was what he was.

He nodded his acceptance.

He felt the mantle of the Marshal settle on his shoulders with surprising ease as Max's power subtly surrounded him. It felt comfortable, like a part of him had been missing and then given back to him. His Puma purred its approval. He now had the authority necessary to ensure not only the safety of his mate, but that of his Alphas and his Pride. Although he knew it was still incomplete; they had no Omega, but unless he missed his guess Max already knew who it was and was just waiting for the right moment to clue the person in.

"Can I ask you something?"

Max shrugged. "Sure."

"Why didn't I feel this when Becky was attacked?"

Max raised one eyebrow and waited.

And it hit him. "She wasn't Pride yet." And because Livia hadn't endangered a Pride member, his "spider sense" hadn't tingled.

"And since she challenged Emma rather than just attacking her, it wouldn't have set you off, either."

"But Emma was in danger, wasn't she?"

Max shrugged. "Not really. It was a dominance challenge. Trust me, if Livia had gone after Emma without challenge, you would have activated."

"Okay, now you make me sound like a Wonder Twin." Adrian shuddered.

Max huffed out a laugh and leaned forward. "Yeah, I can just see you in purple tights. Do you want to know how this works or not?"

"I suppose I'd better. I wouldn't want to be so lame I could be beaten by a mop."

Max grinned. "Okay, relax. Think about the Pride as a whole. Who's in pain right now, and is it natural or something inflicted?"

He frowned. How the hell was he supposed to know that?

Only, he did know. Becky had a toothache; he'd have to let Simon know. Sarah Parker had cut her finger, probably trying to cook. She was a bit clumsy with the kitchen knives, and just about anything else she laid her hands on. Marie Howard had a skinned knee from a fall. Emma also had a cut finger...and she was...

He turned to Max, horrified. "Emma!"

Max was up and out the door before he'd finished. Adrian was right behind him. It was only a few blocks to Wallflowers but they both ran the whole way, jackets left behind in their hurry to get to Emma.

Max stopped outside the door. "Mother fucker."

Adrian growled low in his throat at what had been the glass front of the store. Emma held up a piece of the glass that had been her picture window, some of the old-fashioned gold lettering still visible, blood dripping down her hand from where she'd cut herself. Her eyes glistened with tears as she stared at it. "Max?"

Max was through the door and holding his mate before the first tear fell.

The gold eyes that locked on Adrian's were fierce. "Find him."

Unspoken were the words, *kill him.*

Sheri woke up with the worst headache she'd ever felt in her life. Her head pounded in time to her heartbeat, and nausea danced a tango in her stomach. It felt like something was trying to pry its way out of the top of her head using a jackhammer. "Kill me," she whispered, groaning.

Even that slight sound made her skin crawl.

"Hey, princess. Head hurt?"

She opened her eyes. Adrian leaned down, nose to nose so she could see him clearly. His deep brown eyes were full of concern.

"Owie," she whimpered.

He kissed her forehead, reaching above her to press the call button. "I'll get you some medicine for the pain. Okay?"

She would have nodded but that might have made the top of her head fall off. So she chose not to. She closed her eyes against the minute glare coming through the windows. Adrian must have shut the curtains. Bless the man.

"Okay, sweetheart, the nurse is coming."

She could hear the squeaky shoes of the nurse in the overly waxed hallways before he did, but she didn't say anything. Speaking hurt too much. Even grunting was beyond her at the moment.

If he'd just kill her the pain would stop. She'd be forever grateful to him.

She closed her eyes as he began stroking her hair, careful of the large lump on the side of her head. She heard the nurse enter quietly, and Adrian explaining what was wrong. A few minutes later the nurse injected something into her IV.

"You'll feel better in a few moments, sweetheart."

She couldn't even nod. She sighed, and he seemed to understand.

He left her for a moment. She could hear water running in the bathroom, and a moment later a cool washcloth was draped over her forehead and over her eyes. She moaned as the cold took some of the pain away.

"I don't want you to worry about anything, princess. I have it all under control. Relax and go to sleep."

"Jerry?"

"The vet checked him out. He's fine, just a little banged up. They kept him overnight for observation. He's at my place now."

Her lips twitched up. It wasn't a smile, she hurt too much for that, but it was the beginnings of one.

"Belinda's awake and talking. She's in pain, and she'll need physical therapy, but she'll be okay." His hand moved back to her hair, stroking softly. "Gabe's looking into who hit her, and we've set up security measures for the both of you. Someone will be with you at all times."

She stirred, frowning. Just as she opened her mouth, his finger pressed against her lips.

"No. I need this, sweetheart. Don't fight me on it. I can't be with you all the time, but I need to know you're protected or I'll lose my fucking mind."

She kissed his finger in answer.

"Thank you." His lips gently touched hers, a barely felt caress that didn't jar her head. "I put the same security measures on Belle, just in case."

She bit her lip and tried not to cry. She knew it wasn't her fault, but she couldn't help feeling it was. The medicine the nurse had given her began to work, making her drowsy. She felt herself slipping away again as his lips brushed hers once more.

"Sleep, princess. I'll guard you."

She wasn't sure, but just as she drifted off she thought she heard him whisper, "Love you."

That was good. Because she loved him, too.

"Good morning, sleepyhead!"

Sheri considered keeping her eyes closed just a little bit longer. Maybe four or five hours. Just until Mrs. Anderson left.

"I know you're awake, Missy McFaker! Open those eyes! It's a beautiful day out!"

Oh, dear God, please don't let her have opened the blinds. Sheri cracked her eyes open and shut them with a squeak as ice picks in the form of sunlight jabbed themselves into her eyeballs. *"Please close the curtains!"*

"Dear, you need more sunlight. You're way too pale."

Sheri groped the nightstand, trying to find her sunglasses. "Can you hand me my sunglasses, please, if you won't shut the curtain?"

"Those old things? They're way too dark. You should try using blue blockers. You'll see much better that way."

That would turn the ice picks into broadswords. *No, thank you.* "I have albinism, Mrs. Anderson. Sunlight is dangerous for me," she explained as patiently as she could.

"Oh? OH!" Sheri heard the rattling of the curtains being drawn. As the light dimmed she sighed in relief. She cautiously opened her eyes.

The room was comfortably dim again. Mrs. Anderson stood at her bedside holding her sunglasses. "Sorry, dear. I didn't realize."

Sheri stared at her, totally dumbfounded.

"Yes, I know. I'm not the world's most observant person. Are you hungry?"

"Ah...yes?"

Mrs. Anderson beamed down at her, dark blue eyes

twinkling. "Good. I'll just get you your lunch then." She marched over to the door and pulled it open. "The young lady is awake and we're hungry." She shut the door and marched back over to the bed. "There. Your food should be here shortly."

Sheri tried, and failed, to stifle a giggle. "Door to door service, huh?"

Mrs. Anderson nodded decisively. "Of course. It pays to be the grandmother of the sheriff and the mate of the Marshal, you know." She plopped down into the chair next to the hospital bed, grinning. "So, what is it you want to know?"

Sheri thought about it for a moment. "The secret of immortality?"

One salt-and-pepper eyebrow rose into the air. "When you learn that one make sure you share with the rest of the class."

"How's Belle?"

The smile left her face. "They had to put a pin in her hip."

Sheri winced. "She won't be able to change unless they remove it."

"Which won't be for quite a while, unfortunately. And don't feel guilty, either. Belle said she wants to see you as soon as you feel up to it. She's worried about you."

"Okay. As soon as I'm allowed I'll take a walk and go see her."

"Not without the guards."

Sheri grinned. "Of course not."

"Let's see, what else." Mrs. Anderson tapped her finger against her chin. "Oh! Someone vandalized Wallflowers."

"What?"

"Yup. Threw a brick through the front window. I don't know why they didn't do any other damage, but Emma arrived to find the window totally smashed. Luckily whoever did it wasn't there any longer and no one got hurt."

Sheri knew why no other damage had been done. That was next. If Emma and Becky continued to harbor her, things would only get worse for them.

The older woman chattered, giving her all the Pride gossip. Most of the people she mentioned Sheri didn't know, and she felt her mind beginning to drift back into sleep.

"Lunch!" a male voice announced from the doorway.

"It's about time." Mrs. Anderson got up and got the meal, two nice big bags full of fast food burgers, fries and milk shakes. "I know this isn't exactly the healthiest thing on the planet to eat, but frankly, my dear, I never could resist a Big Mac," she shared with a guilty grin as she handed Sheri her food.

Biting into her own burger, Sheri could only nod in agreement. *Yum.*

Chapter Seven

She had a bruise the size of his fucking head on her hip. The sight of it made him furious again as he gently helped her into the tub. He'd bought several large candles in glass jars, placed them on the counters and the edges of the tub and lit them so she'd have soft lighting for her sensitive eyes. She'd smiled when she'd seen it, and that made the extra trip to the store worthwhile.

"God, that feels so good," she moaned as the hot, bubbly water covered her creamy skin.

She'd been home for maybe an hour, and he couldn't stop touching her. Two days in the hospital; two days of pain Parker needed to pay for. Every bruise, every mark on her was etched into his brain, a visual reminder of the payback he meant to exact. "You need help scrubbing your back, princess?"

She smiled up at him, soft and sweet, her blue eyes languid. "Maybe later. Right now I just want to soak out the aches."

He knelt down and, careful of her injuries, gently pulled her mouth to his. It was the first time since the attack he'd been able to really kiss her, and he took full advantage. He persuaded her lips apart, tasting her mouth like it was fine chocolate, slowly and with exquisite care. He loved the way she tasted, sweet as honey, tart as apples. He could sit there and kiss her all day long.

When he reluctantly pulled way she was panting and her

eyes were glazed. She licked her lips and swallowed. "You know, I feel much better now."

"Do you?"

"Mm-hmm." Wet arms encircled his neck as she tried to pull him back down to her mouth.

"Well, then, if you're a good girl maybe I'll tuck you into bed after your bath," he purred.

Her eyes flashed red as his fingers tweaked one bubble-covered nipple. "What if I'm a bad girl?"

He growled, his eyes flashing gold. "Then I'll just have to punish you." He stood abruptly, lips twitching as she gasped in surprise. "Now be a good girl and take your bath."

"Pig," she pouted.

He laughed all the way down the stairs, his heart lighter than it had been in days as he heard her amused sigh.

As soon as her muscles were all nice and warmly relaxed from her bath he had every intention of seeing his princess safely ensconced in his bed. He then had every intention of licking every inch of her body. And once she was boneless he'd curl up around her and finally get his first night's sleep in days.

He heard the phone ringing and decided to answer it in his office. "Hello?"

Silence.

"Hello?"

Nothing.

That stupid danger sense of his was tingling again. "What the hell do you want, Parker?"

"I think you know the answer to that, Giordano."

Adrian leaned one hip against his desk, every sense alert. He could hear Sheri splashing gently in the tub. Outside the house was silent. He could hear Parker's breath over the phone, and the sounds of traffic in the background. "She's *my* mate, Parker."

Parker laughed. "Sure she is."

"She bears my mark."

"She bears *my* mark," Parker snarled.

"Sorry, Muttley, but you need to back the fuck off. She's all mine."

He could almost feel the other man smile. "Sheridan has the sweetest pussy I've ever fucked." Adrian's Puma growled possessively and his eyes flashed gold. "And she loves taking it up the ass. I bet I'm still the only man who's ever taken her there. She screams so loudly and clamps down so hard around your cock you feel like she's going to squeeze it off."

Adrian snarled silently, his mind racing. There might just be a way to get Parker focused on him and not Sheri. He smiled coldly. "I know," he purred. He could hear the other man's breathing accelerate. "I love it when those sweet lips of hers wrap around my cock. Did you know I was inside her when she marked me?" Adrian laughed softly at Parker's growl. "That's right, Parker. I bear *her* mark."

"I'll fucking kill you," Parker panted.

"She's upstairs, naked, wet, and waiting for me, Parker. As soon as I hang up this phone I'm going to go upstairs and fuck her until neither one of us can see straight."

"You're a dead man!" Parker screamed.

"Then I'm going to curl up around her and sleep with her in my arms. My arms, Parker." Parker's growl wasn't even human anymore. He hoped the man had control of his change, or things could get really ugly really fast. "And do you know what I'm going to do tomorrow night?"

"What?"

The gravelly voice on the other end of the line let Adrian know it was time to end this. "The same damn thing I'm going to do tonight. Fuck my woman."

"I know where you live."

If Parker thought that would scare him, he had another thing coming. "Bring it on. In the end it'll be my cock in her tight little pussy."

He hung up the phone and took a deep breath. It had taken every ounce of his self-control to play that little game with Parker; talking about his princess like that with her fuckhead ex was the hardest thing he'd ever done. He didn't even want the other man thinking her name, let alone spewing his filth about her body.

"You sure that was wise?"

He turned, not surprised to see Gabe standing in the doorway. The other man had volunteered to spend the next few nights with them. He was supposed to be out front in an unmarked car, though, not inside the house where Sheri could see him.

"I want him focused on me. Not Sheri or the Pride."

Gabe nodded. "Yup. Telling him how you like to fuck the woman he's obsessed with definitely grabbed his attention." He shifted uncomfortably. "Hell, it grabbed my attention," he muttered, smiling slyly.

Adrian rolled his eyes. "You have a better idea?"

Gabe shrugged. "Even if I did it's too late now. Odds are good he'll be here before morning."

"When is Richard due?"

"He's already here. He's staying with Mr. Friedelinde."

The Friedelinde mansion was probably the most comfortable place for the visiting Pack Alpha and his entourage. "Give them a call and let them know what happened. I'll call Max."

Gabe nodded and pulled out his cell phone on his way back towards the front door.

Adrian shook his head, still somewhat uncertain how he'd wound up the Marshal and Gabe his Second. The other man radiated authority from every pore. His loose limbed stride and relaxed posture fooled no one. Those dark blue eyes could be cold as an arctic breeze in an instant. That large frame, almost as big as Simon's, moved with a grace and agility only professional athletes could mimic.

But when the other man looked back at him, a question in his eyes, something in Adrian immediately responded. "What's the problem?"

"Richard wants in."

Adrian sighed and pinched the bridge of his nose. He'd planned on meeting with Ben, the Pack Marshal, in the morning over coffee to discuss strategy. Apparently that plan was now in the crapper. "Fuck."

"Yeah. I told him I'd call him back."

"How many does he have with him?"

"Four. His Marshal, the Second and two others."

Adrian stared at a painting on his wall without really seeing it. Plans were busy whirling through his mind. "Van?"

Gabe nodded and grinned. "I'll park them at the corner."

"Get Simon to bring them. I want you here."

"Will do."

He shook his head and picked up the phone. He dialed Max, quickly filling him in on what was going down. Max agreed to have Simon play liaison with Richard, since there was no Omega to do the job.

Then he climbed the stairs to his wet, willing princess.

Sheri was already out of the tub when she heard him coming up the stairs. She'd heard his entire conversation with Rudy, and was ready to kill Adrian herself. She wrapped the robe closer around herself and waited, tapping one foot impatiently.

She wasn't stupid. She knew why he'd said what he'd said. She hadn't needed to hear him explain it to Gabe. But the fact that he was making himself a target for her sake had driven her out of the tub. She wanted to scream at him, rant and rave until he gave up his idiotic plan. But it was too late for that.

Rudy would have him in his sights now, and if Adrian died because of her she'd never survive it. Just the thought of Rudy sinking his teeth into Adrian, pulling away flesh, making him bleed, had her seeing red. She'd kill Rudy herself before letting him hurt her mate.

The man himself stepped into the bathroom, took one look at her out of the tub and frowned. "Why aren't you soaking?"

"I got out because I didn't think there'd be enough room for both me and your fat head."

"Huh?"

The man looked totally clueless. "I heard your conversation with Rudy, Adrian."

He sighed wearily. "Princess—"

"Don't you princess me, Adrian Giordano! How could you put yourself in danger like that?"

He rolled his eyes and took her hand, gently leading her from the room. "I can handle Parker."

"Sure you can. But can you handle him and five of his best friends?"

He led her into the bedroom and stripped the robe off her before she could blink. "Into bed with you." He gently picked her up and laid her down on the bed, careful of her injuries. He snarled when she gasped anyway. "I will be facing Parker. His best friends will be facing Max, Simon, Gabe and Richard Lowell, plus the wolves Richard brought with him."

"Then why don't you leave Rudy to the Pack?"

She watched him strip silently. "Because," he said as he finally climbed between the sheets, "he's mine."

"Adrian."

He put his finger over her lips. "Don't try to talk me out of this. I am personally going to gut him for what he did to you. Every bruise on your skin, every bite mark he placed on you, I'm going to give back to him. And when I'm done making him hurt, I'm going to make him scream. Then I'm going to kill him."

The calm tone of his voice, the factual way he stated everything he had planned for Rudy, made it that much more frightening. "This isn't what I wanted." She sighed.

He rubbed his cheek against hers gently in a gesture meant to comfort her. "I know. You were hoping he'd see you here, safe and surrounded by people, and leave you alone." He looked deep into her eyes, his nose touching hers so she could read every nuance of his expression. "But that's not what's going to happen. He'll hound you, day and night. He knows where you live, what your dog looks like, who your friends are—and you've been here only a week. Once he knows your routine he won't hesitate to use it, or your friends, against you. He'll lure you out into the open where he can grab you. And if he does that, he'll be a dead man anyway. If Max and Simon don't get to him first and hand him over to Richard, who, by the way, plans on killing him, I'll kill him."

"It's not your job to stop him, Adrian."

"Yes, it is." He slid one arm around her carefully. "Max confirmed me as Marshal a few days ago."

She frowned. "Marshal?"

"I keep forgetting you've never been part of a Pride before. The Marshal is the one who sees to the safety of the Pride. Gabe's my Second, like Simon is Max's."

"I thought Mrs. Anderson was mated to the Marshal?"

"Why would you think that?"

"When she sent the guards for McDonald's...uh-oh," she whispered as his furious expression registered.

"She sent the guards out for *McDonald's?*" he growled through clenched teeth.

"We were hungry." He glared at her. "Besides, I don't think both guards went."

"Oh, well that's all right then. Not."

She frowned at his sarcastic tone. "Give them a break, Adrian. It's not like you were dealing with soldiers or cops.

You're dealing with people who have been asked to guard someone, almost a complete stranger, against a threat they've never faced before."

"So?"

"So, take it easy on them because I really like McDonald's?"

He sat up and glared down at her, holding both hands in front of him as if he was weighting something. "Hmm, let me think. Your life, a Big Mac. Your life, a Big Mac." Both hands waved in the air. "Hey, no contest, right?"

She bit her lip to keep from laughing. "It was a really good Big Mac. And we are talking *McDonald's* French fries."

He growled, and she quickly decided to change the subject. He looked ready to climb out of bed, get dressed and hunt down her "guards" to give them the sharp end of his teeth.

"So explain to me again why it's your responsibility to go after Rudy."

He sighed. "It's the job of the Marshal to remove threats to the Pride."

"And Rudy is a threat to the Pride."

"Yes. The moment he went after you *and* Belle, he became a threat to the Pride."

She'd known her decision to join the Pride could have consequences. The price Belle had paid was, in her mind, too high. She closed her eyes as the guilt threatened to choke her.

"Hey."

She opened her eyes and saw the anger in his.

"You better not be blaming yourself."

"And what if I am?" she whispered.

He shook his head. "You are not responsible for the actions of Parker."

"If Belle hadn't volunteered to protect me she wouldn't have been hurt." Relief lit his eyes at her tone of voice, and she knew he understood that she wasn't upset.

She was pissed.

"Belle is going to be fine. I promise you that."

Sheri shook her head. "How can she be? Mrs. Anderson told me they had to put a pin in her hip! If they did she won't be able to change, you know that."

He sighed. "That woman talks too much," he muttered.

"Tell me about it."

His lips twitched, the rest of the anger leeching away. "We're trying to figure that one out."

"And what about Emma's store?"

His eyes widened in shock before dark lashes dropped over them, hiding his expression. "What about Emma's store?"

"I know about the window, Doc Obvious."

He laughed. "That's a new one."

She rolled her eyes. "Stick with me, kid, I've got a million of them."

"I plan on it," he purred, gently cradling her body against his. He reached up with one hand and gently tweaked one of her pale nipples.

"Uh..."

"I know just which part I'd like to stick to, too."

She thought about bopping him on the head, but it hurt too much to move. "First off, I'm in way too much pain for what you have in mind. Secondly, I will not be distracted by sex."

"No?" He pouted down at her, eyes twinkling with mischief.

"No."

"You're sure?" he asked as his hot tongue swiped quickly across her puckered nipple.

"Sure," she gasped, not sure anymore what she was agreeing too.

"Marry me?" he whispered just before he kissed her with mind-bending thoroughness.

"Sure...wait, what?"

"Too late," he grinned triumphantly.

"Hold on there, weren't we fighting a minute ago?"

"Nope."

"But—"

"Hey, no take-backs!"

"*Adrian!*" She laughed, loving the look in his eyes as they twinkled down at her.

He shook his head, clucking his tongue. "That wasn't the kind of screaming I was going for tonight, sweetheart. Guess I'll just have to try harder." He sighed happily.

"Dork." She laughed breathlessly as his mouth landed on her breast again.

He laved her nipple gently, barely sucking it between his lips. "Hey, studies show that orgasms are very good for pain management. It has to do with all those lovely endorphins crashing through your body. Hold very still, sweetheart."

"Not...sure...I can," she panted, desperate to get closer to him. The pain in her body seemed to recede when he touched her like that, so maybe there was something to that endorphin thing, after all.

Or maybe it was just his touch. Everything seemed better when he touched her.

"If you don't hold still I'll have to figure out some other way to help you sleep," he whispered, grinning his wicked grin. He kissed the tip of her nose when she whimpered and froze. "Good girl."

He nibbled his way down her neck to his mark, but didn't bite. She wanted him to, oh, so desperately, but he merely shushed her and moved on.

Butterfly-light kisses worked their way down her body, stopping at each breast to lovingly pay homage. Lips, teeth and tongue came out to play as he did his best to make her forget her pain. He kept his body away from hers, hovering over her as he moved down, almost as if he was afraid to touch her. He lingered on the bruise on her hip, barely breathing on it as he growled over it. The barely there kisses soothed the ache in her heart more than the ache in her hip. She closed her eyes and shivered as he worked his way down one leg. He kissed both of her feet reverently before working his way back up the other leg. He spread her legs apart, softly kissing up the inside of her thigh. She waited for him to nip her there, wanting to feel the bite of his teeth, but again he refused. Instead, he began a long, languid, wet lapping at her pussy that had her drenched in seconds. It took everything in her not to follow that hot tongue as he methodically worked her over, slit to clit, never stopping, speeding or slowing.

Her breath was coming in pants, her hips undulating despite her efforts to hold them still. "So good," she whispered just before the orgasm rolled through her, hot and sweet as candy.

Her eyes opened as he slid inside her. She could feel every rock hard inch of him straining against her as he held himself back. "I love you," he whispered just before he took her mouth with a dominance that left her feeling weak and shaken.

He fucked her slowly, careful not to jar her. She could see the promise in his eyes. As soon as the pain was gone he planned on giving her what they both wanted, a good, hard pounding that would leave them breathless, sweaty and very, very happy.

For tonight, he gave them what they both needed.

She reached up and wrapped her arms around his neck, barely hiding the wince the movement caused. "I love you, too."

His eyes went wide and, as if the words were a trigger she'd pulled, he came with a groan.

He lay there as she slept in his arms and tried to go to sleep, but every little noise in the house had his eyes flying wide open. The creak of the front porch swing had him nearly leaping out of the bed. He knew Gabe was guarding them, but a part of him just couldn't relax. Not after his conversation with Parker earlier. There was no way in hell he was sleeping tonight, and he knew it. He'd be lucky if he dozed.

Sheri snuffled in her sleep and curled in tighter around him. Sighing, she settled back down, one arm draped across his stomach, one leg thrown across both of his.

If they didn't catch Rudy soon he was going to be one massively tired kitty. He kissed his princess on the forehead and resigned himself to guarding her sleep.

Chapter Eight

Richard Lowell was huge and intimidating. The man easily reached six-foot-four. Broad, powerful shoulders matched the massively muscled arms crossed over his chest. Pale blue eyes stared coldly at Adrian from a face that had seen hard times. There was a scar that ran the length of his left cheek, an angry red one that let Adrian know it was still new, probably within the last few weeks. Since he was the new Pack Alpha, odds were he'd received it during a dominance challenge. Long bright red hair was tightly bound by a braid that went all the way to his waist. He wore black jeans and a dark blue sweater that strained against his massive chest. "What do you mean you're leaving to bring back the other female?"

Belinda was being discharged from the hospital. She'd been in a full day longer than Sheri. She'd refused to go to a halfway house, opting instead for physical therapy on an outpatient basis. "Both women are at risk, Belle because she pushed Sheri out of the way of the car. I think it's best to have them both under the same roof, especially since Belle can't protect herself right now. Gabriel will guard Sheri while I fetch Belle."

"I don't think that's wise."

Adrian stared at the huge Pack Alpha. "You're here. Are you telling me that Parker will be able to get through you, your Marshal, his second, *my* second, and two other wolves to get to my mate?"

"I'll send one of my wolves to fetch the female."

Adrian rolled his eyes. "Sure, right. Belle would take one look at your guys and scream her head off. No offense but she doesn't know any of you guys from Adam, and she has reason to be cautious of Wolves right now."

"But she trusts you, since you're Pride." Richard still stared at him coldly. "Then have one of my men go with you, or send your Second."

Gabe flushed. "She won't go with me, either."

Richard looked at the sheriff briefly before returning those cold eyes to Adrian. "Meaning that the female can't trust the peacekeepers of her Pride?"

He pinched the bridge of his nose; the headache he'd woken up with that morning was only getting worse. "Look, there were some issues between Belle and the rest of the Pride that we're still resolving, and none of them are her fault. She trusts very few people right now. I just happen to be one of them." He looked around the room at the five Wolves and three Pumas. "Sheri isn't leaving this house, and she's one of the few Belle trusts. Emma and Becky are dealing with the vandalism of their store. Max and Simon will be going with me to get Belle, and, no, I will *not* send them alone; the threat is to both of them as well. Gabe will protect my mate. I'm asking you to stay here and help him with that. If you can't I'll make other arrangements."

The power rolling off of Richard was different from the power that Max exuded with such ease. The man was incredibly strong, but the difference between the independent, strong-willed power of the Pride Alpha and the dominant hammer the Pack Alpha wielded as he tried to bludgeon Adrian into submission were completely different. Richard didn't give a fuck what Adrian wanted. He demanded obedience with his force of will. He probably always got it, too.

But not today.

Adrian knew he was right. He was acting on his instincts as his Pride's Marshal, not as a Puma with a mate in danger. The thought of sending Max and Simon to the hospital alone gave him a major case of the panics. He stared the Alpha down, not budging an inch as Gabe clutched his head and groaned. Sheri curled up in a ball, whimpering at the power rolling through the room.

"Let it go, Rick, he's not going to budge," the Pack Marshal said with a smile as his second joined in with some head clutching and groaning of his own. The other wolves were all cowering on the floor at their Alpha's display of temper.

The power Richard had been wielding abruptly cut off. "You are a stubborn man," Richard said softly.

"I'm my Pride's Marshal, and every instinct I have says it's dangerous to send Max after Belle without me."

Richard stared at him for a long moment before nodding once. He turned to his Marshal. "Secure the area, Ben. Let me know when the Pride Alpha and Beta arrive."

The man nodded once and motioned to the other wolves. They left the house, presumably to "secure the area" to their Alpha's satisfaction.

"Thank you."

The other man finally smiled. "No problem."

Adrian shook his head and sat next to Sheri. He gathered her close, not surprised when she tucked her face into his shoulder. "As soon as the others get here I'll leave. Belle will sleep here, with us, until Parker's dealt with. You'll be able to fuss over each other to your heart's content. Okay?"

She nodded.

"Head hurt, princess?"

She shook her head.

Richard knelt in front of them, his ice blue eyes soft as he looked at the trembling woman. "I promise you, Parker will not lay a finger on you while you are under my protection."

Sheri looked up at the huge man. She bit her lip, uncertainty in her eyes as she stared at him. "May I see you?"

Adrian started, his Puma snarling. "Seeing" Richard meant nose to nose, not something he felt comfortable with.

Richard looked at Adrian, then looked back at Sheri. "I can understand your nervousness, considering it was Wolves who attacked you. If it will make you feel more comfortable, by all means, um," he frowned, slightly confused, "see me."

Adrian sat back and forced himself to allow his mate to get close to the big, bad Wolf.

Sheri stared at the large red-headed man in front of her and tried to remember that he was there to help. The fact that he smelled of Wolf didn't help much. His coldness and his power only made her more afraid.

But when he'd knelt in front of her and tried to reassure her she'd known he understood. He only *seemed* cold. Every instinct she had told her that this man would sooner gnaw off his own paw than hurt a woman. She didn't know how she knew that, she just did.

Maybe it was in his scent, or the way he immediately grasped her problem and tried to fix it in the only way he knew how. By opening himself up to her examination he allowed her teeth and claws dangerously close to his unprotected eyes and neck, something he would never do if he felt threatened in any way. It reassured her as nothing else could have.

She leaned in close and allowed their noses to almost touch. She felt Adrian's tension and knew he wouldn't appreciate it if she actually made contact with the other man.

Pale blue eyes stared at her from a battle-worn face. The initial layer of frost hid a nature more deeply compassionate and caring than any she'd ever seen before, mixed with a fierce determination to protect those he considered under his care. It was easy to see. She'd seen it in Adrian's eyes once too often to mistake it.

But it was different in this man. Where Adrian was content to slide through until his special abilities were called for, this man was always "on", always aware of what was happening with and to those people he considered his. If her mate hadn't had the threat of Parker to fuel his power, he'd have been groaning right alongside Gabe.

"I can see why she is your mate now," he said, staring into her eyes. What he saw there, she had no idea, but it seemed to reassure him just as much as what she saw reassured her. "She sees deeply, more deeply than anyone I've ever met."

"But I was still fooled by Rudy."

He went cold again, hiding himself behind icy eyes. "Just because you can see deeply doesn't mean you always think to look."

He stood up, towering over them, and stared at their joined hands. "She'll be safe with us. Go get the other female."

And he turned and walked into the kitchen without a backward glance.

Sheri tapped her fingers nervously on her legs. She was watching television, trying to distract herself until the others returned. Richard's utter stillness wasn't helping, either; it wasn't relaxed at all. It was the stillness of a predator waiting for his prey to come within striking distance. He stayed away from windows and doors, making sure she did the same, and he kept between her and the doors and windows the few times she moved. He inspected every room she went into before she entered it. He'd detailed his Marshal and men to outside guard duty. His Marshal had agreed, as he felt it was his job to guard them both. In short, he acted the perfect bodyguard. Gabe was outside with the other Wolves, since he was familiar with the wooded territory behind Adrian's house and they weren't.

Her cell phone rang. An amused chuckle came from over her shoulder as he heard her ring tone. "Where did you find that?"

"On a website that had Looney Tunes sound waves," she answered as she dug her phone out of her purse.

He chuckled some more as Sylvester the Cat's voice said once again, "You're darn tootin', Buster. You *did* see a pussycat!"

"Hello?"

"Hello, Sheridan."

She felt her blood run cold as Rudy's soft, growling voice filled her ears. She looked up at Richard, hoping he could see the expression on her face, but his back was to her. "Hello, Rudy."

"I hear you've been a busy, busy girl, Sheridan."

She licked her lips as Richard moved to look out one of the kitchen windows. "Yes, I have."

"I'd love to get together, discuss what you've been up to. Do lunch, maybe."

"Sorry, my social calendar is booked full through two thousand sixty. Maybe some other time."

"Really? Because Giordano would just *love* it if you joined us."

She froze. "Adrian's not with you."

"No? Have you spoken to him since he left for the hospital?"

Richard turned back to stare at her but was too far away for her to see his expression. "No, I haven't."

"Tell you what, Sheridan. I'm a generous guy. You get on the phone and call him, see how he's doing. I'll call back in five. Just to see if you've been able to get a hold of him."

The connection cut off.

With shaking hands and voice she filled Richard in as she dialed Adrian's cell. No answer. She tried Max's, and then Simon's.

No answer.

Her heart pounding with fear, she started to dial Emma's number. When the cell phone rang again she jumped. She fumbled it open. "Hello?"

"Well, Sheridan? Were you able to get in touch with any of

them?"

"No," she whispered, terrified beyond belief.

"That's odd, because I could have sworn I heard his cell phone ringing."

The gloating triumph in his voice sent shards of terror straight down her spine.

"What do you want?"

"Hmm. Well, my men *are* getting hungry. Are you sure you won't join us for lunch?"

She whimpered. Wolf packs in the wild had been known to eat lone pumas.

"I tell you what, sweetheart. I'll arrange it so you can get away from the Neanderthal who thinks he's guarding you. You leave the house, come quietly with me, and maybe I won't feed Giordano to my packmates. Deal?"

Before she could answer Rudy disconnected.

"Don't even think about it."

She looked up at the large Pack Alpha. Menace rolled off him in waves. "I have no choice."

"Then don't make the mistake of thinking you're leaving this house without me."

The sound of a gunshot cut off anything else she might have said. A cry of agony was swiftly followed by another gunshot.

"Shit! Wait," Richard said. "This must be what he was talking about. Move to the front door, I'm right behind you."

She saw him pull something out from behind his back and figured it must be a gun. At least she hoped it was a gun.

She moved around the couch to grab Jerry's harness but Richard's hand stopped her. "Leave him. He'll be safer." She nodded her agreement and moved to the front door, opening it slowly.

A third shot rang out before it was open all the way, startling her. She heard Richard groan just before the large man fell, knocking her to the ground.

"Get up, Sheridan, let's go."

Rudy grabbed her arm and dragged her to a car. "Be grateful I don't have much time," he said as he shoved her in the car, "or I'd have made sure the big fucker was dead." He got in behind her, crowding in close to her. "Drive," he snarled to the man in the driver's seat.

"Get off me," Sheri said, trying to push him away from her. Another shot rang out, and this time Rudy cursed.

"Not on your life. You're mine again, and there is no way in hell I'm letting you go."

When he began ripping at her clothes she began fighting. A vicious slap stunned her long enough for him to rip away her sweater. She thought briefly about shifting but she was still mostly clothed. Getting tangled in her jeans would merely make her more vulnerable.

So she fought him with teeth and claws as he bit and snarled over her, praying that Adrian would arrive before Rudy got to finish what he'd started.

Max pulled up outside of Adrian's house and snarled. "Problems."

"No shit, Sherlock, what was your first clue?" Simon snarled back, climbing out of the Durango. "What the hell happened here?"

Gabe stepped out onto the porch, gun in hand. "Two shots out back, one out front. Richard's down but not out. One dead, one wounded, both ours."

"Sheri?" Adrian growled.

Gabe shook his head. "Not quite sure what happened but as soon as the shots rang out she took off for the front door. One of Rick's men saw her go but wasn't close enough to get to her. Rick tried to stop her but got taken out. We've got a license plate, and a Wolf followed the car for as long as he could before he had to double back."

"Where the hell were you?"

"Trying to get to the sniper."

"And?"

"He got away when I heard the shots out front. I shot at the car just as they took off, but missed the damn tire."

"FUCK!" Adrian shouted. Both hands clenched in his hair. "What the *hell* was she thinking?"

A pained growl erupted from the Pack Alpha where he sat on the porch floor. "Rudy told her he had you. She couldn't reach you, so she believed it. Is your cell phone on?" A dish towel was pressed against his shoulder and soaked through with blood.

"She is in so much trouble when I find her," Adrian growled as he checked his cell. "Yes, it is."

"Yours too?" Richard pointed with his chin to Max and Simon.

"Yup."

"After what happened at Wallflowers? Damn straight it's on."

"Check in the car, see if there's an RF jammer somewhere," Gabe said to one of the Wolves. The man nodded and went to look.

"What the hell is an RF jammer?" Simon asked.

"Radio frequency jammer. Really illegal just about anywhere, but something a mechanical engineer would know how to build," Gabe answered.

The Wolf came back quickly with a small yellow device the size of a deck of cards. "This is why no one could reach you."

"Okay, Adrian, think! Where is she?" Max demanded.

"How the fuck should I know?"

Max glared at him as Simon went to the Durango and helped Belinda out. "You're the Marshal. She's pride. *Where is she?*"

He concentrated on his mate, his eyes turning gold as he felt where Rudy's hands were on her body. "I'm going to fucking kill him."

"Good. Where are they?"

"In a car, still moving. He's..." Adrian snarled, holding back the primal scream of his Puma with difficulty. "I think he's trying to rape her, and she's fighting him." She'd lost her sunglasses somewhere along the way and the pain of the sunlight in the car was excruciating. He felt like both of his eyes were being stabbed with knives.

"Can you smell anything?"

Adrian found himself belted into the front seat of the Durango. A large red Wolf leaped into the back seat, a shoulder wound bleeding sluggishly all over Max's leather upholstery. Another Wolf, this one smaller and a lighter red (*Ben, the Marshal* his Puma whispered) joined the larger, wounded one. He sniffed, but the smell of blood and Wolf nearly overwhelmed him.

"You have to use her senses, not yours. What does *she* smell?"

"Why don't you try this?" Adrian growled.

"I would if I could but I can't. I'm not the Marshal."

He took a deep breath and tried once again to reach his mate. She could smell Parker, the driver, and her own blood as Parker's claws ripped into her soft flesh...

And the smell of the Susquehanna River.

"Shit. She's about fifteen minutes away, somewhere near the Susquehanna."

Max took off in a squeal of tires. "Think he's heading for Harrisburg?"

"Not sure. If he picks up I76 he could move into Ohio or further east towards Philly."

"Then we have to catch him before he hits the highway."

His cell phone rang. "Gabe."

"I'm on my way, following an alternate route. Consider yourselves escorted by the police."

"Thanks, dude."

"No problem. I can fucking *feel* what he's doing to her. The son of a bitch."

"We're cutting him off before he gets to the highway."

Gabe sucked in a breath. "We'll never find them if he takes her out of state."

"No shit."

"He heads east and he can pick up I95."

"I know."

"I'm calling in a few favors. Trust me, he won't get much further."

Adrian stared at the dead phone in his hands and wondered what his Second was up to.

"God damn it! Stay on the fucking road, Steve!"

"I'm trying, Rudy, but there's a bunch of fucking yahoos with trucks blocking it!"

Rudy lifted his head from her breasts with a growl. He'd just succeeded in getting her jeans off her, leaving her completely naked. "*Go around.*"

"What the hell do you think I'm doing?"

Sheri squealed as shots were fired.

"What the fuck?"

"They're shooting at us!"

Rudy sat up and pulled out his gun. He peeked over the top of the bench seat and stared out the windshield, and the scent of Puma came through. Those "yahoos" were her Pridemates.

Sheri could barely see, so she stayed down. She recognized the sounds of rifles being fired, and did the only thing she could think of. She hit the floor of the car and covered her head with her arms.

Bullets shattered the windshield, raining glass down on top of her. Rudy cursed again and fired back as Steve tried desperately to go around the roadblock.

"Fuck!"

"What?" Rudy snarled at his driver.

"Tire's blown."

She could feel the car fishtail as the driver tried desperately to bring it back under control. "*Adrian!*" she screamed as loud as she could, firmly convinced he was responsible for this and praying he would hear her over the noise of the gun battle.

Because if he didn't get her out of there, her Puma would. And then hell would *really* break loose.

The sound of his mate screaming broke something inside Adrian. "Up there," he snarled, already ripping his clothes off. He knew the men on the road block were Pumas; Gabe had called him back as soon as he'd set it up. They would do their best to hold Rudy in place until Adrian could arrive and kill his ass.

He shifted right there in the front seat, uncaring that his claws ripped Max's leather seat. Max reached around him and opened his door and he leapt out, making a beeline for the car Rudy had his mate in.

The snow-white puma came soaring out of the back window with an effortless grace that burned through him. Her bright red eyes were fixed on him with fear, love, relief and hope. She was almost safe.

A gunshot fired.

She stumbled, and went down.

And his heart, missing its core, stopped beating.

He looked from his fallen mate to the man in the car, the Wolf with his mate's scent all over him, the smoking gun still held in his hands, and realized he had one more task to complete before he joined his mate in death. But even that was denied him as the huge red Wolf sailed past him, leapt into the car and in one strike ripped out the throat of the rogue.

Adrian crawled to his mate and nuzzled at her wound. To his relief she grumbled, and his heart started beating once more.

She lived.

He curled up around her and allowed the Wolves to deal with the remaining rogues. He had more important things to do.

Epilogue

"Your heart stopped."

"I thought my mate was dead. Of course my heart stopped."

"What happened to those wonderful Marshal powers? You'd think they would have told you I was mostly stunned."

Adrian cuddled her closer. "Yeah, well, I wasn't exactly thinking at that point in time."

He hadn't been able to let her go in hours. They sat on the front porch, curled up in his swing, enjoying the night air. He barely felt the chill. He had his snow princess safe and in his arms, keeping him warm. The four blankets he'd wrapped around them didn't hurt either. She'd mentioned something about buying a chiminea for the front porch. She'd had to explain what that was to him, since he didn't have a clue. When she told him it was an outdoor Mexican-style fireplace, his Puma had purred its approval of that idea.

After all, his snow princess only liked to come out at night, and he had to keep her warm. He couldn't wait until summer, when she said she'd show him the joys of "moon bathing".

She nuzzled his neck, planting a tiny kiss. "I'm fine. Once I shifted back to human the bleeding stopped. It was just a flesh wound. Although I admit it stung like hell."

He pulled her even closer with a low growl.

"Can't. Breathe."

He loosened his hold on her with a huffed laugh. "I don't

think I'll be able to let you out of my sight for a good long while, sweetheart." Hell, if he could he'd rig a papoose and carry her everywhere.

"What happened to the rest of Rudy's Pack?"

Adrian snarled. "Dead." And a good thing, too. Adrian had been damn near feral by the time they got Sheri back home. If any of the rogues had been alive, he'd have eaten them. Literally.

"You shouldn't be walking," a deep, cold voice said. They turned to look and realized the window behind them had been left cracked open, probably in an effort to remove the blood scent. They looked at each other, pretty sure they knew who Richard was growling at.

"I'm sorry, do you have a medical degree? No? Shut up." Belinda's voice panted, pained and pissed at the same time.

"You're in pain."

Belinda gasped mockingly. "I am? Really? I never would have guessed."

"Then you shouldn't be walking."

"My doctors told me to move around as much as possible, as it will speed the healing process."

"Heart-stopping agony speeds the healing process? In that case I'll break out the red hot pokers. You'll be better in no time."

"Look, *Dick*, I'd much rather be riding the morphine train right now, but if I ever want to shift again then I need to get the goddamn pins out of my hip. If I ever want the pins out, I need to heal. My doctors told me to walk in order to heal. So sit. Stay. Good dog. Arf."

Adrian and Sheri shared a wide-eyed glance. Belle was giving the huge Pack Alpha grief?

"She must be in an awful lot of pain," Sheri whispered.

"Sit down before you fall down!" Richard bellowed.

"You lay one single paw on me and I will bite it off! Got it,

Dick?"

"Stop calling me that!"

"Then stop acting like one! I hate to tell you this, Dick, but you ain't the boss of me!"

"Oh, really?" There was a brief silence, and then Richard howled. "Ow! You *bit* me!"

Adrian started to laugh, his shoulders shaking silently. Sheri had one hand over her mouth, her eyes filled with horrified amusement.

"Back off, Fido. Don't say I didn't warn you."

When the big Alpha growled, Adrian found himself in the house before he could blink. "Back off, Richard."

The Pack Alpha glared at him. "I'm not threatening her! Not much, anyway," he muttered as he glared at the blonde trying to walk around Adrian's living room. She was using the wheeled walker the hospital had recommended. Pain etched fine lines next to her lush mouth and her green eyes glared right back at the big redhead. She was dressed in the rattiest blue robe he'd ever seen, with blue bunny slippers on her feet.

Ben, the Pack Marshal, was standing near his Alpha, one hand over his mouth as he tried to stifle his own laugh.

"Isn't it time for you to toddle on back to your den, Dick?"

Richard's smile was coldly sensual. "Not without my mate."

Belle narrowed her eyes at him. "Someone actually has the misfortune of being mated to you? Poor bitch. Give her my condolences."

The smile slipped off his face. Sheri made her way into the room and to Adrian's side, her lips quivering.

"Belle?" she said. It sounded like she was choking on a laugh.

"What?" Belle snarled, her eyes turning gold as her Puma surfaced.

"I think he means you."

Belle's eyes widened as the big Pack Alpha nodded once.

"Look on the bright side, Belle," Adrian choked as he tried not to laugh. Belinda looked like she'd swallowed a live fish. "This should solve your Pride problems."

"You'll be telling me all about those. *Won't you.*" The Alpha crossed his massive arms over his chest and glared at Belle.

It wasn't a request, it was a demand, one that had Belle stiffening in outrage. Adrian decided it was time to get out of the line of fire. Shaking his head, he grabbed Sheri's hand and began tugging her up the stairs to their bedroom.

"Where are we going?" she whispered as the argument erupted downstairs once more.

"Bed. Duh," he whispered back.

"Are you sure it's safe to leave them alone together?"

"Don't worry, sweetheart," he said as he shut the door, "I'm pretty sure Belle can hold her own." He began undressing her. "Besides, I have more important things to worry about."

"Like what?" She was trying not to smile, but her eyes had gone red.

"Petting my kitty."

"Pig," she sighed.

He cupped her cheek. "I love you," he whispered, totally serious. He'd nearly lost her today and though he hid it well he was still shaken.

With a small sigh she wrapped her arms around his neck and snuggled close. She buried her face in his neck, and Adrian closed his eyes, enjoying her scent and softness so close to his own. He began stroking her back, trying to soothe her, knowing that after her ordeal she had to be just as shaken as he was.

Just as his hand reached her ass his eyes flew wide. A startled laugh boomed out of him as, very softly, she began snuffling his neck and oinking.

"Oh baby," he said as he swung her giggling form into his arms, "You are in trouble now."

"Oh goody," she replied as he fell on top of her and began

nuzzling her neck, "because I've been a very bad kitty."

As he stilled above her, his cock throbbing between them even through both their jeans, she sighed. Arching up into him, she purred, "A *very* bad kitty."

He stared down at her, eyes wide and gold as she raked her claws down his sides. When they dug into his ass he bit her again, right through her shirt as his own claws came out and ripped her jeans away. His jeans were quickly opened and his cock rammed home, both of them groaning at the sensation of hot steel encased in wet velvet. He held her down with his teeth as he fucked her, pounding into her with enough force to rock the oak headboard. It banged rhythmically against the wall, letting everyone in the house know what they were up to, but she couldn't muster the energy to care.

He was snarling against her shoulder, his teeth still deeply imbedded into her. The combination of pain and pleasure was too much, and she came screaming around him. He stiffened above her, his own orgasm tearing a groan from him as he poured himself into her.

"Vegas sound good to you? I have a yen to visit the Elvis chapel there," he panted a few minutes later.

She pried open one sleepy eye and glared at his dark head where it rested against her breast. "I am not going to be married by a fat man in sequins. Dork."

He sighed and snuggled closer, a happy grin on his lips. "God, I love it when you talk dirty." He opened his eyes and watched in satisfaction as she collapsed into giggles again. Not even the ongoing argument between Richard and Belle could dampen his mood. With the threat to the Pride eliminated, and his mate happy and in his arms, Adrian finally allowed himself to sleep.

About the Author

Dana Marie Bell wrote her first short story when she was thirteen years old. She attended the High School for Creative and Performing Arts for creative writing, where freedom of expression was the order of the day. When her parents moved out of the city and placed her in a Catholic high school for her senior year she tried desperately to get away, but the nuns held fast, and she graduated with honors despite herself.

Dana has lived primarily in the Northeast (Pennsylvania, New Jersey and Delaware, to be precise), with a brief stint on the US Virgin Island of St. Croix. She lives with her soul-mate and husband Dusty, their two maniacal children, two evil ice-cream stealing cats, and a bull terrier that thinks it's a Pekinese.

You can learn more about Dana at: www.danamariebell.com

She's everything a big bad wolf could want.

Steel Beauty
© *2009 Dana Marie Bell*
A Halle Puma Story, Book 4.

Coping with a devastating injury is hard enough for Belinda "Belle" Campbell. Forced separation from her destined mate while she heals is almost more than she can endure. Until she is strong enough to take up her duties as Luna of the Poconos Wolf Pack, however, the safest place for her is Halle. Now, after months of being alone, she is more than ready to be claimed. But is the pack ready for a Puma Luna?

Rick Lowell has waited long enough to bring Belle home where she belongs. He's aware of the danger, as well—and it isn't long before a bitch with an eye on Belle's position issues a challenge. The only way to put down the threat is for Belle to defeat the usurper in combat.

There's only one problem. Thanks to the pins in her broken hip, Belle can't shift. Without that tactical advantage, it won't be a fair fight. With his new mate's life on the line, Rick is forced to make a decision that will change everything.

That is, if Belle gives him the chance to make it.

Warning: This title contains explicit sex, graphic language, lots of doggie (or is that kitty?) style and some songs Rick will never want to hear again. Ever.

Available now in ebook from Samhain Publishing.

Her destiny rests in their hands…

Very Much Alive
© 2009 Dana Marie Bell
A True Destiny Story, Book 1.

Kiran Tate and Logan Saeter have been on the run from Oliver Grimm for so long they've forgotten what it's like to be free. Ending Grimm's power games won't be easy, but this time they have an ace in the hole. PI Jordan Grey, Guardian Investigation's resident hot shot—and Grimm's step-granddaughter.

Jordan Grey has her doubts when Logan and Kir show up in her office with a tall tale of how her step-grandfather has framed them for murder. And to top it all off, they're claiming that they're really the ancient Norse gods Loki and Baldur, and that Grimm is Odin!

When the two lovers see the sexy detective for the first time, stopping Grimm suddenly takes a back seat to seducing her into their arms. But Grimm never rests, and when his anger spills over onto Jordan, it sets them all on a collision course with a destiny that will rock their world…

Warning: This book contains explicit sex, graphic language, some violence, and hot male/male/female action. In fact, it could be considered a religious experience.

Available now in ebook Samhain Publishing.

GREAT CHEAP FUN

Discover eBooks!

THE FASTEST WAY TO GET THE HOTTEST NAMES

Get your favorite authors on your favorite reader, long before they're out in print! Ebooks from Samhain go wherever you go, and work with whatever you carry—Palm, PDF, Mobi, and more.

Samhain Publishing, Ltd

WWW.SAMHAINPUBLISHING.COM

LaVergne, TN USA
31 May 2010
184489LV00009B/2/P